DZUR

BOOKS BY STEVEN BRUST

THE DRAGAERAN NOVELS

Brokedown Palace

THE KHAAVREN ROMANCES

The Phoenix Guards
Five Hundred Years After
The Viscount of Adrilankha,
which comprises
The Paths of the Dead,
The Lord of Castle Black,
and
Sethra Lavode

THE VLAD TALTOS NOVELS

Jhereg	*Athyra*
Yendi	*Orca*
Teckla	*Dragon*
Taltos	*Issola*
Phoenix	*Dzur*

OTHER NOVELS

To Reign in Hell
The Sun, the Moon, and the Stars
Agyar
Cowboy Feng's Space Bar and Grille
The Gypsy (with Megan Lindholm)
Freedom and Necessity (with Emma Bull)

STEVEN BRUST

DZUR

A TOM DOHERTY ASSOCIATES BOOK

NEW YORK

DZUR

This book is printed on acid-free paper.

Edited by Teresa Nielsen Hayden

A Tor Book
Published by Tom Doherty Associates, LLC
175 Fifth Avenue
New York, NY 10010

www.tor.com

Tor® is a registered trademark of Tom Doherty Associates, LLC.

Library of Congress Cataloging-in-Publication Data

Brust, Steven, 1955–
   Dzur / Steven Brust.— 1st ed.
      p. cm.
   "A Tom Doherty Associates book."
   ISBN-13: 978-0-765-30148-2
   ISBN-10: 0-765-30148-2 (acid-free paper)
   1. Taltos, Vlad (Fictitious character) —Fiction.   I. Title.
PS3552.R84D98   2006
813'.54—dc22

                                          2005036186

First Edition: August 2006

Printed in the United States of America

0 9 8 7 6 5 4 3 2 1

For Mark and Guin

Acknowledgments

Paul Knappenberger helped me with some research, and various computer problems (and they were legion this time) were solved by Aaron Thul, Graydon Saunders, Berry Kercheval, Kit O'Connell, and Bill and Anne Murphy. Jason Jones of The Four Queens, Las Vegas, was my food consultant on this one. Terry McGarry did her usual outstanding copyedit. My thanks to you all.

DZUR

PROLOGUE: PEASANT'S PLATTER

Vili glanced up, turned his head back toward the interior, and said, with no particular inflection, "Klava with honey for Lord Taltos." He then turned back to me and said, "Your usual table is available, m'lord."

If Vili wasn't going to make any observations about the fact that I had been gone for years, was missing a finger, and had a price on my head sufficient to make every assassin in the city drool with greed, well, I certainly wouldn't either. I followed him inside.

Valabar and Sons is in a part of Adrilankha that looks worse than it is. The streets are narrow and full of ruts winding among the potholes; the dwellings are small and most of them show their age; and the population there—urban Teckla with a few Chreotha—give no appearance of wealth, or even comfort. But, as I say, it looks worse than it is. Few who live there are actually destitute, most of them being tradesmen or those employed by tradesmen and most of the families having lived there for millennia, some for Cycles. Valabar's fit right in.

You walk down three shallow steps, and if you're Dragaeran (which I am not) or an exceptionally tall human (which I am not), you duck your head. When you raise it again, you're immediately ambushed by the aroma of fresh-baked bread—ambushed, and you surrender. Why it is that with all of the scents inundating the place it's the bread you smell, I don't know; there are myriads of other smells that you notice when you're outside. But inside, it's the bread.

You're in a room with eleven tables, the largest of them big enough to seat a party of six. There is a great deal of space between the tables. The walls and tablecloths are white, the chairs a sort of pale yellow. On each table is a yellow flower, a small white dish with finely ground salt, and a clear glass jar with powdered Eastern red pepper.

I followed Vili to the other room, much like the first, but with space for only nine tables. Those two rooms were all there was; most evenings both were full. We reached my favorite table, a deuce in the back corner that I liked not for any reasons of security, but just because I enjoyed seeing what everyone else was eating.

The chair felt good—familiar. I salivated and my stomach rumbled. As I sat down, Mihi came by with my klava, and I drank some, and right away I have a problem: I could spend so much time telling you about just the klava that I wouldn't get anything else done. It tasted of cinnamon and monra and honey and heavy cream and I found myself smiling as I sipped it. Loiosh and Rocza, my familiar and his mate, were quiet out of respect for my pleasure—a rarity in Loiosh's case especially.

Next to my chair, carefully positioned so I couldn't bump it by accident, they placed a small brazier. In it were wine tongs, carefully kept heated. Next to the brazier was a bucket of ice water, and in the ice was a single, long white feather.

There would be wine tonight. Oh, yes.

I'd come early; there weren't many diners at this hour, just a quad and a stiff. The quad—all Chreotha—spoke quietly. Valabar's seems to encourage quiet conversation, though I don't

know why. The stiff looked like a Vallista. He gave me a glance as
I entered, then went back to his Ash Mountain potatoes. A good
choice. But then, so far as I knew, Valabar's didn't have any bad
choices.

I had made a good choice by accident, showing up as I did in
the early afternoon. I enjoyed Valabar's when it was full of people, but being almost alone fit my mood. I sipped my klava, and
found that I'd closed my eyes for a moment, savoring what was,
and what soon would be. I smiled.

An hour earlier, I had been in Dzur Mountain. An hour before that, I had been fighting for my life and the soul of a friend
against—

Now, right away, I have a problem. You see me, but I don't see
you. I don't know who you are. You're there, but invisible, like
Fate if you choose to believe in it; like the Lords of Judgment
even if you don't. Do you know me? Have we met? Do I need to
explain who I am, or shall I assume you're the same individual
who's been listening to me all along?

Well, I guess there's no point in telling you about what happened before either way. If you've been with me before, you know;
if you haven't, you'd never believe it. I just barely believed it. But
I touched the hilt of Lady Teldra hanging on my left hip, and
there was such a keen sense of her presence that I couldn't doubt,
no matter how much I wanted to.

But then that was ages before—hours, as I've said. Now life
was klava, and the klava was good, so life was good.

Klava had been part of what I now thought of as my "old
life." Every morning I'd gone into my office, had my first cup of
klava brought to me by my secretary, Melestav, and begun planning what crimes I'd commit that day. After Melestav was killed,
Kragar, my associate and, if you will, lieutenant, who didn't know
how to brew klava and could just barely make coffee, would order
it from a place down the street.

I look back to that now as a good time in my life. I was respected, I had power, I had money, I was happily married (at least, I thought I was), and, if every so often someone tried to kill me, or the Phoenix Guards would beat me bloody, well, that was just part of the game. At the time, I suppose I wasn't so aware of being happy; but then, spending your time asking yourself if you're happy is as good a way to be miserable as I know. If you want to be happy, don't ask yourself difficult questions, just sit in a quiet, peaceful place and enjoy your solitary klava.

I was not, however, destined to enjoy my solitary klava for long.

"M'lord," said Vili. "A gentleman wishes to be brought to your table."

Loiosh gripped my left shoulder a little tighter.

"If he were coming to kill me, do you think he'd ask?"

"No, Boss. But who knows we're even here?"

"Let's find out."

Before Loiosh could reply, I said, "What sort of gentleman, Vili?"

"A Dragaeran, m'lord. He would appear to be of the House of the Dzur."

I frowned. That was certainly unexpected.

"Bring him over."

Young, was my first reaction. I'm no great judge of ages of Dragaerans, but if he'd been human, he'd have barely needed to shave. He also had that sort of tall, uncoordinated lankiness that spoke of someone who hadn't quite settled into his body yet. His House was no mystery at all: Only Dzurlords have ears like that and eyes like that, and think that black on black is the ultimate of fashionable color combinations. And if that wasn't enough, there was the hilt of a sword sticking up over his shoulder—a sword that was probably taller than I was; a very Dzur-like sword, if you will.

The expression on his face, however, was very un-Dzur-like. He was smiling.

"Hi there," he said, all cheerful-like. "My name will be Zungaron someday, but for now it's Telnan."

It took me a moment to manage a reply. For one thing, I'd never had anyone introduce himself in quite that way. For another, Dzurlords are . . . well, some of them can be . . . you might find some who . . .

You don't expect to find a cheerful Dzurlord.

I stood up. If he'd been a Jhereg, I'd have remained seated, out of courtesy, but he was a Dzur so I rose and gave him a half bow. "Vladimir Taltos," I said. "Call me Vlad." I sat down again.

He nodded. "Just checking. Sethra sent me."

"I see. Why do they call you Telnan?"

"Sethra says I haven't yet earned the name Zungaron."

"Oh. What does 'Zungaron' mean?"

"She hasn't told me that, either."

"What does Telnan mean?"

He thought about that. "I think it means 'student' but I'm not sure. May I join you?"

I held up two fingers to Vili, who nodded and went back about his business. Telnan sat. I don't know how he managed with that thing slung behind his back that way, but it seemed easy and natural. Maybe that's something Dzurlords study. He said, "Sethra was worried about you."

"That's a kind thought on her part, but are you trained to handle Jhereg assassins, assuming one shows up?"

He smiled like he'd just been ordered into battle against overwhelming odds with half the Empire watching. "Not yet."

"Oh. So this is training for you?"

He nodded.

"I don't know about you, Boss, but I feel worlds better."

"Uh huh."

Mihi brought klava for Telnan. I drank some more of mine.

"Have you known Sethra long?" I asked Telnan.

"No, not really. Around twenty years."

Not long. More than half of the time I'd been alive. "Odd I've never met you before."

"It was only a year and a half ago that I was permitted above the dungeons."

I blinked. "Uh, if you don't mind my asking—"

"Yes?"

"What did you do in the dungeons for most of twenty years?"

He frowned. "Why, I studied wizardry of course. What else?"

I nodded. "Yes," I said. "Of course. What else?"

He nodded agreeably.

"You know, Boss, I don't think this one is the brightest candle in the sconce."

"That looks like a sort of uniform you're wearing."

He lit up like the skies on Ascension Day. "Oh, you noticed?"

"I picked right up on it," I said. From his reaction, I knew I was supposed to ask, and the klava had temporarily removed my normal contrary streak. "What sort of uniform is it?"

"The Lavodes."

Well, that *was* interesting.

Presently Mihi, a pleasant, chubby Easterner with great, gray bushy eyebrows, approached again. This time holding a large, wooden platter that I knew well. He gave me a sort of conspiratorial smile, as if he knew what I was thinking. I imagine he did. The platter contained a block of granite, smooth, about a foot round, and heated in a bread oven. Mihi set the platter on the table, and took a small stoneware pitcher from his apron. He gave it a quick, practiced shake, then removed the cork from the pitcher.

The bottle had oil—a mixture of grape-seed, olive, and peanut oil to be precise. The aroma it gave off as it spread over the heated granite was mild, slightly musky. I sat back in my chair. It had been so long. The last time I was at Valabar's, I was—

I was still married, but let's not go there.

I wasn't yet on the Organization's hit-list, but let's not go there either.

I still had all ten fingers, but let's &c.

Years. Leave it at that.

Telnan gave the platter a curious glance, as if wondering what was to come. Around it were leafs of lettuce—red, green, and yellow. Between the lettuce and the granite were thin strips of raw beef, smoked longfish, raw longfish, poultry, lobster, and a small pair of tongs for each of us. All of these except the tongs had been marinated. Hey, they marinate the tongs too, for all I know. I'd give a lot to know what's in the marinade, but it certainly contains lemon.

Also on the platter were three dipping sauces: hot mustard, sweet lemon sauce, and garlic-horseradish-crushed-mustard-seed sauce. I don't generally use the sweet lemon sauce; something about that combination of flavors bothers me. The other two I alternate between.

You take beef, or the fish, or whatever, and move it to the middle of the granite, where it cooks in about ten seconds on a side—the waiter will do that for you, if you wish. Then you take it with the tongs, dip it in the sauce of your choice, and go to work. With the beef, I wrap it in a piece of lettuce. I started to show Telnan how to do it, but Mihi was faster and better. Telnan paid close attention to Mihi's instructions.

"You know," said the Dzur, "this is really good."

"You know," I said, "I believe you're right."

"Don't forget to save some for the Planning Committee, Boss."

"Do I ever forget?"

"About half the time when you eat here."

"You have a long memory for wrongs."

"Just looking out for the lady, you know."

"Think Rocza will appreciate the food?"

"I'll let you know."

Telnan was frowning at me. "Are you talking to the, uh, to the jhereg?"

"Yes," I told him.

"Oh."

He had no more to say about it, but I enjoyed giving him something to think about.

When we were just finishing up the peasant's platter, I got two things: The first was a basket of what in my family we called "langosh," which is an Eastern garlic bread. The second was another visitor.

I really liked the bread; I'll get to the visitor in a moment.

As I reached for a garlic clove, a little tingle went up my left arm—the lingering effects of a recent injury, even more recently healed by an expert. That was fine; five hours earlier I hadn't been able to use the arm at all; I'll take a little tingle.

Telnan and I didn't talk for a bit. I was concentrating on the process of rubbing garlic on bread when Loiosh tightened his talons on my right shoulder, followed almost immediately by Rocza tightening her claws on my left. I looked up, which gesture alerted Telnan, who turned his head and half turned his body, while reaching for his sword. An elderly, plainly dressed Dragaeran was walking up to the table, with no hint of effort at concealment or speed. If he had hostile intentions toward me, he wasn't very good; I had time to drop the bread, wipe my fingers, and take a dagger from my boot. I kept the dagger under the table. Telnan must have reached a similar conclusion because he didn't draw. I studied the fellow as he approached.

He was a bit small for a Dragaeran, and, though I'm not all that good at their ages, I'd have put him at over twenty-five hundred years. I couldn't identify a House either from his clothing, or from his features.

He showed none of the signs of being a Jhereg—by which I mean that I got no sense that he knew how to handle himself, or was looking around for danger, or that, well, he was anything except an elderly merchant. Naturally, I assumed he was there to kill me.

It took him something like six seconds to get to my table, which gave me time to remember Lady Teldra, so I pushed myself just a bit back from the table, re-sheathed the dagger in my boot, brought my hand back up, and let my right forefinger rest against the hilt of Lady Teldra on my left hip. Lady Teldra is—but we'll go into that later. For now, let me say that, as before, touching her hilt gave me a comforting sense of her presence. The thought came to me that if this individual was going to disrupt my meal, I would be more than a little annoyed.

Vili frowned and started to approach but I waved him off—I'd hate myself forever if Vili got himself shined trying to valiantly defend my right to a quiet dinner.

It's funny how time seems to stretch out when you think you're about to have to defend your life. As he came closer, I was able to make a few more snap observations about him—he had a pleasant, slightly round, almost peasant-like face in spite of the noble's point, with bright, friendly eyes and thin eyebrows. His hands were the only thing that struck me as dangerous, though I can't say exactly why I thought so; they were just hands: neatly trimmed nails, fingers about average, though perhaps a bit stubby. I stood; Telnan did as well. If it was rude, I didn't especially care.

The visitor didn't keep me in suspense. In a pleasant baritone, he said, "My name is Mario Greymist. May I join you, Lord Taltos?"

When I could talk again, I said, "So, correct me if I'm wrong: You're not a myth, then?"

"Not entirely, at any rate. May I join you?"

Telnan hadn't appeared to recognize the name.

"By all means, if my friend doesn't mind. His name is Telnan, by the way." I trust my voice was even, and I sounded sufficiently calm.

"Hi," said Telnan, smiling.

Mario Greymist inclined his head and smiled back.

I addressed my familiar: "*Loiosh, you're about to draw blood.*"

"*Sorry, Boss.*"

He relaxed his grip on my shoulder. Vili shuffled a chair over from another table, placing it to my left and Telnan's right. If Mario Greymist decided to join us for dinner, the table would be crowded. The three of us sat down.

"*Boss, if he'd wanted to kill you—*"

"*I know, I know.*"

"I take it," said Mario, "that you've heard of me?" He smiled. The smile of a downstairs neighbor who has just thanked you for loaning him half a pound of coffee.

"Yeah," I said. I was at my cleverest.

"I haven't," said Telnan.

Mario and I looked at the Dzurlord. I said, "Uh . . ."

"Never mind," said Telnan.

"Don't let me interfere with your meal," said Mario.

I looked at him. He seemed to be sincere. I said, "Feel like having something to eat?"

"No, thank you. I won't be here that long."

I almost said, "Good," but caught myself. Mihi approached and asked the same question of Mario, and got the same answer. He then asked me if we'd care for wine. We would. He could recommend—fine. I trusted him, just bring whatever he thought best. He bowed.

Mario.

He was to assassins what Kieron the Conqueror was to soldiers. Except that Kieron was dead. Mario had assassinated an Emperor before the Turning of the Cycle, at least according to the stories. When the Phoenix Guards couldn't solve a murder, they'd say, "Mario did it," meaning the case would never be solved. There is a story (probably not true) of a guy who was told that Mario was after him who simply brought himself to Death-gate and threw himself over the Falls.

And Mario was sitting across the table from me, and smiling a friendly sort of smile.

It was almost enough to put me off the food.

"Hey, Boss."

"What?"

"How do you know he's really Mario?"

"Hmmm . . . good point. But do you know anyone who'd claim to be Mario if he wasn't?"

"Well, no. But still."

"Yeah."

He leaned back in his chair and folded his arms over his chest. It was about as non-threatening a position as he could take, without making it painfully obvious that he was trying to look non-threatening. He said, "Of course, you're aware that you've annoyed some people."

"Yes," I said. "That's been made clear to me."

Telnan turned to me. I didn't feel like giving explanation to a Dzur, so I didn't.

Mario said, I guess to both of us, "There are two things you don't do: talk to the authorities about the association, and—"

"Association?" I said.

He smiled. "An old term. The Organization? The—?"

"I see."

"I don't," said Telnan.

"Tell you what, Loiosh. You take the Dzur out and explain to him."
"Uh huh."

Out loud, Mario and I ignored him. I nodded. Mario continued, "Talk to the authorities about us, and interfere with our Imperial representative. You did both. Well, one and a half, anyway."

"I didn't tell the Empire anything about the, uh, Association. Not really."

"Close enough to annoy people."

"I suppose."

"But you know that."

I nodded. "In the last few years of wandering the world dodging them, it's become more-or-less clear. I assume, at some point, you were offered the job?"

He looked directly at me. At the same time, I felt an odd little twinge from somewhere in the back of my head, as if there were a voice whispering just too softly for me to hear. I decided now wasn't the time to think about that twinge, and what it implied.

"Sorry," I told Mario. "Improper question."

His nod was barely perceptible. He said, "You're taking something of a chance coming here, aren't you?"

Loiosh shifted slightly on my shoulder; in response, Rocza shifted on my other. Telnan said, "I'm here."

"Yes," said Mario. "Of course."

"Not so much," I said. "You know how we . . . that is, you know how things are done. By the time word gets out that I'm here, and someone sets something up, I'll be far from the city."

"That's why you were so relaxed when I walked in."

"Yeah, that's why."

He nodded. "There are rumors that you've acquired a rather formidable means of defending yourself."

I felt the length of Lady Teldra hanging from my left hip, just in front of my rapier. I didn't touch her, though I wanted to. "No," I said. "They aren't rumors. You were flat out told, and from a reliable source."

"Well, that too."

Which, I figured, was as close as I was ever going to get to confirming the stories I'd heard—that the most famous assassin in the history of the Dragaeran Empire was the lover of Aliera e'Kieron, second in line as Dragon Heir, and head of the most prestigious line of the House of the Dragon. It was amusing. Or something.

So as I sit here, between Valabar's *Kermeferz* and the Jhereg's Mario Greymist, and await my wine with a strange Dzurlord for company, maybe I should tell you a little bit about myself. Hmmm . . . then again, maybe not.

Mihi showed up with the wine, asking me to approve the bottle. I nodded. I was sure it was a bottle. He used the feather and, with the aid of a thick glove taken from his back pocket, the tongs. He opened it and poured without flourish. Jani, my other favorite waiter, always made it look like opening the bottle was an occasion for major triumph. It's the little stylistic things that differentiate us, don't you think?

I leaned back in the chair like I didn't have a worry in the world and said, "Care for some wine?"

Telnan did, Mario didn't. Mihi poured and left the bottle.

I nodded, sipped, and waited for Mario to go on.

"Good wine," said Telnan. I doubted he'd know the difference. But I could be wrong.

Mario shifted in his chair, and, for just a moment, looked uncomfortable. Before the shock really had time to register, he said, "You know Aliera."

Well, yes, I knew Aliera. That is, I knew her as well as any "Easterner" (read: human) could know a "human" (read: Dragaeran). I knew she was short, as Dragaerans go; not much over six feet tall. I knew she had a lethal temper and the skill in sorcery to back it. I knew, well . . .

"Yeah," I said. "I suppose, in some measure, anyway."

He nodded. "She asked me to speak with you."

That was certainly worth an eyebrow. "She's concerned about my safety?"

He frowned. "Well no, not really."

"That's reassuring."

"There are others she's concerned about."

"Are you going to make me guess?"

He sighed and looked unhappy.

"Okay," I said. "I'm guessing. Since she sent you, it has to have something to do with the Organization, since Aliera would never publicly demean herself by admitting she had anything to do with criminals."

Telnan and Mario both glanced at me, and I felt myself flushing. "Uh, I hadn't meant to exactly include you in that," I told Mario.

He nodded. "Continue, then. You're doing well."

Unfortunately, having gotten that far, I drew a blank. If Aliera was in trouble with the Organization, which I couldn't imagine, Mario could do anything I could do. And if the Organization was in trouble in some way, it was no longer a concern of mine; I no longer had any interest or connections in their doings, with the possible exception of—

"Cawti," I said.

He nodded, and something slammed down in the pit of my stomach.

"South Adrilankha," I said.

He nodded again

"My fault, then."

He nodded again.

"Uh . . . care to explain?" said Telnan.

"No," I said.

I made a few other remarks, these with more emotional than rational content.

"I suppose," said Mario. Telnan looked puzzled.

I felt Loiosh's presence in my mind, the way I sometimes do when a spell threatens to get out of control. I concentrated on my breathing, like during a fencing exercise.

In case we haven't met before, I used to run a small area of Adrilankha. That is, when anything illegal happened there, I either got a piece of it, or made arrangements for someone to regret that I didn't get a piece of it. I also, eventually, acquired some similar interests in the Easterners' Ghetto, what was called South Adrilankha. At this time, I was happily married. To the left, my wife, Cawti, was unhappily married at the same time, mostly because she had some sort of moral objection to making money off Easterners the same way we made it off Dragaerans. Who knew?

Then she was in danger, and I heroically saved her and all like that. In the course of doing so, I made a few enemies and a quick escape. The last thing I did before leaving my career, my friends, my wife, and everything else, was to give Cawti all my interests in South Adrilankha as a kind of going-away present.

At the time, I thought it was funny, in a sick sort of way.

Now it was sounding sick, in a funny sort of way.

Mihi wanted to know if I was ready for—no, I wasn't. He could return after our guest left, as our guest didn't care to dine. Mihi understood and vanished into that place waiters and creditors go when they aren't in front of you.

"Okay," I said. "Let's hear it."

He nodded and smiled. Like the guy who lived downstairs, as I said before. Or else maybe the old man who pinches the pretty girl in the market, but she smiles back instead of smacking him. That guy.

"The Dagger started out by—"

"She isn't called that anymore."

He gave me an odd look, and said, "That's what I call her."

"Eh," I said. "Okay."

"She started out by trying to dismantle the Organization in South Adrilankha entirely."

I nodded. "And, of course, it popped back up, only outside of her control."

"Yes."

"I could have told her that would happen."

He tilted his head a little. "Some things are easy to see when you aren't in the middle of them."

"I suppose. What next?"

"She managed to get back some control of the area, and tried running it—" He frowned. "More gently, I suppose you'd say."

I grunted. "That's what I'd have tried first."

"It didn't work either. As I understand it, debts went uncollected, profit margins were too small—"

"I get the idea."

He nodded. "So, well, various individuals started smelling opportunities. You know how that works."

"Yeah."

"I don't," said Telnan brightly. We ignored him.

Mario said, "She tried to hang on to what she had, but, really, she didn't have an organization; just herself and her reputation. That only goes so far."

I nodded.

"Then she started getting help. A few button-men turned up dead, and—"

"Help from whom?"

"That's the big question."

I gave him a look.

"No," he said. "I had no part in it."

"Then who . . .? Oh."

He nodded. "Her old partner."

"The Sword of the Jhereg."

"Yes," he said. "At least, that's the rumor."

"The Sword of the Jhereg, now Dragon Heir to the Throne."

He nodded. "And not just her personally, but she included various friends and retainers."

"Aliera?"

"No. Just some Dragonlords who felt obligated to help her, no matter what."

"That could get ugly."

"Yes," he said.

"If word gets out that the Dragon Heir is involving herself in—"

"Exactly."

I rubbed my chin. "They've just gotten over the last near-scandal with her. But I can see it. Norathar and Cawti—" it still gave me a twinge to say her name—"are friends. Norathar can't just let it alone."

"Precisely. And it's upset Aliera more than a little."

"She mentioned nothing about it to me."

He frowned. "I don't know the whole story, but it seems to me that when you last saw Aliera—"

"About two hours ago," I said.

He nodded. "It seems she had other things on her mind."

"Yeah, I suppose she did."

"And then you left rather abruptly."

"I suppose I did. Has anything been heard from Kiera the Thief in all this?"

His brows came together. "Why would it concern her?"

"No reason that I know of. Just wondering."

He shook his head.

I leaned back in my chair. "So, Aliera would like me to see if I can help out."

Mario nodded. "As long as you have returned to the area anyway."

"Yeah, as long as I'm here." I didn't quite roll my eyes. I said, "I admit that, in some ways, I'm in a position to help. At any rate, I know the principles rather well."

He nodded again.

"And I can't argue that the whole situation isn't my fault."

He nodded again, which was uncalled-for.

"But there's the issue that, if I stay around this area for more than a few hours, my life isn't worth a rusted copper."

"That's where we come to the new resources you are reputed to have."

Telnan twitched a little when he said that. He had, it seemed, mostly been lost during the entire conversation, but he must have guessed something about what we spoke of there.

I ignored him and said to Mario, "Not enough to take on the whole Jhereg, thank you very much."

"And an additional resource you may not know about."

"Oh?"

"Me," he said.

I stared off into space for a while. Then I said, "Sure you don't want something to eat?"

"Positive."

I nodded, and cleared my throat. "Uh . . . shall I call you Mario?"

"It's my name."

"Okay. Look. I have some idea of how good you are, but—"

"But?"

"We're talking about the whole Jhereg being after me."

"Not the whole Jhereg. Just the Right Hand, as it were."

"Oh, well, that's all right, then."

"And it's the Left Hand that is moving on South Adrilankha."

I stared at him. "The Bitch Patrol?"

He chuckled, as if he'd never heard the term before. "If you like."

"What do they want in South Adrilankha?"

"You'll have to ask them that."

I sat back, remembered my wine, and drank some. I don't remember how it tasted.

Loiosh said, *"Boss, this is all kinds of not good."*

"Thank you," I said, *"for the profound observation."*

I sat there and considered what I knew about the Left Hand of the Jhereg, which was not nearly as much as I should have known. The Right Hand, what I usually just called "the Jhereg," or "the Organization," was almost entirely male—Kiera, Cawti, and Norathar being exceptions—and it was involved in, well, all the stuff I knew: untaxed gambling, unlicensed prostitution, selling stolen goods, high-interest loans, and other fun things. I had known that the Left Hand, mostly women, existed; but I'd never been exactly clear on what they did. Well, that isn't completely true; I mean, I know if you need to purchase some artifact of Elder Sorcery, they're the ones to see. If you need a quick bit of sorcery to help you make someone dead or insure that he stays that way, you go to them. And if you need a piece of information that is only stored inside someone's head, then a Jhereg sorceress is your best bet.

But I also knew that couldn't be all the extent of their interests. What could they want in South Adrilankha?

"What else can you tell me?" I said at last.

He sighed and shook his head. "It's unfortunate, how little the Right Hand knows what the Left Hand is doing. I wish I could tell you more."

"Whatever details you have."

"Yes. Well, at this point, we know that the Dagger has been given warnings to leave South Adrilankha alone. So far as we know, they've taken no particular steps."

"How do you know it was the Left Hand delivering the warnings?"

He reached into his cloak. I tensed involuntarily and my hand twitched toward the stiletto I'd replaced in my boot. Telnan seemed to tense as well. Mario pretended not to notice, and emerged with a neat little square of paper, which he passed to me. The handwriting was simple and clean, almost without personality. It read, "We thank you for your interest in and contribution to this part of our city. Now that your work here is done, we hope you will accept our kind wishes for your continued good fortune and good health." It was signed, "Madam Triesco," and had the symbol of House Jhereg at the bottom.

"Madam Triesco?" I said. "Never heard of her."

"Nor have I." He shrugged.

"Yeah, well, I agree. It seems clear enough."

He nodded.

I drank a little more wine.

He said, "So, are you in?"

"Of course I'm in."

He nodded. "Aliera said you would be." He stood up. "Where will you be?"

"I could go to Castle Black, but I'm not in the mood to start another Dragon-Jhereg war. So how about Dzur Mountain?"

"That will be fine."

"Umm. . . ."

"Yes?"

"If I should wish to get in touch with you, is there any—?"

"Aliera will be able to find me."

"Uh, it is unlikely that I'll be able to reach Aliera."

"Oh?"

I tapped the chain I was wearing around my neck. "Well, as I see it, I won't want to remove these—"

"Oh, right."

He frowned for a moment, glanced at Telnan, then leaned across the table and whispered in my ear. Telnan politely pretended not to notice.

I sat back and stared at him.

"You're kidding."

He shook his head.

"Uh . . . I'm not sure if I need to kill someone."

"It would probably be a bad idea," he said.

"Yeah, well. All right. I have it. If I need to reach you, I know what to do."

He nodded and stood up. "I'll be in touch," he said. And, "Enjoy your meal," he added to both of us.

"We'll try," I answered for both of us. Telnan gave him a friendly smile.

As he walked away, Mihi approached, appearing from that place where waiters and creditors &c. There being nothing else to do at the moment, I turned my attention back to food.

1

DRY RED WINE

When Mario was gone I was able to concentrate on the wine. I will
deny being any sort of wine expert, but I liked it. It was dry, of course,
because sweet wines are for dessert, but it had all these hints under-
neath that made me think of grassy hills with orchards and wind
blowing through them and poetical stuff like that. Knowing what was
coming later in the meal, the wine was setting me up, trying to tell me
my mouth was safe, and that I shouldn't worry. Nasty, evil wine. I
don't know what Telnan thought about it; he didn't say anything at that
point, and I wasn't interested in conversation.

I had told Mario that he could find me at Dzur Mountain; now I
considered that. Did I have any other options? My grandfather was no
longer in the city, and I wouldn't have wanted to stay there anyway,
with the whole Jhereg after me. I'd been right about Castle Black. And
the idea of clapping at Cawti's door and saying, "Mind if I sleep on the
couch for a few weeks?" made my skin crawl. No, Dzur Mountain was
my only option.

Dzur Mountain.

Home of Sethra Lavode, the Enchantress, the Dark Lady. I don't
know, we'd always gotten along pretty well; she likely wouldn't mind.
And Telnan hadn't responded when I'd suggested it. It would at least
give me a safe place to stay while I figured out what to do.

*I'd do what I always did: figure out what was going on, come up
with a plan, and carry it out. No problem.*

Nasty, evil wine.

Some hours later, I got up from the table feeling pleased. More
than that, satiated, the way only an exceptional dinner, where all
the pieces come together, and each piece by itself is a work of art,
can make you feel. As I remarked to Loiosh, if they got to me
now, at least I'd managed to get in one good last meal. A very
good last meal. Loiosh suggested that that was just as well, as I
was too slow at the moment to save myself from an infant who attacked me with a perambulator. Uphill. I suggested he shut up.

Besides, Telnan was there to protect me, if he wasn't in the
same state.

I sent Loiosh and Rocza out the door ahead of me, to make
sure no perambulators were waiting. None were, so, after giving
and receiving warm good-byes from several of the staff and after I
paid the shot, including Telnan's, we stepped outside.

Nope, no one tried to kill me.

I looked around. It was late afternoon, and the world was
quiet and peaceful. Telnan said, "You're going to Dzur Mountain?"

I nodded.

"Shall I—?"

"Please."

I removed the chain from around my neck (long story), slid
it into a small box I carry just for that purpose, and nodded to
the Dzur. He nodded back, and then there was a slight tingle at
the base of my spine, accompanied by the odd sensation you always get when, in the space of a blink, the world looks different
around you. I stumbled a bit as the chill hit my skin and the
scent of evergreens filled my nose. Dzur Mountain was all about
me. A few years earlier, I wouldn't have been able to have that

spell performed on me without undoing everything that I'd just accomplished in Valabar's. But now—nothing but a bit of a stumble and a twitch. I replaced the chain around my neck, and when the stone lay against my skin pulsing in time to my heartbeat, I relaxed a bit. Safe.

Relatively safe.

Comparatively safe.

Safer.

"No one's around, Boss."

"Okay. Thanks, Loiosh. I guess Telnan didn't accompany us."

"I guess not. Uh, I know we're safe, Boss, but let's get inside anyway."

There was a slight coating of snow on the ground, so I left footprints leading up to the door. My friend Morrolan had doors that opened as you approached them. It was very impressive. I've never figured out about Sethra's doors: sometimes they opened, sometimes you had to clap, sometimes you had to search just to find them. On one occasion, I'd waited outside like an idiot for an hour and a half. I had intended to make some comment to Sethra on the subject, but somehow I never got around to it.

This time, the door didn't open, but neither was it locked. I walked in. I had been there just often enough to make me think I could find my way in without getting lost, but not often enough to actually do so. Loiosh, fortunately, had a better head for such things, and after a few twists and turns and smart-ass remarks from my guide of the moment, we were in one of Sethra's sitting rooms; the one where I'd first met her, in fact. It was a dark-painted, narrow room, remarkably bare, with comfortable chairs set at odd angles, as if Sethra preferred her guests not to look directly at each other. As I was coming in, I heard what sounded like bare feet running away, and I almost thought I heard a giggle, but I didn't give it too much of a thought. This was Dzur Mountain, where anything might happen and you could hurt your brain trying to figure out the little mysteries, let alone the big ones. I picked a chair and settled into it with a sigh.

Sethra's servant, whose name was Tukko, showed up, glanced at me with an expression that fell somewhere between disdain and disinterest, and said, "Would you like something, Lord Taltos?"

"No," I said. In the first place, I had the feeling that I would neither eat nor move again as long as I lived. And in the second, I wanted nothing to interfere with what was still lingering on my tongue. "But can you tell me if Sethra is about?"

He grunted. "She'll be along presently."

Tukko shuffled off, fingers twitching, without giving any sign that he cared either way. He was slightly bent as he walked, and there was a twitch in his right shoulder as well as his fingers. Every once in a while I wondered if it was all an act; if the old bastard was actually in perfect health. I'd never seen any indications of it, but I wondered from time to time. I closed my eyes and spent a while in happy reverie, recalling all of what Valabar's had just done for me.

I heard Sethra's footsteps, but didn't open my eyes. I knew what she looked like well enough that the only question would be the expression on her face, and if I guessed somewhere between sardonic amusement and mild surprise I'd probably have that down, too.

"Hello, Vlad. I hadn't expected to see you back so soon."

"I hope it isn't a problem," I said.

"Not in the least. How was Valabar's?"

"You can't improve upon perfection."

"And you made good decisions?"

"Easy decisions, all of them."

"I take it you decided to honor me with your presence while you recuperated?"

"Not exactly." I hesitated, not sure quite what I wanted to say.

I opened my eyes. Sethra was in front of me, looking like Sethra.
I was right about the expression, too. "You sent me protection."
      "Yes. I hope you aren't offended."
      "You know me better than that."
      She nodded. "I trust he was a good dinner companion."
      "An interesting one, certainly."
      "Oh?"
      "Dzurlords are more complex than I'd thought they were."
      "Vlad, everyone—"
      "Yeah, I know. But still."
      "What did you talk about?"
      "Many things. The food, for one. But also . . . Sethra, you
know Dzurlords."
      "I would say so, yes."
      "What I didn't get is, I don't know, how much work goes into
it all."
      "Yes. Don't feel bad, though. That confuses almost everyone
who isn't a Dzur. They think the Dzurlord only wishes for the excitement, or for the chance of a glorious death against impossible
odds. As you say, it's more complex."
      "Can you unravel the complexities?"
      "Why the interest?"
      "I don't know. Your friend, or rather, student, Telnan—he in-
terested me."
      She pulled one of her inscrutable Sethra smiles out of her
pocket and put it on.
      "So," I said, "if it isn't the excitement, or a chance for a glori-
ous death, what is it?"
      "Depends on the person. Some enjoy the righteous feeling of
being in a small minority."
      "Yeah. Those are the ones I want to smack."
      "And some just want to do the right thing."

"Lots of people want to do the right thing, Sethra. I try not to let them bother me too much."

"Dzurlords won't bother with the right thing unless everyone else is against it."

"Hmmm. I'm surprised I didn't see one or two defending the Easterners during the excitement a few years ago."

"In fact, it wouldn't have been impossible. What's so funny?"

"The idea of the Dzur hero defending the Teckla. The Empire would have hated it, the Guards would have hated it, the House of the Dzur would have hated it, and the Teckla would have hated it."

"Yes," said Sethra. "That's why it could have happened."

I mulled that over, then, "So," I said, "how is everyone else handling the aftermath of the excitement?"

"Who in particular?"

"Morrolan."

"Living, breathing, and returned to Castle Black."

"How did he take the news?"

"About Lady Teldra? Not well, Vlad."

I nodded and touched my fingers to the hilt again. And again I felt something—a presence that was at once comforting and distant.

"And Aliera?"

"She left with Morrolan."

I cleared my throat. "And the Empress?"

Sethra frowned. "What of her?"

"I was just wondering if she wanted to give me an Imperial dukedom for my heroic—"

"None of this is what you returned here for, Vlad."

"Yeah." Eventually I managed, "Something has come up."

"Oh? Tell me."

"I'm not certain I can."

She nodded. "The Northwestern tongue—that is, what we are at present speaking—is a head-last uninflected language, not perfectly capable of expressing all the nuances of emotion and familial connection that, for example, Seriolaa is; yet it can express fine distinctions in its own right, and, with time, a skilled speaker can usually convey the sense of his intention."

It took me a moment to realize that she was turning my bait; I suppose the meal had slowed my thinking some. Eventually, I said, "It's a Jhereg matter, and a personal matter."

Living as long as she had, she had somewhere learned the value of silence. I thought I had, too, but she was better at it than I was.

At last I said, "Cawti. South Adrilankha."

"Ah," she said. "Yes. I think, with what my sources in the Jhereg tell me, I can start to put it together."

I didn't make any remarks about what her "sources in the Jhereg" might be. She said, "How did you hear of it?"

"Mario," I said.

She gave me an eyebrow. "I see."

Of course, she must have made the same connection I did: Mario to Aliera to Norathar to Cawti; but she saw no reason to mention it. "What are you going to do?"

"I'd ask for your advice, except I don't think you'd give me any, and I'm probably too stubborn to take it even if you did."

"Correct on both counts. Have you been in touch with any of your people?"

"Sethra, you *are* my people now. You, and Morrolan, and Aliera. And Kiera, of course."

Sethra Lavode looked vaguely uncomfortable for a moment. This doesn't happen every day. "You must have some contacts in the Jhereg who are still willing to talk to you."

"The ones I could trust are the ones I wouldn't do that to."

"Do what to?"

"Put in an awkward position by asking them to help me."

"Even with information?"

I grunted. "I'll think about it. Where did you find the Dzur?"

"Telnan? Iceflame found him."

"Oh."

"Or, rather, Iceflame found his weapon."

"Do I want to know?"

"Yes, but I don't want to tell you."

"What if I torture it out of you?"

"That isn't as funny as you think it is."

"But you are resurrecting the Lavodes, it seems?"

"Slowly, yes. Why? Think they might be useful for your problem?"

I gave her a short laugh. Loiosh was strangely silent; I guess he knew what was going on better than I did. So did Sethra. Chances are, so did the owner of the pawnshop on Taarna Road.

"So, how are you, Sethra?"

She said, "Vlad, I've been alive for a long, long time, however you choose to measure time."

"Well, yes."

"I have learned patience."

"I imagine so."

"I can sit here as long as necessary, but don't you want to get around to asking about whatever it is that's on your mind?"

I sighed and nodded.

"Tell me about Cawti," I said.

"Ahhh," she said.

"You didn't know what I was going to ask about?"

"I should have."

I nodded.

"Well, what do you want to know, exactly?"

"Start with, how is her health?"

She frowned. "I don't see her often. Fine, so far as I know."

"Who does see her?"

"Norathar."

"That's all?"

"At least, among those I know."

I nodded. "And who sees Norathar?"

"Aliera."

"Okay. And I suppose, if I'm going to see Aliera, there's no way to avoid Morrolan?"

"You wish to avoid Morrolan?"

I touched the hilt of Lady Teldra by way of explanation. As I did so, I felt something, like a pleasant breeze with a hint of the ocean blowing across the face of my soul. And, yes, I know how stupid that sounds. Well, you try getting that feeling and see if you can do a better job of describing it.

"If you'd like, I will ask the Lady Aliera if she is available to visit me."

"I'd appreciate that."

She nodded, and her face went blank for about a minute.

"Well?" I said when she looked at me once more.

She nodded.

About two minutes later Aliera came floating into the room. Well, walking or floating or some combination; her gown, a silvery one with black lacing about the neck and shoulders, dragged along the ground, so I couldn't tell if her means of locomotion were a graceful walk or a jerky levitation. On her lips was a smile. At her side was Pathfinder. In her arms was a fluffy white cat.

She kissed Sethra on the cheek, then turned to me. "Hello, Vlad. How good to see you. How long has it been? Four, five hours?"

"Thanks for stopping by, Aliera. Did she tell you what I wanted to ask you about?"

"No," they both said at once.

I nodded. "I need to find my . . . I need to find Cawti."

"Why?" said Aliera. She was still smiling, but a bit of frost had crept into her voice.

"Jhereg trouble," I said. "You don't want to know about it. You know, Dragon honor and all that."

She ignored the barb and said, "Cawti is no longer involved with the Jhereg."

"Actually, she is. That's the trouble. Or maybe she needs to be involved in them to keep from being involved with them; that might be a better way to put it."

She frowned. "Vlad—"

"Here it comes, Boss. Her hands would be on her hips if she weren't holding that cat."

"I know, I know."

"You vanish for years, then suddenly show up, lose our friend's soul in a weapon, make my mother fear for her existence, threaten the very fabric of creation, and now you want to stir up trouble between the woman you walked out on and the gang of criminals she's managed to extricate herself from? Is that what I'm hearing?"

Well, I suppose some of that was partly true, from a certain perspective. From my perspective, of course, it was so far wrong that you couldn't find right on the same map.

"That's about it, yes," I said.

"Okay. Just checking," said Aliera. She stroked her cat. Loiosh made some sort of remark in my head that didn't quite form itself into words.

I said, "Does that mean you'll tell me how I can reach Cawti?"

"No."

I sighed.

"However," she said. "I'll let her know you wish to speak with her."

"When!?"

"Is it urgent?"

I started to say something witty, tossed it away, and said, "I'm not sure. There are things going on, and, well, they could take forever, or blow up an hour from now. That's part of the problem; I don't know enough."

She nodded. "Very well. I'll be seeing her and Norathar later this evening. I'll mention it then. But how can she reach you when you're wearing that, that thing you wear?"

She was referring, of course, to my Phoenix Stone, hanging from the chain about my neck. "If Sethra doesn't mind, I'll just stay here, and she can let Sethra know."

Sethra nodded.

"Very well," said Aliera. Then she said, "Sethra, there are things we should discuss."

I moaned softly, and they both looked at me.

I said, "If you're implying I should move, I'm not certain I can."

Aliera frowned again; then her face cleared and she said, "Oh, Valabar's. How was it?"

"Beyond all praise."

"I should eat there sometime."

She had never . . . ? I stared at her, but words failed me. Maybe she was lying.

"Come, Aliera," said Sethra. "Let's take a walk."

They did, and I took a nap—one of those naps where you don't actually fall asleep, you just lie there, filled with food, a stupid smile on your face.

Yeah, sometimes I love life.

"Hello Vlad," said Cawti. "I'm sorry to wake you, but I was told you wished to speak with me."

"I wasn't sleeping," I said.

"Of course not."

She looked good. She'd gained a few pounds here and there, but they were pleasing pounds. She was wearing a gray shirt with long, sharp collars, and maroon trousers that tapered down to her pointed black boots. She carried a dagger with a plain leather-wrapped hilt, but no other weapons that I could spot. And I'm good at spotting weapons.

"Mind if I sit down?"

"Uh, I hadn't known you needed my permission."

Loiosh and Rocza were both twitching.

"*Go ahead.*"

"*You sure?*"

"*Yeah.*"

He flew over to her hand and rubbed his face on hers. She smiled and said hello to him. After a moment, Rocza flew over and landed on her shoulder. She scratched and cooed at them. It was obvious she'd missed them. I could have felt good and sorry for myself if I'd wanted to.

She said, "I heard about your hand."

I glanced at it. "From?"

"Kiera."

I nodded. "Nice to know you're still in touch with her."

She nodded. "How did it happen, exactly?"

"Kiera?"

"The finger," she said, without cracking a smile.

"I went back East for visit, and forgot to pack it when I returned."

"Have you actually been back East again?"

I nodded. "I learned to ride a horse, but not to enjoy doing so."

That got a bit of smile. Then she said, "So, what's on your mind?"

"South Adrilankha."

"You've heard about that?"

"Yeah."

"From Aliera, no doubt."

"Indirectly."

"So, let me guess, you're going to come into town and save me like a Dzur rescuing a helpless maiden."

"That isn't exactly what I had in mind." Actually, it had been pretty much spot-on, damn her. "Are you going to claim that everything is fine, and you don't need any help?"

"Just what help can you offer, Vlad? And I don't mean that rhetorically."

She called me "Vlad." She used to call me "Vladimir."

"I know people. Some of them will still be willing to do things for me."

"Like what? Kill you? You know how much of a price the Jhereg has on your head?"

"Uh . . . no. How much?" Odd that it hadn't occurred to me to wonder at the exact amount.

"Well, I'm not sure, actually. A lot though."

"I suppose. But, yeah, there are people I can ask questions of, at least." Before she could answer, I said, "So, how are things with you?"

"Well enough. And you?"

I made a sort of non-committal sound. She nodded, and said, "Have I grown a wart?"

"Hm?"

"You keep looking at me, and then looking away."

"Oh."

Loiosh flew back to me. Cawti scratched Rocza behind the head.

"You're in trouble," I said.

She nodded.

"I can help."

"I hate that. What?"

"Nothing. I thought you'd been about to say . . . never mind. The fact is, I *can* help."

"I don't hate you, Vlad."

"Good. Does that mean I should go ahead?"

Tukko came in then, and asked if we wanted anything. We both said, "Klava," and Cawti said, "Extra cream in his, but not much honey. You know how I take mine."

Tukko grunted as if to say either he knew how we both took ours, or that we'd take them as he made them and be happy.

"I hate it that I need your help," she said.

"You said that already. I understand."

I got up and paced, because I think better that way. She said, "What is it, worried, or unhappy?"

"Because I'm pacing?"

"Because your shoulders are hunched forward, and you're slouching. That means worried or miserable."

"Oh." I sat down again. But she could probably tell things about how I sat, too. "Both, I guess. Worried about whether you'll let me help you, unhappy that you don't want me to."

"I don't suppose I could convince you to charge me for the service?"

I started to laugh, then stopped. "Actually, yes. There is a fee I could suggest."

She gave me the look someone gives you who knows you very well, and she waited.

"A piece of information," I said.

"And that is?"

"Tell me what that look meant."

"What look?"

"When I mentioned South Adrilankha."

She frowned. "I can't imagine what look I could have given you."

"It looked like relief."

"Relief?"

"Yes. Like you were afraid I was going to mention something else."

"Oh," she said.

For a while, neither of us spoke.

Tukko returned with our klava. Once, long ago, I had asked Sethra how old he was, and she'd said, "Younger than me."

He set the klava down and turned away. I said, "Tell me, Tukko, how old *is* Sethra, exactly?"

"Younger than me," he said, and shuffled out again.

I should have predicted that.

Cawti drank some of her klava.

"Do you wish payment in advance?" she said at last.

"It doesn't matter."

She bit her lip. "What if I say it's too much?"

I shrugged. "I don't know. I'll do it anyway."

She nodded. "Yes, I expected that's what you'd say."

Loiosh rubbed his head against my neck.

Three sips (for her) later, she said, "All right. Go ahead."

Suddenly, I had something to do. Maybe, if I were lucky, I'd have someone to kill. I felt better right away.

"Let's start with names," I said.

"Name," said Cawti. "I only have one."

"Madam Triesco."

She stared at me. "Aliera didn't know that."

"I said the information came from her indirectly. My source—"

"Who?"

"Does it matter?"

She continued staring at me in that way she had—not squinting, but with her eyelids just a little lowered. I knew that look.

"Okay," I said. "It matters. But I'd prefer not to say just now."

"Was it your friend Kiera?"

"As I said, I'd just as soon not say."

After a moment, she gave me a terse nod. "Okay," she said. "Yes. Triesco."

"What do you know of her?"

"The name," said Cawti.

"Do you know she's Left Hand?"

She shrugged. "I assumed, just because it's a she."

"Okay. Where, exactly, do operations stand in South Adrilankha?"

She winced. "Out of control," she said.

"You have people?"

"No, I let them go. I tried to shut it down, and—"

"Yeah, I heard. Any of them you can get back aboard?"

"None that I'm willing to."

I knew that tone; I didn't even consider arguing. "Okay," I said. "I'll do a little checking around."

"If you were to get yourself hurt doing this, I would hate it a lot."

"So would I."

"Don't joke about it."

"You know, that's a much more difficult request than merely taking on the Left Hand of the Jhereg."

A corner of her mouth twitched a bit.

"One small victory, Loiosh."

"If you say so, Boss."

She said, "I've been hearing stories."

"Of?"

"You. Jenoine. Lady Teldra."

Almost involuntarily, my hand brushed across the hilt of the long, slim dagger at my side. Yes, she was still there. "They're probably true," I said. "More or less."

"Is Lady Teldra dead?"

"Not exactly."

She frowned.

"You were involved in a battle with Jenoine?"

"More of a scrap than a battle," I said. "But yeah, I guess that part is true."

"How did it happen?"

"I've been wondering the same thing. A series of accidents, I suppose."

She drank some more klava, and gave me her slow, contemplative look. "I'm not sure what to talk to you about anymore."

"Oh, I don't know. It shouldn't be that difficult. Say something about oppressed Easterners to put me on the defensive. That should work."

Her eyes narrowed, but she didn't say anything.

"Okay," I said. "Maybe I should just be about this business. That will give you time to think up a subject of conversation."

She didn't say anything.

I stood up. Even now, hours later and after a nap, it was something of an effort. I hoped no one attacked me; I'd be slow.

"You're always—"

"Shut up, Loiosh."

"Okay, Cawti. I'll be in touch."

"Do," she said.

I left the room without ceremony, or a backward glance, mostly because I didn't trust myself to say anything. After a bit of searching, I found Tukko. "Would you be good enough to ask Sethra if she'll do a teleport for me?"

He didn't quite scowl.

I have a small backpack I travel with, which contains a spare shirt, some socks, undergarments, and a couple of different cloaks that I switch between depending on the weather and other factors. I unrolled the gray one, and filled it with a few weapons that Morrolan had dug up for me the day before. I put it on, made sure it was hanging right, and took a deep breath.

Sethra came in and nodded to me. I took the amulet off and put it away.

"Good luck," she said.

I nodded.

An instant later I was standing at the east end of the Chain Bridge, in South Adrilankha.

2

GARLIC BREAD

Mihi told me what Mr. Valabar had prepared that evening. *Of course,
that evening was early afternoon, but let's not worry about trifles. It
was house pepper stew, brisket of beef, Ash Mountain potatoes, roast
kethna stuffed with Fenarian sausages, anise-jelled winneasourus steak,
and triple onion beef. Then he stepped back a bit and waited. I had always been puzzled by this behavior, until I realized that he was giving us
time to think about it, while being available to answer questions.

"What do you recommend?" Telnan asked me.

"Anything. It's all good."

I ate some of the garlic bread.

"Langosh" isn't like anything else in the world. My grandfather
makes it too. Loyalty demands I say my grandfather makes it better, but
we won't stress the point.

It consists of a small, round loaf of slightly, very slightly, sweet
bread that has been deep-fried. It's served with a clove of garlic. You
bite the garlic in half, then coat the bread with it, burning your fingers
just a little. Then you take a bite of the garlic, then you wait, and, as
it's exploding in your mouth, you take a bite of the bread. It's all in the
timing.

I decided on the brisket of beef, Telnan ordered the roast. We told
Mihi, who smiled as if we were the cleverest two customers he'd ever

had. Telnan studied my technique with the bread, copied it, and broke out in a delighted grin.

A Dzurlord with a big grin on his face. Very odd. But I was glad he liked the food.

"So," I said, picking up the conversation from some time before. "You're studying wizardry? Good. Maybe you can tell me just what a wizard is, then. I've been wondering for some time."

He grinned like his schoolmaster had just asked him the very question he had prepared for. "Wizardry," he said, "is the art of uniting with and controlling disparate forces of nature to produce results unavailable from, or more difficult to obtain with, any single arcane discipline."

"Ah," I said. "Well. I see. Thank you very much."

"You're welcome," he said, sounding sincere. "What do you do?"

"Hmmm?"

"Well, I'm a wizard. What do you do?"

"Oh." I thought about it. "I run in terror, mostly."

He laughed. Evidently, he didn't believe me. Probably just as well; if he had, he'd have been required to be scornful, and then I'd have been required to kill him, and Sethra might not like that. It did, however, effectively kill the conversation.

I took another bite of garlic, waited for the explosion, then the bread. Perfect. Each bite of garlic was like a new discovery, exciting even in its confusion; each bite of bread the epiphany that completes it. And the combination took me away from all that had happened in the last few years, and into that time when things were simpler. Of course, they were never really simpler, but, looking back on them now, my senses filled with garlic and fresh bread, it seems like things were simpler then.

$\mathcal{B}$

Stepping off the Chain Bridge was also a step into the past, as it were. It made me think of a time before I had met Cawti, before I had begun working for the Jhereg, when I was just an Easterner, living along Lower Kieron Road, but walking across this bridge, or else along the waterfront to Carpenter, several times a week to visit my grandfather. My grandfather no longer lived here; now he lived in a manor house just outside of the town of Miska, near Lake Szurke. I'd visited him once a couple of years ago; I decided I should probably do so again, if I could get this matter settled without becoming dead.

My memory told me that all of South Adrilankha stinks all of the time. That isn't really true. You have to reach the Easterners' quarter to get the smell, and the Easterners' quarter is a large part of South Adrilankha, but by no means all of it.

I took the roads that were as familiar to my feet as langosh was to my tongue, though nowhere near as pleasant.

It was a little chilly in Adrilankha, but the cloak kept the ocean breeze off me. Loiosh and Rocza shifted on my shoulder; I could feel them looking around.

I tapped the hilt of my rapier, just to reassure myself that it was there. Lady Teldra hung just in front of it.

My boots were a fine, soft darr skin; quite comfortable, and good for walking across grasslands, and even feeling your way carefully along rocky mountain passes; but they didn't suit the stone streets of Adrilankha. My old boots, however, were gone with my old life.

I made it to Six Corners, which is as much the heart of the Easterners' district as anywhere, and looked around. I was surrounded by humans, by my own kind; I felt the easing of a tension I hadn't known was there. Even being by yourself isn't quite the same as having your own people around you.

Now, it's never been all that clear who my *own people* are, but I'm telling it to you as it felt at the time.

Six Corners is, as they say, no place to found a dynasty. I'm told that, before the Interregnum, it was an area frequented by the higher class of merchant, but it was destroyed by fire and never rebuilt. As no one wanted it, the Easterners moved in, migrating from, well, from the East. After that, it was built up slowly and haphazardly; no one cared what happened there, or what things looked like. Or, for that matter, who did what to whom. The patrols by the Phoenix Guards were cursory during the day, and non-existent at night. Not, I suspect, because they were scared to be there; just because they didn't much care what happened.

A few walls that had once been painted green, a roof that was sagging in the middle, and a doorway covered by a torn burlap curtain led the way into the abode of the finest bootmaker in South Adrilankha, maybe in the Empire. Since this wasn't Valabar's, Jakoub stared at me with undisguised astonishment, before saying, "Lord Taltos! You're back!"

I agreed that I was. "How are things, Jakoub?" I knew it was a mistake the instant the words were out of my mouth.

"Well enough, Lord Taltos. We've had a bit of rain, you know, and that always means an increase in custom. And Nickolas injured his hand, a few weeks ago, and still isn't able to work, so most of his regulars are coming to me now. Of course, Lady Ciatha has chosen to let half her land lie fallow for the season, so I'm not getting any—"

"Good to hear," I said, before he could get really warmed up.

He took the hint, praise be to Verra. "How are you, my lord?"

"Well enough, thanks."

He glanced down at my feet. "What are those?"

"Darr skin," I said. "I've been spending a lot of time walking through wilderness."

"Ah, I see. And, because it's the wilderness, your arches won't collapse? Your heel won't callus? Your instep—"

"Do you still have my measurements?"

He looked hurt. "Of course."

"Then make me something suitable for travel outdoors or on paved streets."

He looked thoughtful. "For the soles, I can—"

"I want to wear them, not hear about them." I tossed him enough silver to make up for the second hurt look.

He cleared his throat. "Now, uh, your special needs. . . ."

"Not as much as in the past. Just a knife in each, about this size." I made one appear and showed it to him.

"Can I keep it?"

I set it on the counter.

"Nothing else? Are you certain?"

"Nothing else for the boots, but I also need a new sheath for my rapier. The last one you made for me was, uh, damaged."

He came around the counter, bent over, and inspected it. "It's been horribly bent. And the tip's been cut off. What happened?"

"It got stuck in me."

He stared at me, I think wanting to ask how that had happened but not daring. I said, "It was an apprentice physicker, and I have no clear memory of just what he did or why, but I guess it worked."

"Eh . . . yes, m'lord. The new sheath—"

"Use the same design."

"And all of the additions?"

"May as well."

"Very good, m'lord." He bowed very low.

"How long will it take?"

"Four days."

I raised an eyebrow.

"Day after tomorrow."

I nodded. "Good. Now let's chat."

"M'lord?"

"Close up the shop, Jakoub. We have to talk."

He turned just the least bit pale, though I had never, in our long acquaintance, either harmed or threatened him. I guess word gets out. I waited.

He coughed, shuffled past me, and hung a ribbon across the door. Then he led the way into his back room, filled with leather, leather smells, oils, and oil smells.

Jakoub had a full head of black hair, brushed back like a Dragaeran trying to show off a noble's point (which Jakoub didn't have). I've never been able to determine if it's a hairpiece, or his own hair that he dyes. He was missing a couple of lower teeth, which was made more noticeable by a protruding jaw. His eyebrows were wispy gray, in sharp contrast to his hair, and his ears were small. His fingers were short and always dirty.

He pulled out the one stool and offered it to me. I sat down. He said, "My lord?"

I nodded. "Who has been running things, Jakoub?"

"My lord?"

I gave him Patented Jhereg Look Number Six. He melted, more or less. "You mean, who collects for the game here?"

I smiled at him. "That is exactly what I mean, Jakoub. Well?"

"I deliver it to a nice young gentleman of your House. His name is Fayavik."

"And who does he deliver it to?"

"My lord? I wouldn't know—"

He cut off as I leaned toward him just a little.

Before I'd shown up to run things, Jakoub had had a piece of everything that happened around Six Corners, and had ears that extended even farther. His piece might be smaller now, but it was still there. And his ears would still be in place. I knew it, and he knew I knew it.

He nodded a little. "All right," he said. "A few weeks ago, everything changed. More of you—that is, more Jhereg showed up, and—"

"Men or women?"

He frowned. "Men, m'lord."

"All right."

"And they started, well, just being around more. It made all of my friends nervous, so I started asking questions."

"Uh huh."

"It seems there was someone else in charge. Someone from the City."

I nodded. "The City" was how people in South Adrilankha referred to the part of Adrilankha north of the river. Or, well, west of the river.

"I've heard," he said, "that there is some group called the Strangers Group that gets the money."

"Named for Stranger's Road, or some other reason?"

"Stranger's Road. They work out of a private house there."

"Whose house?"

"I don't know."

I gave him the narrowed-eyed quick glance, and he said, "I really don't. It used to belong to an old lady named Coletti, but she died last year, and I don't know who bought it."

"Okay," I said.

It's funny how my mind works: it at once jumped to who I could get to bribe the appropriate clerk to check ownership records, forgetting that, well, I didn't have any "who"s anymore. After being gone for years, I was only back for one day and I was thinking like a Jhereg again.

This could be good or bad.

All right, now I knew the place. What next? Check it out? Sure, why not? What could possibly happen?

"*You're starting to second-guess yourself, Boss. Careful.*"

"*Yeah. I'm not used to this sort of thing anymore. Crime requires constant practice.*"

"*Write that down to pass on to your successors. In the meantime—*"

"*Yeah.*" Point taken.

"What about collections?"

"My lord?"

"Do runners go to them, or do they send a bagman?"

"Oh. Runners go to the house. That's what I do."

"Are runners going there every day, or just once a week?"

"Every day, m'lord."

I nodded and considered a bit more. They certainly weren't making a secret of what they were up to. Did they want someone coming after them, or was it just that they felt so secure that they didn't care? Or were they doing it in order to be seen to be doing it?

That way lieth the headache.

"Okay," I said. "Oh. About those boots. . . ."

"Yes, m'lord. Warm in the cold, but let the air in. Soft, comfortable above all, good support. I can put in enchantments to ward against blisters as well. That will help when you break them in."

I nodded.

"Day after tomorrow, my lord."

I touched the hilt of Lady Teldra and gave him as warm a smile as I could manage, which probably wasn't very. Hey, I get credit for trying, don't I?

Jakoub held the curtain aside for me. Loiosh flew out and scanned the area quickly, let me know it was safe, then returned to my shoulder as I stepped outside. The curtain closed behind me, taking away the smells of leather and oils and returning the smells of South Adrilankha, about which the less said the better.

The walk to Stranger's Road was short. I stopped in front of a dirty gray pawnshop forty or fifty yards shy of the place, and looked it over. The house was a three-story old red stonework thing, with a wraparound wooden porch that seemed to have been an afterthought. It had a pair of glass windows on each of the first two floors, and a single one on the top story.

I leaned against the pawnshop and practiced patience. It was evening, just shy of darkness. Over at Six Corners, things would be just starting to get busy with the usual nighttime activity; here there were few pedestrians, just an old man walking a short, ugly dog and a few children kneeling on the street intent on some game or another.

"Loiosh?"

"We're on our way."

They left my shoulders and flew up, making a spiral above the house, then slowly circling around it, lower, then lower again, then returned.

"No activity, Boss. And all the windows are curtained." He sounded mildly offended.

"I'll speak to them about that."

The "no activity" part changed abruptly. The door opened, and someone in Jhereg gray—someone Dragaeran and female—stepped onto the porch. She stood there, with something like a rod in her right hand, and looked about the street. I pulled myself in close to the pawnshop, so I could no longer see the house, which meant she couldn't see me. Loiosh peeked his head out from around the corner.

"What's she doing, Loiosh?"

"Just looking around. Oh, and now she's making gestures with that stick."

"What sort of gestures?"

"Small ones. She makes a little circle, changes direction a bit, then—she's moving around the side of the porch now. She's out of sight."

"Well, I think we've established two things, at any rate. The Left Hand is, indeed, controlling this area, and they can tell when I'm nearby. Unless you want to chalk it up to coincidence that she came out right now."

"How could they tell, Boss? They shouldn't be able—"

"Lady Teldra," I said.

"Oh."

Even I am aware whenever a Morganti weapon is nearby, unless it is in a sheath that dampens the psychic effect of the thing. With a weapon as powerful as Lady Teldra, yeah, any skilled sorcerer would be sensitive enough to at least be aware that there was something in the area.

"You know, Boss, this is going to mess with your general sneakiness."

"Yep. I'll have to see about an improved scabbard for her, or something."

"Another one just came out. Time to make an exit?"

"Or an entrance."

"Boss?"

"Don't worry. It's tempting, but not yet. I need to know more."

"Good. I was going to start worshiping Crow."

"Crow?"

"His dominion is things that fall."

"Where did you pick up that bit of information?"

"A few minutes ago, passing by a shrine. I heard some people talking."

"I never knew."

"You're pretty distracted."

"I prefer to call it 'concentrating.' "

"Whatever you say, Boss."

"Okay, let's move."

We didn't speak during the long walk across the river. I suppose the visit had been productive; I'd at least confirmed that the Left Hand was, indeed, running things. And I'd ordered boots and a new scabbard for my rapier.

I walked along the right-hand side of the Chain Bridge while the water swirled under me. I glanced upriver, speculating on who and what might live there; all of those people being born, living, and dying along its banks. Maybe, if I lived through this, that's where I'd go next; just follow the river and see where it brought me. The East Bank, of course.

When the two miles or so of the bridge were behind me, I found a cabriolet and had myself brought north to a district that overlooked the docks. A few miles away, on the other side of the river, were the slaughterhouses; on this side were houses: public, private, and ware, as well as the stalls of the poorer craftsmen and the shops of the more prosperous ones.

It was becoming dark as I entered a house whose sign depicted a ship's lantern hanging from a mast. There would, I suspected, be a lot of Orca in here. There were a lot of Orca in all the taverns in this part of Adrilankha, so it wasn't a terribly daring guess.

It was a long, narrow room. I spotted a door on the far end that would, no doubt, lead to smaller rooms. Near the door was a small raised area for musicians. And standing near it was a pale-looking Dragaeran in blue and white, holding some sort of instrument with lots of strings and an oddly curved body.

Years before I had made a deal with the Minstrels' Guild; expensive, but one of the smarter things I'd done. You don't need to hear the whole conversation. I showed him a ring I carry, asked him a couple of questions, got a couple of answers, and slipped him some coins. Then it was out the door quickly, before some of those looks I was getting from the assembled Orca turned themselves into action which would result in more attention than I cared for.

I followed the musician's directions, which took me west a bit less than a mile. I want to say something like, "No one tried to kill me," just to let you know that the whole being killed thing was never far from my mind; but it'll be played out pretty fast, so if I don't say anything about it, you can assume I didn't get killed.

This house, marked by a newly painted sign showing a sleeping dog, was a bit larger than the last and more nearly square. The stage was off to the left, and the fellow I was looking for was standing next to it, holding a wide, curved drum.

"Aibynn," I said after the twenty steps or so between the doorway and the stage.

He blinked a couple of times, as if the word were in some foreign language, then gave me a smile. "Hey, Vlad," he said. "I got a new drum."

"Yeah," I told him. "That's why I came back."

"Oh? You've been away?"

"Uh, yeah."

Aibynn was thin even for the thin Dragaerans, and as tall as Morrolan. He was not native to the Empire; I'd met him on an island while involved in a complicated business involving a god, a king, an empress, political conspiracies, and other sundry entertainments. Of all the Dragaerans I'd ever met, he was the one I understood the least, but also one of the few I was certain had no interest in using me for his purposes.

We found a table and sat down. A barmaid gave him something clear, batted her eyelashes at him, and then remembered to ask if I wanted anything. I didn't.

Aibynn said, "You sticking around for the show? I'm playing with this guy—"

"Probably not," I said. "To tell you the truth, I don't actually like music."

"Yeah, neither do I," said Aibynn.

"No, I mean it," I said.

He nodded. "Yeah, me too."

Aibynn was a musician. I wasn't.

I said, "It's not like I'm tone-deaf or anything. And, I mean, there are some things I like. Simple tunes, that you can hum, with words that are kind of clever. But most things that people call real music—"

"Yeah," said Aibynn. "Sometimes I want to be just done with the whole thing." As he spoke, his fingers were drumming on the tabletop. I don't mean tapping, like I might do if I were bored,

I mean drumming—making complex rhythms, and doing rolls, and trills. He seemed entirely unaware of what his fingers were doing. But then, Aibynn usually seemed entirely unaware of most of what was going on.

"I don't think he's going to get it, Boss," said my familiar.

"I think you're right, Loiosh."

"Anyway," I said, "I actually came because there are some questions I wanted to ask you."

"Oh." He said it as if it had never before occurred to him that he might know the answer to any conceivable question. "All right."

"You used to go to South Adrilankha fairly often. Do you still?"

His eyes widened slightly, but from him that didn't mean much. "Yes, I do. The Easterners have an instrument called—"

"Is this guy bothering you?"

We both glanced up. A particularly ugly specimen of Orca-hood was speaking to Aibynn. Funny how differently people react to you when you aren't dressed as a Jhereg.

Aibynn frowned at the fellow, as if he had to translate. I reached for my rapier, but my hand came in contact with the hilt of Lady Teldra instead. I leaned back in my chair, and waited for Aibynn to answer.

He said, "No, no. We're friends."

The Orca gave him an odd look, started to say something, then shrugged and shuffled off. Five years ago, there would have been blood on the floor. Ten years ago, there would have been a body. I guess I'd changed.

I returned my attention to Aibynn.

"Do you know the area called Six Corners?"

He nodded. "I used to play at a place there called, uh, I don't know what it's called. But, yeah."

"Good. That was going to be my next question."

"What was?"

"Never mind. Tell me about the place."

"Well, the acoustics are really nice because—"

"No, no. Uh . . ."

Eventually I managed to get the information I wanted, and even to communicate what I wanted him to do. He shrugged and agreed because he had no reason not to. I got out of the place without any untoward incidents, and slipped around behind it to give myself time to figure out my next move.

"Think that's going to do any good, Boss?"

"Any reason not to have it set up, just in case?"

"Well, no, I guess not. Rocza is hungry."

"Already?"

"Boss, it's been hours."

"But it was Valabar's. Doesn't that count extra?"

"I'm sure it does in some ways they've found you, Boss."

"Huh?"

"Boss, someone just found you."

"How . . . what?"

"I don't know. I felt something. You're being looked at."

"Through you?"

"I don't know."

As we were talking, I was moving—walking as quickly as I could without appearing to rush. I passed a few tradesmen and Teckla, none of whom paid any attention to me. I turned right onto a street whose name I didn't know.

I carried a charm that prevented anyone from finding me by sorcery. I was also protected against witchcraft, just on the off-chance the Jhereg would use it. There are other arcane disciplines, to be sure, but could they be used to track me? I wished I knew more.

Sethra Lavode had once located Loiosh. That was one possibility. But there weren't many Sethra Lavodes in the world. Could they have tracked Lady Teldra, even inside her sheath? If I were given to muttering, I'd have muttered.

Loiosh and Rocza took off from my shoulders, to keep an eye on things from above, and so that, if it was Loiosh who had been located, I wouldn't be in his immediate proximity. I guess it was having the Bitch Patrol on my mind, but I kept seeing visions of some sorceress showing up in front of me and blasting me to pieces before I could move.

Okay, I had three choices. I could find an alley where they had to come at me from one direction, and wait. I could gamble that I could remove the amulet and complete a teleport before they showed up. Or I could keep moving until I thought of something else.

I went for option three.

I took another street to the left, and wished I still had Spellbreaker.

Well, that was silly. I did still have Spellbreaker.

I reached past my rapier, gripped Lady Teldra, and drew her.

Then I stared at her.

Like me, she had changed.

3

SHAMY

I slipped Loiosh and Rocza the remains of the bread (neither expressed any interest in the garlic) as Mihi brought the shamy. I've never come across shamy anywhere but Valabar's, and I have no clue how it is made. It is mostly ice, crushed or chopped very fine, flavored, and with, well, with something else in there so it holds together. Maybe a cream of some kind, maybe egg. The flavor is very subtle, but reminds me of certain wines that Morrolan favors—wines that tingle on your tongue. Shamy has no such tingle, but it does have just a bit of the flavor.

"Who was that fellow, Vlad?"

"Hmmm?"

"That fellow who came in before and sat with us."

"Oh. That was Mario."

"I got his name, but who is he?"

"Mario Greymist. You never heard of him?"

He shook his head.

"He, uh . . . he's a Jhereg."

"I saw that. But I was polite to him. Did you notice?"

"Yes. It showed great restraint."

Telnan smiled.

"You notice I kept my face straight, Loiosh?"

"Yeah, Boss. It showed great restraint."

"So, why would I have heard of him?"

"The story is, he assassinated the Emperor right before the Inter-regnum."

"Oh! That Mario." He frowned. "I thought he'd been killed."

"I guess not. Or else it didn't take."

He nodded.

The shamy melted on my tongue, taking with it the taste of the garlic, but not the memory.

The idea, as Vili explained it to me long ago, is to keep your mouth from lingering too long on what has just happened; to prepare your senses for what comes next.

Telnan seemed to like it. I know I did.

A good meal, you see, is all about unexpected delight: it's one thing for food to simply "taste good," but a real master can make it taste good in a way that surprises you. And for that to work, you have to start from a place where you can permit yourself to be surprised. And, interestingly enough, the person eating has to cooperate for that to really be successful.

I'm a decent cook. I'm an outstanding eater.

ᛒ

For a long time—say, three or four seconds—I forgot that I was being pursued, and just stared at Lady Teldra; even the sensations that rushed through me from having her in my hand took second place to looking at her.

A long, long time ago—about thirteen hours, more or less—I had held in my hand a long, slim Morganti knife, and with it, I had undergone, uh, certain experiences that had transformed it into what those with a flair for the over-dramatic called God-slayer and I called Lady Teldra. But it had been a long, slim Morganti dagger.

She didn't *feel* any different; she still caressed my hand the way shamy caressed my tongue. But she was no longer a long knife; now she was a smaller knife, about ten inches of blade, wide, with a slight curve to her; a knife-fighter's weapon. I'm no knife-fighter. Well, I mean, I can defend myself with one if I have to, but—

"Boss!"

Someone was standing about thirty yards in front of me. How she'd gotten there, I don't know; there is slight shimmering in the air the instant before an individual arrives from a teleport, and a sort of aura effect for a second or two afterward. I didn't see anything like that. Maybe I was distracted by staring at Lady Teldra. But there she was, in Jhereg gray, and she was pointing a finger at me, as if accusing me of something.

There was this knife in my hand. I couldn't reach her from here, and if there was ever a knife that wasn't designed to be thrown, this curving thing was it. So I spun it in my hand, which I'd learned as a trick for impressing girls back when impressing girls was the entire goal of my life. Once, twice around, much like in the old days, when I'd had a gold chain I'd called Spellbreaker, and a very familiar tingle ran up my arm, just like the old days. Two spins, then I held it out in front of me, and the sorceress crumbled and dropped to the ground.

There were wisps of smoke coming from her clothing.

My goodness.

I wasn't exactly sure what had happened, but whatever it was, I felt neither the deep weariness that accompanies witchcraft, nor the momentary disorientation that often goes with casting a sorcerous spell.

"Boss, what just happened?"

"I didn't get killed."

"Okay, I think I understand that part."

"Beyond that, I'm not sure. Except I'd like to get somewhere safe."

"Good thinking, Boss. Dzur Mountain?"

"Just my thought."

I stared at Lady Teldra, then glanced at the sheath. It had changed too; it looked just right to accommodate a curved knife with about an eleven-inch blade. I put the one into the other and resolved not to think about it just then. I removed the amulet from around my neck, put it into the box I carried at my hip, shut the box, and performed the teleport as quickly as possible without risking turning myself into little pieces of Easterner scattered all over the landscape.

It was chilly on Dzur Mountain, but once the amulet was around my neck again, I felt safe.

The door was unlocked. I let myself in and eventually made my way to the sitting room. I badly wanted something to drink, but there was no sign of Tukko. I sat down and considered what had just happened, and what I had yet to do, and all I didn't know. In particular, all those things I didn't know that might make the difference between living and dying.

In the midst of my pondering, Sethra came in.

I stood up. "Sorry, Sethra. I had some trouble and needed a place—"

"You know you are welcome here, Vlad."

"Thank you. Uh . . ."

"Yes?

I cleared my throat. "Do you know how, uh, how I might be able to reach Kiera the Thief?"

She raised both eyebrows. I didn't answer all the questions she didn't ask.

After a moment, she gave an almost imperceptible shrug, and said, "I expect her to be by shortly."

"Thank you," I said.

"For what?"

There was no possible way to answer that, so I didn't. Sethra left, and I sat there being bored and restless for about half an hour. I passed the time as well as I could by recalling details of the meal at Valabar's, at the end of which time Kiera slid into the room.

"Hello, Vlad."

"Kiera. I appreciate you stopping in to see me."

"It was no trouble; I was in the neighborhood. I assume you wish something stolen?"

"Actually, no. Not this time."

"Then what's on your mind?"

"The Left Hand of the Jhereg."

"Oh? You thinking of joining?"

"Not this week. But I think one of them just tried to send me to that place from which none return except for those who do."

"Hmmm. You've annoyed someone."

"I've annoyed just about everyone in the Jhereg. That is, our side. Would the Left Hand care?"

She frowned. "Now that, Vlad, is a splendid question."

"Hey, thanks. Now I feel all smart."

"I don't know as much about the relationship between the two organizations as you might think I do."

"You know more than I do; that's good for a start. For example, you just spoke of two organizations; they really are entirely separate?"

She nodded.

I said, "What about the Imperial Representative?"

"Officially, he represents the House, not any organization."

"And unofficially?"

"I'm not sure. He may represent both sides, or the Left Hand may have another representative in the Palace that I don't know about."

"If he represents both sides, that would explain why the Left Hand just tried to kill me. The—"

"You're sure it was them?"

"Female, Jhereg colors, sorcerous attack."

"That's pretty conclusive, yes."

"So either they want me for the same reason the Jhereg wants me, someone in the Jhereg hired them, or they already know what I'm up to, which is awfully fast work."

"What you're up to?"

"Uh . . . yeah. I may be bumping heads with them over South Adrilankha."

"Ah. I see. When did this come up?"

"A few hours ago. I got a, uh, request."

"And you've already been attacked? By a sorceress?"

"Yes."

"What happened? How did the attack take place?"

"I don't know, a spell of some kind." I shrugged. "Lady Teldra handled it."

She frowned. "Lady Teldra? But I heard she—"

I tapped the weapon. I kept expecting Kiera to know things she couldn't, even though she did.

She nodded. "Ah. Yes, that's right. I heard something about that."

"In any case, I find that I need to know more about the Left Hand than I do. One way or another, I seem to be involved with them."

She nodded. "I wish I could tell you more." She frowned. "Well, as you said, the attack on you may have simply been hired, by the Council. You know the Left Hand does that."

"Yes, I know. It's possible. Only the Council wants it Morganti."

She shuddered. "Yes, that's true. And, so far as I know, there's no way to achieve that effect with sorcery."

"I'm sure some Athyra somewhere is working on it."

"No doubt. But in the meantime, we'll assume it wasn't at the order of the Council."

I liked it that she'd said "we." That was first hopeful thing I'd heard in some time. A lovely word, "we."

Tukku finally showed up, and set something recently dead on a table in the corner. My familiars flew over and began eating. I hadn't mentioned anything about them being hungry to either Sethra or Kiera, and I hadn't seen Tukko. Sometimes I wonder about these people.

Then he asked us if we wanted anything. "No, thank you, Chaz," said Kiera. I asked for wine. He shuffled off.

"The Left Hand," she said softly, almost under her breath. "I've tried to stay away from them, you know."

"Me, too," I muttered.

"They began recently, as I understand it. That is, recently in terms of Imperial history. Perhaps in the Fourteenth Athyra Reign, when sorcery took such large leaps, and when the Jhereg—the Right Hand, if you would—was relatively impoverished."

I nodded, and listened.

"Five women, sorceresses, started it. The odd thing is, they were not women associated with the Organization before, as far as I know."

"Interesting."

"Yes. Why women? I don't really know. I'm inclined to think it was more than coincidence, but I've never heard a good explanation for what else it could be."

Tukko showed up, set a glass of wine down next to me, and left.

"Moreover," she continued, "they were not Jhereg. I mean, not only were they not in the Organization, they weren't even in the House."

"Eh?"

"I believe two were Athyra, two were Dragons, one a Dzur."

"But—"

"All thrown out of their Houses, of course, once their activities were discovered."

"And, what, they bought Jhereg titles?"

She nodded. "They'd been working together, studying, and so on, and their work led them into illegal areas. Pre-Empire sorcery, and a few other things the Empire isn't fond of."

"And they weren't arrested?"

"They were. And tried. That's mostly how I know about it, it was a very famous trial."

"Well?"

She shrugged. "The Empire was unable to prove their guilt, they were unable to prove their innocence. So they were all expelled from their respective Houses, and were given various punishments from branding to flogging. Of course, without proof of guilt, they could not be put to death."

"Right. And so, they just went back to work?"

"One of the Athyra, the leader, I believe, suggested they join House Jhereg, and tried to interest the higher-ups in the idea that there was money to be made in illegal sorcery. Those who ran the Jhereg weren't interested, but she kept trying until she died. Then—"

"Died? How, exactly?"

"Indigestion."

"Uh huh. Arranged by whom?"

"No one. It really was just indigestion."

"You're kidding."

"Not at all. Chronic indigestion, of all the deaths there are, and no other."

"If you say so."

"I do. And, after she died—"

"Let me guess: The remaining four gave up on joining the Jhereg, and just set up on their own. I see."

She nodded. "Exactly right. And they've been around ever since."

"What a charming story."

"They have their own structure, about which I know nothing. And their own enforcement arm, about which I know little. And, really, they have almost nothing in common with our side."

"Except that they've taken over South Adrilankha."

"Yes. Which makes no sense to me. I've never heard of anything like it."

"Well, what is the gossip about it in the Jhereg? I mean, in the Right Hand."

"No one has ever heard of anything like it. Everyone is upset, and no one is too certain what to do about it, if anything."

I nodded. "If anything. Okay, seems like I've landed in the middle of something interesting, doesn't it?"

"As usual."

"As usual."

"Is there talk of war?"

"War? You mean, between the Left Hand and the Right Hand? No, there's no talk; everyone is too scared of it happening to talk about it."

I sipped my wine. I don't recall what it tasted like.

"So, I need to find out what they're after in South Adrilankha. And I need to do it without any way to get inside information on them, and while both sides of the Jhereg want me dead. Is that pretty much it?"

"Sounds like it, yes."

I drank some more wine. "No problem."

"Would you like some help?"

"Thanks, Kiera, but this is likely to be . . . no thanks."

She nodded. "So, what's your plan?"

"Plan. Yes. Good idea. I should come up with a plan."

"*How about the one where you stumble around until something happens, Boss? And then you almost get killed, and have to be rescued by—*"

"How about the one where you shut up and let me think."

He could have made a number of responses to that, I suppose, but he just let it lie.

"So, Kiera, if you needed to find out what was going on in the Left Hand, how would you go about it?"

She frowned. "I have no idea."

"I was afraid you'd say that."

"What are you thinking, Vlad?"

"Thinking? I'm trying to figure out what to do."

"I'm just wondering if . . .?"

"Yes?"

"If you're going to do something foolish."

"Me?"

"Uh huh."

"What I'm going to do, is try to learn something about what I'm up against. Once I know, I'll be able to figure out if there is a sensible way to go about doing what I have to do."

"And if there isn't?"

"I assume the question is rhetorical."

She sighed and stood up. I stood as well, and sketched her a sort of bow.

"Thanks for taking the time, Kiera."

She smiled—a distinctly Kiera smile, that didn't look like anyone else's. "You're most welcome, Vlad. Be careful."

"Yes. I'll try."

She drifted out. I sat down and realized that I'd finished my wine. There was no sign of Tukko. I cursed.

"Yeah, Boss. It's rough when you have a city full of sorceresses trying to kill you, and you have no idea what they want or what they can do but you have to stop it, and there's no one around to bring you more wine."

"Exactly."

By the time Tukko showed up again, I hadn't solved the other problems, but shortly thereafter I had more wine. This didn't cheer me up as much as it might have.

Presently Sethra returned. "Did you see your friend?"

"Yes, I did."

"And was she helpful?"

"Somewhat."

She nodded.

"Tell me something, Sethra. Does Iceflame ever, uh, change?"

"In what sense?"

"In any sense."

"Certainly. My weapon—" she touched the blue hilt at her waist—"is very sensitive on certain levels, and will respond to a number of different . . ." Her voice trailed off. "I believe you lack the vocabulary."

"Yeah, I'm sure I do."

"Why do you ask?"

"Earlier, when I was attacked, I drew Lady Teldra, and she was different."

Sethra frowned. "Different how?"

"Size. Shape. Weight. She was a small curved knife."

"Now that *is* interesting," said Sethra.

"I thought so, too."

"Judging by the shape of the sheath, she isn't anymore."

"No, at some point she changed back. I didn't notice either change. The sheath changed as well."

"The sheath changed?"

"Yes, to fit the new shape of the weapon."

"Where did you get the sheath?"

"The Jenoine gave me the knife in the sheath."

She considered. "The most obvious explanation . . . would you mind removing your amulet for a moment?"

"Uh, sure." I did so. "What are you doing?"

What she was doing was making small, subtle gestures in my direction. Then she shook her head.

"No," she said. "So far as I can tell, you've had no illusion cast on you."

"Well, that's good." I replaced the amulet.

"I don't know what to tell you, Vlad."

"Okay."

"Well, I can tell you one thing, as a piece of advice."

"Oh?"

"Keep that amulet on."

"Uh, I do."

"During those few seconds you just had it off, someone attempted a sighting."

"Oh, good. Did it succeed?"

"I can't be sure, but I think so."

"Great. So they know where I am."

"They'll not find it easy to get to you while you're here, you know."

"That's something, anyway."

"But—"

"Yes?"

"Vlad, consider what it means that, just in those few seconds, they found you. They are very, very determined."

"Yeah. Well, that just brightens the hell out of my life."

She let a smile flick over her lips, probably for form's sake.

"What could you tell about the sighting?"

"It was sorcerous." She shrugged. "Fairly straight-forward."

"Dzur Mountain has no protections against that sort of thing?"

"I've never needed any."

"Uh. I suppose not."

"I've never seen you do that before, Vlad."

"What?"

"Chew on your thumb."

"Oh. I must have picked up the habit from my friend Kiera. She does that when she's thinking."

"Ah," said Sethra. "I see."

That was utterly untrue, and Sethra knew it, but she couldn't admit she knew it.

"You're a real bastard, Boss."

"Uh huh."

"Speaking of the amulet . . ."

"Yes?"

"How strong is it?"

"What do you mean?"

"How much protection does it give me? I mean, could you blast through it, with sheer strength?"

She frowned. "I'm not sure. Shall I try?"

"Uh, no thanks."

"All right."

I cleared my throat. "We were discussing Lady Teldra."

"We were?"

"I was. Or, rather, Great Weapons in general. It's slowly dawning on me that I have one."

"Yes, you do indeed."

"Ummm . . . what can they do?"

She frowned. "They are different, of course."

"Yes, but they have certain things in common."

She nodded. "They can all kill Jenoine. Also, gods."

"Right. Well, killing gods and Jenoine is not a big priority in my life. What else?"

"They will act to preserve your soul, and possibly your life."

"Possibly?"

"Possibly. But, in your position, with what the Jhereg wants to do to you, a weapon that will preserve your soul should be of some comfort."

"True enough. You said 'act to preserve.' There's an implication there it will try."

"Yes."

"How reliable is that? I mean, can I count on it?"

"Well, if you know it's coming, and the weapon has time to prepare, it's more likely. You remember the incident with Aliera in Castle Black."

"It would be hard to forget."

"But don't bet your life on it. I know of at least three times when the wielder of a Great Weapon had his soul taken by a Morganti weapon."

"All right."

"Also . . . I'm not certain exactly how to say this." She chewed on her lower lip. I keep forgetting how sharp her teeth are. "Also, by possessing a Great Weapon, you have a connection, if you will, to something that goes beyond this world. Does that make any sense?"

"I'm not sure. You mean, another world in the sense that the Necromancer means it?"

"Do you understand how the Necromancer means it?"

"Well, no."

"I mean something that you might term 'fate.' "

"I hate that word," I said.

"I'll try to find another, if you like. It refers—"

"I hate the whole concept behind it, so another word won't help. It implies that I'm not free to do as I wish."

"It isn't that simple," said Sethra.

"Nothing ever is." I sighed. "I really just want to know what I can expect from Lady Teldra. What she might do, what I can try with her that I couldn't before, what chances it might be reasonable to take with her that I wouldn't have taken before."

"Oh? Are there chances you wouldn't have taken before?"

"Funny, Sethra."

She shrugged. "As for your weapon, well, there are stories and legends, but I don't actually know anything."

"Leaving me pretty much where I was before."

"I'm afraid so. Although—"

"Yes?"

"I've never heard anything that would account for the strange behavior you referred to."

"Wonderful. Well, would you care to let me in on the stories and legends?"

"Are you sure you want to know? The things I've heard all have to do with destiny."

"Wonderful. Yeah, I guess I'd like to know anyway."

"Very well. The weapon is supposed to destroy Verra."

I nodded. What with one thing and another, that didn't surprise me.

"Hmmm. Sethra, could the Jenoine know about that?"

"Certainly, Vlad."

"Okay, that would explain a couple of things. Anyway, what else?"

"There is also something I heard years ago, all wrapped in metaphor, that implies Godslayer is designed to, uh, cut out the diseased flesh in the world."

"Okay, well, that's clear enough. Any idea what it means?"

"Not really."

I sighed. "Okay, mind if I change the subject?"

"Go ahead."

"Do you know anything about the Left Hand of the Jhereg?"

"I thought you wanted to change the subject."

"Eh?"

"Never mind; it was a joke." She considered. "I've had a few encounters with the Left Hand over the years."

"What can you tell me?"

"They're very secretive, as you probably know."

"Yes."

"They do have magic no one else has. I know that the Athyra in particular are always attempting to insinuate someone into their organization, just to discover how some of their spells operate."

"Attempting?"

"They haven't had much success, so far."

"So far is a long time, Sethra."

"Well, yes. From what I've picked up, those in the Jhereg—that is, the Left Hand—rarely even tell each other how to perform some of the more obscure and difficult magics."

"I think I might have seen one of those."

"Oh?"

"You know how much I know of sorcery, so I could be wrong, but the one who attacked me, when she appeared, well, it didn't look like any teleport I've seen before."

"Interesting. What was different about it?"

I described what I'd seen, and what I hadn't seen, as best I could. Sethra looked thoughtful.

"I don't know what that could be. I wish I did."

"If you ask nicely, maybe she'll teach you."

"I'll keep that in mind. Would you like to sleep here tonight?"

"Please, and thank you. And, yeah, I'm pretty tired. It's been quite a day."

She nodded. "Tukko will show you to your room."

Tukko appeared and led me to a room where once I had awoken after death; he left a candle burning and shut the door. I laid myself down in a very soft bed—the kind that wraps you up like a blanket. Not my favorite sort of bed, but I appreciated the feeling just then.

The only decoration in the room was a painting, which showed a battle between a jhereg and a dzur, in which they both looked pretty banged up. I'd never seen a jhereg like that in real life; it was smaller than the giant ones that hover near Deathgate Falls, but much larger than any of those that scavenge in the jungles and forests and even sometimes in Adrilankha. Maybe the nameless artist had never seen a real one. I couldn't say about the dzur, I'd never seen one close up. Nor was I in any special hurry to; they were larger than the tiassa, black, wingless, and, by all reports, very fast. And they had claws and teeth and were reputed to fear nothing.

Things that fear nothing scare me.

When I'd studied the painting before, I had been pulling for the jhereg to win. Now I wasn't sure. Now maybe I was for the dzur.

I blew out the candle, and let a good night's sleep clear my mind the way a good shamy will clear the tongue.

4

Mushroom-Barley Soup

There were several different soups that could have appeared at this point, of which I passionately enjoyed all except the beet soup. Today was one of my favorites; I smelled the mushroom-barley before Mihi arrived with it. The bowls were wide, white, and there was wonderful steam coming out of them.

Valabar's mushroom-barley soup is something I can almost build. At least, I can come closer to achieving the right effect than I can with most of their menu.

First, I quarter a whole chicken. Then I throw the carcass into a pot with onion, garlic, celery, salt, pepper, and a bit of saffron. I clean the stock and dust it with powdered saffron. I cook the barley in the same pot (which took me a bit to figure out), and throw in some chopped garlic and shallots that I've sauteed in rendered goose fat until they're clear, and wood mushrooms, nefetha mushrooms, or long mushrooms, whatever looked good at the market that day. Then I just cook it until it reduces.

That's almost like Valabar's. I've never quite identified the difference. I mean, I've found some of it. I tried sea-salt instead of mined salt, and got closer. Then I used white pepper instead of black pepper, and that helped too. I had to play with the amount of saffron, and I think I finally got it about right. But there's still something that isn't

quite the same. It might be how they sauté the onions: a subtle difference in time there can change a lot.

It was a bit of an annoyance, but not enough to prevent me from enjoying what was in front of me. That first taste just hits you, you know,
and as the aroma fills your nose, the broth—just the tiniest bit oily from
the goose fat—rolls around on your tongue.

It's wonderful.

"This is really good," said Telnan. "How do they make it?"

"I have no idea," I said. "Glad you like it, though."

"So, you live around here?"

"I used to. Why?"

"Well, just because it seems like you know this place."

"Ah. Yes, I've eaten here many, many times."

"Where do you live now?"

"Hmm. An interesting question. I own some land around Lake
Szurke, but I don't live there. I live . . . uh, nowhere, really."

"Nowhere?"

"I've been doing some traveling."

"Oh, I see. I've always wanted to do that."

"Much joy may it bring you."

"Thank you."

"You're welcome."

"Where is Lake Szurke?"

"East. Near the Forbidden Forest."

"I've heard of that place. Why is it called the Forbidden Forest?"

"I asked Sethra about that once. She said it used to be owned by
a duke who was especially snotty about poachers."

"Aren't they all?"

"I guess he was particularly determined about finding and prosecuting them."

He nodded.

"But then," I added, "Sethra might have been lying."

The point of the soup, at this stage, is, I guess, like the final setup.
You aren't in desperate need of food, because you've had the platter and
the bread. And then you're prepared yourself for what is to come with
the shamy. Now the soup appears, and as you linger over it, it just
starts to dawn on you what sort of experience you have entered into.
You are simultaneously anticipating more than ever what is to come
next, and are able to await it more patiently. The soup is warm, and
it's, if I may, sensual, and it provides a certain amount of comfort.
And as it vanishes, spoonful by happy spoonful, you discover that you
are in the perfect condition for whatever might come next. All is now
ready.

Vili brought us a bottle of wine, showed it to me, opened it, and
poured us each a glass. We hadn't made more than a dent in the last
bottle, but I learned long ago that it is a mistake to try to finish all the
wine. Sometimes, a certain amount of waste is just a necessary part of
maximizing one's pleasure.

βɔ

While I slept, I had a confusing dream, in which Valabar's was all
mixed up with the Left Hand, and parts of Six Corners appeared
in the courtyard of Castle Black. Other than a general feeling that
I was in danger, with no specific cause that I noticed, or at least
that I remembered after waking, there wasn't anything to connect
the dream to what I was involved with. And if the dream intended to let me know I was in danger, it was a wasted effort; I'd
already figured that part out.

I woke up and blinked away the dream. The painting reminded
me that I was at Dzur Mountain, and I gradually recalled what I
had agreed to do. I thought about getting up, decided I'd rather
lie there and plan the day, realized I couldn't make plans without
some klava in me, and grumbled to myself about the necessity of
finding klava in someone else's house.

I am, you see, a lousy houseguest, mostly because I have a terror of being a lousy houseguest. I worry about whether I'm going to dirty a towel unnecessarily, or move someone's footstool, or empty someone's boiler, or use the last of the kerosene. I can't really relax. Once, I found myself traveling with a young Dragaeran, and when I returned him to his family they insisted I stay with them for a few days on the floor of their little cottage, and I hated the experience more than I've hated several attempts on my life, including one or two successful ones. This was Sethra, whom I called a friend, but I still dreaded the thought of getting up and rummaging through her kitchen for klava.

So I remained in bed for a bit, giving myself a few minutes to remember yesterday's meal, which put me in a better mood. Then I rose, dressed, and shuffled off through the corridors of Dzur Mountain, in search of the elusive Tukko, which was known to dwell near klava nests.

"You're really weird when you wake up, Boss."

"It's taken you how many years to figure that out?"

I eventually treed the Tukko near the kitchen, and mumbled the secret password that would produce klava. As I stumbled back to the sitting room, I realized I had been hearing the sputter of the klava-boiler before I asked. The sitting room became brighter as I entered, though I could not identify where the light was coming from. That's another one of those tricks I really like, although it was a bit brighter than I'd have chosen.

Ten very long minutes later a cup was in my hand, the steam coming up as wonderful in its own way as Valabar's soup. Ten minutes after that, I realized that I was beginning to wake up.

"We going back to South Adrilankha today, Boss?"

"I don't see any way around it."

Rocza launched herself from my shoulder (I hadn't even been consciously aware she was there, but that's just because I'm used to her) and flew around the room a couple of times, before perching on the back of a chair.

"Loiosh?"

"She's just restless."

"Okay."

I took a moment to recall what weapons I had secreted about my person. It wasn't like years before, when I had dozens and knew exactly what and where each was without thinking about it, nor the more recent period when I carried only a couple of knives. This was an uncomfortable in-between time.

I drank klava and considered my next move, which led inevitably to a consideration of everything I didn't know. My hand caressed the hilt of Lady Teldra; like before, a certain sense of her calm, warm presence made its way up my fingertips. Of all the things I didn't know, she was, perhaps, the most important. One part of me believed that, so long as she was with me, I could walk anywhere in safety, that the Jhereg couldn't hurt me. But there were Sethra's words from yesterday, and, more than that, my memory kept returning to the sight of Morrolan, lying dead on the floor of an Adrilankha public house. He carried Blackwand. He'd been assassinated.

By a sorceress from the Left Hand.

And Aliera had been killed by a simple, old-fashioned dagger to the heart, while Pathfinder was with her.

And Sethra herself had returned, undead, from beyond Deathgate, so something must have killed her at some point.

These statistics were not entirely encouraging.

To the left, there were those remarks Telnan had made, which kept going through my mind. He seemed much too simple to have been dissembling. Yes, I know, it could all be very clever deception. But I didn't think so.

"Tell me, Teldra. Just what can you do?"

She didn't answer. I'm not sure what I'd have done if she had.

Okay, best to assume, in spite of yesterday's experience, that I was on my own as far as getting out of trouble was concerned. That way, any surprises would be pleasant ones, which I've always felt are the preferred sort.

I finished the klava and looked around for Tukko so I could ask for more. He wasn't around. I made my own way to the kitchen, found what I needed, and engaged in the klava-preparation ritual, then returned to the sitting room, sat, and pondered the immediate future.

I moved away from grand strategy, as it were, and considered practical details for a while.

"Good morning, Vlad. I'll get Tukko to clean that up and bring you some more. Did you burn yourself?"

I put my dagger away. "Good morning, Sethra. Not noticeably, and thank you."

"You were quite lost in thought there. Or just jumpy?"

"Both," I said. I sat down. Loiosh returned to my shoulder. Rocza gave me an offended look and remained perched on a chair. "Yeah, I was trying to figure out how I'm going to leave here. I don't really want to remove the amulet while they're looking for me, and that means I can't teleport."

She frowned. "I hadn't thought of that. Morrolan's window can get you back to Adrilankha easily enough."

"How far is Castle Black from here?"

"A day's ride."

"Ride?"

"I keep a few horses stabled here. You're welcome to borrow one."

"Ah. Yes. Horses."

"Shall I have your trousers cleaned?"

"No, thanks. It's just klava."

"And klava stains don't count?"

"You know, Sethra, sometimes I forget that you're a woman."

"There is no way I can possibly respond to that."

"Um. Yeah, forget I said it."

Tukko showed up with another cup, set it down next to me, gave me a look, and began cleaning up the broken crockery.

"Whatever you do, it might be easier if you made Castle Black your base of operations, though you're certainly welcome here any t—"

"I won't do that to Morrolan."

"Do what?"

"A Jhereg, on the run from the Jhereg, taking refuge at Castle Black. Does that sound familiar, somehow? If not, ask Kiera. She'd understand."

"Oh." She frowned. "Yes, I see the problem."

I nodded.

"She's right, Boss."

"About what?"

"You have started chewing on your thumb."

I stopped chewing on my thumb.

"Sethra, can you do, I don't know, something to keep them from spotting me for a bit while the amulet is off?"

"What did you have in mind?"

"Getting back there without spending weeks at it, and without being killed the instant I appear."

"You mean, teleport you somewhere, and leave them confused about your location long enough for you to wear it again?"

"Well, long enough for me to wear it, and then get some distance from where the teleport landed me, yeah."

"How much time are you thinking?"

"Twenty minutes?"

She looked doubtful. "I might be able to do that."

"How about ten?"

She nodded. "I can give you ten."

"That should work, then."

"Where do you want to go?"

"I need to think about that. Somewhere where I can be hard to find ten minutes later."

"But South Adrilankha, I presume?"

"Yes. Somewhere with a good supply of shops, but not Six Corners, because that's where I'll probably end up."

She nodded as if she understood. Most likely she did.

I rubbed the purse I carried inside my cloak, feeling coins there. Yeah, I was okay; it would be embarrassing to run out of money, and gaining access to the rest of my hoard would be at least annoying, and maybe problematical. So, all right.

"Yeah, I know a place."

"Whenever you're ready, then."

"Okay. When I finish this klava. Either drinking it, or spilling it."

"Have you thought about getting back here?"

"I don't believe I can do that safely anymore. I plan to remain in town until this is settled."

"Is that safe?"

"I think I can manage to make it safe. I hope so."

"Ah. You have a plan."

"Yeah, something like that."

"All right."

I drank my klava. Sethra was silent while in my mind I went through every step of the few minutes I'd have available to me once I arrived. Then I went through it again, reconstructing the look of the doorways I'd have to cross. I had killed people with less planning than this. It was late morning, not a terribly busy time in South Adrilankha. That should work to my advantage.

Tukko hadn't stirred the klava thoroughly; some honey had accumulated at the bottom of the cup. I set the cup down and stood up. I took a couple of knives out of my cloak, putting one of them in my boot-top; the other I set on a table. I took my purse out and tied it to my belt. I ran my hands over the cloak to make sure I hadn't left anything in it, then bundled it up and set it next to the knife.

"Okay," I told Sethra. "I'm ready."

She nodded and drew Iceflame. I almost flinched, out of reflex, because being in the presence of a naked weapon like that does things to one's mind. And, indeed, it did things; but this time it was a different sort of thing than it had been before. In the past, it had been a naked threat, the feeling of being in the presence of some hostile and unbelievably powerful force, as if a dragon were charging me, with me unarmed and with nowhere to run.

But now I felt something different. No less powerful, the threat was still there, but now it wasn't directed at me. I knew it, felt it, but it was like a guard dog in the home of a friend you've known for years; you give him a sniff of your hand, then you stop worrying about it.

More than that, though, there were overtones, subtleties of flavor. I could feel, albeit from a distance, Iceflame's connection to Sethra, to Dzur Mountain. It was, well, it was all very confusing for a simple Eastern kid.

I got so involved in trying to sort out these strange sensations, that I pretty much missed what Sethra was doing, which I believed involved making twitching motions with her fingers and muttering under her breath. Then I was suddenly very much aware that Iceflame had gotten involved in the proceedings, and the next thing I knew Sethra was saying, "Here we go, Vlad."

"All right."

"Vlad, that means you need to remove the amulet."

"Oh. Right."

"Now, concentrate on the place you want to end up. As clear a vision as possible, and any other sensory impressions you have of it—smells, sounds, anything. With the interference I'm generating, I need it especially clear to make sure you don't end up a thousand feet under the ocean, or somewhere else you'd prefer not to be."

Very convincing, is my friend Sethra.

I slipped the amulet over my head, paused briefly to make sure the plan was still in my head, muttered a thank-you to Sethra, and put the thing into its spell-proof receptacle. Then my vision blurred. At least, I thought my vision was blurring, but after a moment, it became apparent that it wasn't my eyes, but rather something was happening to the light in the room. At the same time, I became aware that I was hearing odd noises, like a low-pitched "thrumb" accompanied by some very faint squeals.

I stood outdoors in a small market area in South Adrilankha. I stumbled a bit but recovered quickly. I think a couple of people—humans—glanced at me as I appeared, but I couldn't see well enough to be certain.

"*Directly behind, Boss.*"

"Okay."

I put the Phoenix Stone amulet back around my neck, waited until I felt it pulsing, then turned around and began walking quickly. Loiosh guided me; either he was unaffected by Sethra's spell, or he was able to use other means.

"*I just have better eyesight than you.*"

"Shut up."

I had almost reached my destination when my vision abruptly cleared, and the sounds disappeared from my ears; whatever Sethra had done had worn off.

I pushed past the curtain of a doorway to my left, took a quick look around, and grabbed a long brown coat with big pockets. I also picked up a beret. I tossed the shopkeeper a coin, told him to keep it, and left. It took about a minute. The next shop was about ninety feet away and supplied me with a white shirt and some baggy pale green breeks. The public house next to it had a private

outhouse that stank horribly but was big enough for me to change
clothes. I transfered a few things into the coat, then changed. My
shirt went to where I'd never want to retrieve it again. The spare
knife went from my boot-top to a pocket of the coat. My purse
went into the inner pocket.

"No one's around, Boss. I think it worked."

I pulled the beret down so it almost covered my eyes, and
stepped out, taking a grateful breath of the rank-but-less-rank
air of South Adrilankha.

Vlad Taltos: Master of Disguise.

"Okay, Loiosh. You and Rocza need to keep overhead. Or at least
not with me. You're too recognizable."

"Check, Boss. We'll be around."

They flew off as I stepped back onto the street.

I was able to relax a bit now, so I strolled over toward Six Corners, stopping just across a narrow street from a place I knew well.
It had changed: the little porch with rugs on the floor and partly
surrounded by curtains was gone, and there was a new door into
the shack. It had also received a new coat of paint. There was
nothing, really, to say who now lived there.

I didn't doubt that if I were to make my way inside, or even
over to where the porch had been, I'd feel psychic traces of my
grandfather; he'd lived there many years before I managed to
convince him to relocate to lands I'd never seen. I wondered if he
missed being surrounded by his own kind, or if he was enjoying
playing the part of lord of the manor. That's the tricky part of doing a kindness for someone; you can't always be sure it really is a
kindness.

"Boss, what, exactly, are we doing here?"

"Feeling maudlin."

"Oh. Good. How long are we planning on doing that?"

"Don't you ever miss the days when you used to be nostalgic?"

"What?"

"Never mind."

I turned away, feeling pleased that I had finally gotten one past Loiosh. I headed toward Six Corners, then skirted it to the north on a small street with no name. In a few hundred feet, I came to a two-story wood house with a small sign hanging over it. I squinted at the sign. Yeah, something had once been painted on it, and I suppose it could as easily have been a horn as anything else. I went in. I'd have blended in effortlessly with the customers, except that there weren't any customers.

The host was a dumpy fellow sitting behind a sort of counter, his head down, and a large lower lip protruding as he snored. I cleared my throat. He sputtered, opened his eyes, wiped some saliva from the corner of his lip, and said, "Yes?"

"My name is Sandor. You have a room for me for a night or so?"

"We don't usually rent them by the night."

"I said, my name is Sandor."

"Eh? Oh. Yes. That's right." He considered. "No playing of instruments after dark."

"Of course."

"Three and three per night."

I gave him enough for a couple of nights, and suggested he let me know when he needed more. He grunted an agreement and closed his eyes again. I cleared my throat, and he opened them.

"The room?" I suggested.

"Oh." He frowned. "In back, up the stairs, second door on the left. Do you need help with bags?"

"No. Thank you," I said. "Sleep well."

I followed his directions, and arrived in the room that would be my home for at least the next few days.

There was a small window. Loiosh and Rocza flew in and landed on my shoulders. I looked around the room to see what else was there.

"It has a bed, Boss. That's something."

"And a washbasin. That implies there may be water somewhere. An actual door would have been nice, though."

Rocza shifted uncomfortably on my shoulder.

"Tell her to get used to it, Loiosh."

"I already did, Boss."

I looked out the window. The view was of the blank wall of the house next door, about three feet away. It had once been painted red. On the ground below were various bits of wood that seemed to have once been a chair, the remains of an old mattress with signs of having been burned, and various other things I didn't care to investigate too closely. I'd have drawn the curtain if there had been one.

"I think next time I'll have to give Aibynn more specific instructions."

"Next time, Boss."

"In the meantime, it'll do."

"It will?"

"It will. We're going to be heading out now. You two need to still keep your distance from me while we're out."

"Admit it, you're just ashamed to be seen with us."

I left the room without touching anything, and spent the day buying a few extra changes of clothing and hiring a couple of boys to give the room a good cleaning. I had a local witch drive out any small animal life that might have taken up residence in the bed. I bought a cheap chair, mostly to give Loiosh and Rocza a perch, and a little end table to set the washbasin on, and a whetstone and honing oil.

As much as anything else, I wanted to practice my new look and new personality. I worked on walking differently, holding my head differently, and above all, trying to look harmless, cheerful, and a bit timid. I had a few conversations with people in the neighborhood, and discovered because I heard myself saying it that I was a clerk for one of the slaughterhouses. I wasn't exactly sure what a clerk for a slaughterhouse did, but I knew there were such things, and I didn't expect it to be a profession that would generate a lot of questions. Staying? At the Hunting Horn for now, because there had been a fire in my old rooms. I'd either be moving back there soon, or find a new place. Do you know of any rooms for rent? I require it be clean, you know, and not too far from the slaughterhouse district, because it is amazing how it can eat into one's income to have to be conveyed to and from work every day, like I am now. Married? No, I have not yet met the right woman. Why, do you know someone? I've always felt a man ought to have a family, don't you think?

And so on. I smiled at everyone, and put on Sandor like a suit of clothes.

I picked up some bread and sausages and a jug of cheap red wine from a street vendor. Hauling the chair and other things through the jug-room didn't earn me so much as a raised eyebrow from the host (now vaguely awake) or the two Easterners he was speaking with. I put the chair near the doorway and the end table below the window.

I shared the bread and sausages with my familiars when they came in the window and settled on the chair.

"Not bad, Boss."

"Kind of pales next to mushroom-barley soup, though."

"You never gave me any of the soup."

"You wouldn't have appreciated it."

"No, I wouldn't have. Barley isn't food. Barley is what food eats."

"Uh huh."

"Rocza agrees with me."

"Well, that settles it, then."

"Good sausage, though. And I like the bread, too."

"Yes. Very good bread. I wonder if there's barley in it."

"You're just really funny, Boss."

"Part of my charm."

I took out the whetstone and oil and put an edge on all my knives, more to be doing something than because they needed it.

"What's the plan for now, Boss?"

"I'd rather surprise you," I said.

"Uh, Boss! Are we really safe here?"

"I wish I knew. We're safer than if I weren't disguised, didn't have the Phoenix Stone, and were in the heart of Adrilankha. More important, though, we have a place to attack from."

Loiosh flew over to the window, stuck his long, snake-like neck out, then turned around and gave a sort of hop back over to the chair, settling in next to Rocza. Their necks twisted and they looked at each other. I wondered what they were saying. Probably best I didn't know.

I took a good couple of drinks of the wine. It was different enough from what Valabar's served that it seemed wrong to use the same term to describe them. But Sandor wouldn't have been able to tell the difference, so I pretended I couldn't, either.

I put on my ugly coat and hat and, as Loiosh and Rocza went through the window, I pushed the curtain aside and went out into the evening.

About half a mile away was a red brick house on Stranger's Road. Sandor headed in that direction as if he had not a care in the world, and certainly no reason to anticipate danger.

5

WHITE WINE FROM GUINCHEN

To give credit where it is due, my father did know a great deal about wine; certainly more than I know. He once explained to me that anyone can find good wine—all you have to do is pay a lot of money. The reason for learning about wine is so you can find a wine you like without paying a lot of money. The curse of the small businessman, I guess: everything is expressed in terms of making or losing a few coppers.

But still, he's right.

Mihi knew my taste in wine probably better than I did. Properly (as he once explained) mushroom-barley soup was served with a white wine like a Doe Valley Bresca or a Pymin; the trouble with those is that I don't care for the hint of sweet apples that goes with a Bresca or of apricots that goes with a Pymin. When I'm eating, any trace of sweetness is too much, even when dominated by that pleasant acidity that the real wine experts love so much. So what he brought was a Lescor from Guinchen. To me, the traces of goslingroot and of green pepper, of all things, made it fit perfectly with the soup. That's me, though. Mihi knew, so he brought it. That's Mihi.

Telnan just drank it, and I believe never gave it a thought. Well, in fact, there's no reason he should have; it's supposed to make the experience more enjoyable, not provide a topic for hours of conversation.

Unless you don't have anything else to talk about, and Telnan appeared to have a never-ending supply of things to talk about. After discussing where I lived, he proceeded to give me more details than I wanted about living in Dzur Mountain, and what the food was like there (compared to Valabar's mushroom-barley soup) and the difficulties—primarily boredom—of Lavode training. The subject of food (ever on my mind) brought up the issue of who did the cooking there. I asked him, and he gave me a puzzled look and said it had never occurred to him to wonder.

"How many of you are there?" I asked him.

"Hmm? I don't understand."

"Are there other Lavode candidates, or trainees, secreted away in the bowels of Dzur Mountain?"

"Oh. No, just me." He drank some wine, frowned, and added, "As far as I know. She's only training me because of, well, my weapon. And I don't think there are that many around."

"Your weapon. Yes." I glanced at the hilt sticking above his shoulder, and wondered again how he managed to sit, with all appearance of comfort, with that massive thing strapped to his back.

"Maybe there's no sword at all, Boss. Just a hilt that he wears to look good."

"Uh huh. Think I should get one?"

"Oh, certainly."

"What is it about your weapon?"

His eyes widened a little, and he suddenly reminded me of Aibynn. "You don't know?"

Several remarks came and went, but, in the interest of a companionable meal, I said, "No, I don't."

"Oh. It's one of the Seventeen." He frowned. "Are you familiar with the Seventeen Gr—"

"Yes," I said. "I've heard of them."

He nodded. "Like Iceflame."

"Yes."

"You know much about them?"

"I'm not sure what qualifies as 'much,' but I'm pretty sure the answer is no however you mean it."

"Ah. Too bad."

"Why? You thought maybe I could tell you things Sethra can't?"

He grinned. "That Sethra won't. And I was hoping."

"Oh. Well, I'm pretty sure you know more than I do."

We eat some soup, drank some wine. A couple more people, Lyorn, drifted into Valabar's and took a table at the far end of the room.

"I don't know much," said Telnan, "except what everyone knows. I mean, that they have their own life, and you have to come to an agreement with them, and at some point there will be a test of wills, and that if you have one it is a bridge between you and the powers beyond the world."

"Uh. Yes. Certainly. Um, everyone knows that?"

He nodded, looking very sincere.

"What does 'powers beyond the world' mean?"

"Just what it says."

"You asked for that, Boss."

"I suppose I did."

I tried again. "I'm not familiar with powers beyond the world, or even what world we're talking about being beyond, and what is beyond it."

"Uh, I didn't quite follow that."

"I don't blame you."

"Um."

"Your phrase about 'powers beyond the world' leaves me confused, that's all. I'm not sure what that means."

"Yeah," he said. "Neither am I."

I wasn't certain what to say, so I drank more wine. It was good wine, providing a nice counterpoint to the conversation, as well as to the soup. No question, Mihi knows what I like.

The house on Stranger's Road hadn't changed. I studied it from a little farther away than I had last time, to see if they became aware of my presence from here. Loiosh and Rocza circled above it, then perched a short distance away.

Let's say some time passed here. Then some more time. And still more time.

"Boss?"

"Yeah, okay. I'm pretty well convinced they haven't detected me."

"Good. What now?"

"Now we get to wait some more."

"Oh. Do we know what we're waiting for this time?"

"Yes."

Whatever was going on in South Adrilankha, it either had its center there, in that house, or at least that was the nearest tendril. Since I'd first seen the place, I'd had the urge to draw Lady Teldra, walk in the door, and just start cutting. Loiosh had felt that urge in me, and was afraid I'd give in to it. But I didn't survive as hired muscle, a hired knife, and eventually a low-level boss by giving in to urges like that. Especially when I had no way of knowing if, in the unlikely event that I survived, it would get me any closer to solving the problem.

"So, uh, care to let the reptile in on the warm-blooded secret?"

"I'll tell you when it happens."

"Oh, good."

It was about five minutes after that conversation that it happened: A pale little Easterner, about my age, came walking almost right past me, and up the stairs of the house. He was carrying a small satchel. He started to pound on the door with his fist, stopped, set the satchel down, and clapped his hands. The door opened, and he entered.

"So, was that what we were waiting for, Boss?"

"Yep, that was it."

"It was very exciting."

"*I thought so.*"

"*Well, good. Now what?*"

"*We wait some more.*"

"*I was expecting that.*"

The Easterner was still holding the satchel when he left, just a couple of minutes later. He walked past me again.

There is an art to following someone, and I'm afraid I've never mastered it. I've done it, and done all right, but I haven't gotten exceptionally good at it because I've never had to.

"*Okay, Loiosh.*"

"*On it, Boss.*"

"*Can Rocza stay here, and keep watching the house?*"

"*Sure.*"

Loiosh followed the runner, and I followed Loiosh. We skirted Six Corners, taking Stranger's Road as it meandered northeast past shacks and cabins and small markets. Few people paid any attention to me. I got a hopeful look from a skinny, dark-haired beggar who was sitting on the ground next to a pastry shop holding a tin to collect coins in and a small frying pan whose purpose was known only to himself. A stooped old man whose head was wrapped in a scarf leaned on a walking stick and looked like he was going to speak to me, but he must have changed his mind because he turned away and yelled something unintelligible to a fat woman on the other side of the street. Without turning her head, she called him something that sounded like a "fits" and made various obscene suggestions to him. Their conversation continued as I followed Loiosh's directions and soon I couldn't hear them anymore. A small group of street dancers danced for tips; the musicians, with violins and pipes, played a fiery *chardosh* that brought me back to the East for a while. The girls were pretty. I didn't stop to tip them.

The runner eventually made his way into a hatter's shop. I didn't follow him in because I didn't want him to see me, and I already had a hat.

"Now we wait some more, right?"

"No, let's head back."

"I don't know if I can take the excitement, Boss."

"Nothing going on there, right?"

"No one in or out, so far."

We returned to Stranger's Road, and waited some more, and eventually another runner entered the house with another satchel, then came out, and I followed him, and got another place.

By the end of the day, I had reacquainted myself with much of South Adrilankha: Potter's Gate, the Drumhead, Donner's Court, the Round. I had also identified six runners, and six locations they lived in, worked out of, or at least visited. I had no idea if this information would be useful, but it at least gave me some vague idea of the amount of money involved in the operation. That's one nice thing about the Jhereg: Almost all the time, you can measure the importance of any activity by its weight in gold and be pretty sure you're right.

How big was this operation?

I'd seen six runners, all carrying satchels that were moderately heavy, no doubt with silver. Six a day, five days a week . . . yes, that was a big enough operation to be worth a life here and there.

And, yes, the Left Hand was now very definitely involved in an operation that had, until now, been reserved for the male side of the Jhereg.

I picked up different bread and different sausages from a different street vendor, returned to my room, and shared the meal with my familiars while I considered matters. The sausage was greasy, but I kind of like it that way.

Loiosh and Rocza daintily picked up the last of the bread-crumbs with their feet, balanced on the other foot, and brought them to their mouths. It's the least reptilian thing they do. I love watching them eat.

"We done for the night, Boss?"

"Not quite. I want to get an idea of how much action is going down in Donner's Court. There didn't used to be any at all."

I felt something like a psychic sigh.

"Yeah, I know. You're worked to death. Shut up."

I put Sandor back on and walked through the doorway as they flew out the window. Donner's Court was a fair walk from my place, and most of it mildly uphill. The streets twisted here, but were generally wider than in much of Adrilankha, and it had a more prosperous look. This was where Sandor, were he really a clerk for a slaughterhouse, would be dreaming of living, in his own house purchased with his own money, with a tiny garden. He'd grow carrots, peas, and onions, and he'd find a fat little wife and raise children whom he would teach to respect the Empire above all. If rebellion should happen to break out, he would hide under his bed and he would never exactly tell his children that the poverty all around them was the fault of the poor, but he would talk a great deal about personal responsibility. Not, you understand, that I particularly give a damn about the poor; but at least I can be a bastard without hypocrisy. Sandor, though, would be extremely proud of his peas, terrified of everything beyond the confines of his yard, and I'd hang myself within six weeks.

These, at any rate, were Sandor's thoughts as he made his way up the gentle inclines of South Adrilankha to the Donner's Court district. There was little street traffic, and most of that by footcabs, because footcabs are seen as a sign of almost-wealth, lying somewhere between walking and owning a coach. The almost-wealthy are always more concerned with appearances than either of the extremes.

The Donner's Court area takes its name from a fairly small courtyard which is all that is left of what was once a sizable temple to Barlen, built, oddly enough, by an Easterner named Donner. A street named Harvoth leads into the court, and various shrines and altars to different deities line the quarter of a mile between the court and Donner's Circle, where the local market is. This evening, there were a few people praying or making small offerings at these altars, and that seemed to be almost the only activity in the area. If the Left Hand was making money from this district, which they must be because I'd seen the delivery, then I had no idea where it was coming from.

I walked along near the shrines, trying to look respectful, and trying to figure out what big moneymaking operations for the Jhereg could be. There was a sudden movement behind me and to my left, and my hand slipped under my coat to touch the hilt of Lady Teldra, but even as that pleasant, reassuring warmth went through me I saw that it was only a bird taking flight, and relaxed. I kept my right hand on Lady Teldra's hilt under my coat, just because it was pleasant to be in touch with her. I had seen Morrolan and Aliera caressing the hilts of their Great Weapons fairly often; now I understood why.

There was a small icon next to me, about four feet in height, in the form of a rounded tower of black marble. I rested my left hand on it while I considered matters.

This is not important, Taltos Vladamir, let her touch your thoughts as she will. However it may look, it doesn't matter; let it drift into the shadows where your own demons dance about spots of light like the laughter of innocence. It doesn't matter, because it is not real—

It isn't real? What did you mean when you said it wasn't real, Goddess? I remember now; I remember your voice that went past my ears into my head, echoing there, and I don't think you ever intended me to. But I remember the sounds that came like water, to drown me, and I was screaming denials inside my head, and you just kept droning on and on.

Bitch.

It was strange seeing Morrolan on his knees. It was stranger when there came a flicker, too clear to be my imagination, running along the

*length of the sword at which he stared; a sword made of marble, and
held by a marble hand—*

Yes. That's right. The statue had its own kind of life, and I intended to ask Morrolan if the spirit of Kieron dwelt within the marble, or if it was a life of another sort. But I never did ask him. Because of that voice? Yes, because of that voice. And there was another voice, too, only for a moment.

*I'm sorry Uncle Vlad. I have to. But it isn't lost, and you'll have
it all back someday—*

Yes. There it was. And who do I trust now? She sounded so harmless; the epitome of all that could be trusted: sweet and innocent. But she was older than I, and she was Verra's granddaughter. I had other memories of her, too, and many of them came rushing back, begging to be reinterpreted, with all my natural cynicism let loose on them. And I could feel the part of myself that wasn't crippled fighting it, wanting to believe, fighting through those images as a swimmer fights a strong current—

*There is pool of clear water in the Paths of the Dead, before the tall
arch that leads to the Halls of Judgment, and you must immerse yourself in it before you pass through, as if to be purified. But it does not purify you; it just removes from you that which might balk at accepting
what you have just seen as real. It holds the secrets of the Paths, which
is why you are warned not to swallow any of the water. By the time you
are dry, you have forgotten how you got wet—*

Yeah, that's how it began. There, in that pool. Perhaps a natural part of that place, only now I knew that it hadn't been operating alone. The Goddess had dipped her hand into it, and into my head, and done what she had chosen to do for her own reasons. Maybe I wasn't supposed to have remembered that pool, either. Maybe I only remembered it because she had tried to make me forget so many other things. Maybe she was being undone by her own deviousness.

*Around me are walls of white, white, white. I'm wondering why
they are white, when I suddenly realize that the question should be:
Why do I perceive them as white? And to ask it that way is to answer
it, and then comes the touch again—*

That's right! I had returned to her halls. I could hear myself
asking her questions, demanding answers, and she just shook her
head and started talking; I was seeing her distorted, as through
a rippling pool, and as she spoke, I realized that how I was hearing
her had nothing to do with my ears. I felt myself trembling all
over again. Yes, it was coming back. I squeezed my eyes tightly
shut, and opened them again, trying to remember.

Several people were staring at me, some of them asking if I was
all right.

"*Boss? Say something, dammit!*"

"Uh . . ."

"*That's a start.*"

I was on my back, and the people around me were standing,
looking down.

"*What happened, Loiosh?*"

"*I have no idea.*"

Someone else asked if I was all right. I nodded, because I
wasn't sure if I could speak.

"What happened?" said someone.

I closed my eyes.

"He's been touched by the Demon Goddess," said someone
else, a touch of awe in his voice.

"Drunk, more likely."

"Are you drunk?"

"He doesn't look drunk."

"Who is he?"

"Who are you?"

I opened my eyes again, looking up at the circle of half a

dozen faces staring down at me with expressions ranging from
worry to suspicion.

Who was I? Okay, that was a good place to start. I was Vlad,
only I was calling myself Sandor right now, while involved in a
tricky business to get Cawti out of trouble. The Left Hand of the
Jhereg. Lady Teldra. I'd had a meal at Valabar's yesterday. All right,
my memory still worked.

"Sandor," I said. "My name is Sandor."

My voice still worked too.

"And I'm not drunk," I added.

"What happened?" said one of the faces.

"I don't know."

I struggled to my feet, receiving kindly assistance I didn't want,
but at least learning that, yes, my legs were working. I smiled as
pleasantly as I could, and slipped away, moving back toward Six
Corners.

Someone yelled for me to wait a minute. I chose not to.

"Is anyone following me?"

"No, they're just staring."

"Good. They can stare."

I made it back to my room without incident, though my head
was spinning to the point where it was a bit tricky to keep my eyes
focused, and to remember where to go. When I finally made it, I
threw off my coat and flopped on the bed as Loiosh and Rocza
came through the window.

"You okay, Boss?"

"I'm not sure."

"What is it? What happened?"

"I'm not sure. Something. My head. In my head."

"I know," said Loiosh. *"Me, too."*

There was an edge of panic to Loiosh's voice. I tried to think
of something reassuring to say, but I was having trouble focusing

my thoughts. Loiosh perched on the chair, and either there was something in the way he held himself that made him appear pensive, or else I was just picking it up from him. Rocza perched next to him, rubbing her neck against his.

"*What happened, Boss?*"

"*I don't know. I'm trying to make sense of it.*"

Sethra once told me that, when overwhelmed by the mystical, start with the physical and mundane, and work both inward and outward from there. I never did understand the "inward and outward" part, but the advice still made sense.

"*Okay, the last thing I did was touch an altar of the Demon Goddess.*"

"*You've done that before, Boss.*"

"*Yeah.*"

"*This didn't happen before.*"

"*Yeah.*"

"*What was different?*"

"*I didn't have Lady Teldra.*"

"*Yes, but were you touching her when you touched the altar?*"

"*No, but—wait. Yes, I was.*"

"*You were?*"

"*Yes. I'm sure of it.*"

"*Oh. Well. Isn't it nice when we can solve mysteries so easily, Boss?*"

"*Yeah. It's great.*"

I relaxed onto the bed and closed my eyes. The bed was both lumpy and too soft; they must have paid extra for it.

"*Okay, I know some of what just happened: I just got some memories back.*"

"*Boss, that's . . . I don't know what that is.*"

"*Yeah.*"

I tried to concentrate; to work it out.

Verra, the Demon Goddess, patron of my ancestors, had

arranged for my perceptions to be altered, and for some of my memories to be suppressed. The best way to control someone's actions is to control the information upon which he makes his decisions. Some methods of controlling someone's information are nastier than others.

None of which addressed the questions of what she wanted me to do, or to not do, and I wanted to know so that I could cross her, just out of spite.

I realized that I was shying away from considering exactly which memories had been taken and were now restored, I guess for the same reason that, on a long-ago occasion when I'd been stabbed, I had tried not to picture the piece of steel that was inside of me. The whole idea was—

"You're trembling, Boss."

"Yeah, well. How are you doing?"

"Not so good. What they did to you, they did to me, too."

"Not they. Her."

"That doesn't help."

And the other thing was, I didn't know which memories were taken, and which had come back. It's been weeks now, and I still don't know. Memory doesn't work like that. Sometimes you can dig around in your memory looking for something the way you'd dig through a desk drawer, and maybe even find it. Sometimes you can just explore your memories like going through the old trunks in an attic, and find interesting things. Sometimes you can follow memories, one to the other, like a twisty corridor, just to see where they lead.

But you can't investigate your own memory to see what is there that used to be missing.

And in a way, that was the horror of the whole thing; that's what still is. What memories, or memories of memories, are back, waiting to bite me? And what is still missing?

I brought myself to a sitting position, lit a candle, found the jug of wine, and drank some. It had that taste that reminds me of old shoe leather. I'm told that wine experts really like that taste, when there's only a little of it. That isn't as silly as it sounds; there are any number of things that are good when you have a little, and bad when you have too much; like the way we sometimes forget things that are either unpleasant, or not worth remembering. A little bit of that is okay.

There was way too much taste of old shoe leather.

I set the jug down.

"*Not getting drunk, Boss? I'm impressed.*"

"*Loiosh, when was the last time you saw me drunk?*"

"*Yesterday, when you left Valabar's.*"

"*I wasn't drunk, I was just happy.*"

"*So happy you almost passed out right outside of Sethra's door.*"

"*I don't remember that.*"

"*I'm not surprised.*"

"*Okay, other than that. No, never mind.*"

I sat back on the bed again, leaning against the wall. I had touched the altar. Okay. I'm no expert on how those things work, but I could believe that this would give me some sort of connection to the Goddess. Only I was wearing the Phoenix Stone amulet, which ought to make that impossible. And, even if it wasn't, what sort of contact with the Goddess could restore memories she had taken away?

It was hard to concentrate on that. The idea of her messing around inside my head like that was—

"*You're grinding your teeth, Boss.*"

I stopped grinding my teeth, sat back again, and tried to relax. I cursed Verra under my breath for a while. That helped. Besides, if the Phoenix Stone was working, she couldn't hear me.

I wanted to get up and walk somewhere, because I think better that way. I also didn't want to leave the safety of my room. Or maybe I should say the security.

I took a knife from my boot and threw it into the wall. I made a loud, echoing "thunk." I hoped I'd get some complaints from management. Then I could slap management around and explain what I thought about the quality of the room. That would make me feel better. I found another knife, and sent that one to join the first. It landed about four inches away. I used to be better.

I got up, retrieved the knives, sat on the bed, and threw them again. The results were about the same, but now there were four nice gashes in the wall. By the time the count was up to a score, I had improved a little and become convinced that no one was going to complain about the noise, so I stopped and replaced the knives. I had another sip of wine, then threw the jug out the window. It made a good crash when it hit the ground. Someone yelled something unintelligible. I would have answered, but I didn't have anything unintelligible to say.

"*Not thirsty anymore, Boss?*"

"*That really was terrible wine.*"

"*I see.*"

"*Remind me not to buy it again.*"

"*All right.*"

"*It has to be Spellbreaker.*"

"*Boss?*"

"*Spellbreaker. It's now part of Lady Teldra. And I was touching Lady Teldra, and the altar at the same time. Somehow Lady Teldra broke whatever enchantment was messing up my head.*"

"*How could it do that?*"

"*I have no idea.*"

"*Oh. Well, good then. That's settled.*"

I lay back on the bed and stared at the ceiling. I should have paid the boy to clean the ceiling, too. Shadows from the chair, and Loiosh, and Rocza all flickered across the walls as the candle flame danced. Loiosh must have blown it out. Or maybe flapped it out. All of which means that eventually I must have fallen asleep.

6

SERTALIA CHEESE

You make cheese out of the milk of some animal like a cow or a goat.

Okay, now you know everything I know about cheesemaking.

No doubt there is a whole art to it, and I'm told that the Teckla in every region of the Empire have their own special sorts of cheese, but for the life of me I have no idea what the subtle differences are, or how they might go about flavoring them, or why one sort crumbles when you look at it funny, while another hangs together like roofing mud.

What we were served after the soup was a Valabar tradition called Sertalia—a very soft cheese that you spread, rather than slice, and that had a flavoring reminiscent of wild savory, and a bit of sweetness. It also produced just the least tingle on the tip of the tongue.

It was served on a cracker about which nothing can be said, because it had no flavor at all—it was a blank slate upon which could be written whatever sort of cheese one wished.

They placed the crackers, on their little plates, and the cheese in their little tubs with little knives, on the table right before the fish; in other words, right before the first real, substantial part of the meal— before the meat, if I might use a metaphor in an almost literal sense. It's your last, deep breath before the plunge, and it comes just when you've adjusted to the water.

But don't eat very many. There is a great deal left to come, and you can't fill up now, or you'll have no room to be surprised by what is surprising, and delighted by what is delightful.

I slept badly, waking up several times. This is unusual for me, but I was in an unusual situation. However, each time I woke I felt Loiosh and Rocza's presence, which was reassuring. At some point, though I don't remember doing it, I must have removed Lady Teldra's sheath from my belt and set it next to me on the bed. When I finally woke to see morning filtering in through the little window, my hand was on the hilt, and my thoughts were of the time she had found me in the middle of nowhere, asking for my help, and setting off the train of events that had led to her death.

There was a terrible sadness there, but it didn't come from her; it was all mine. While I felt her presence, it wasn't as if she had any thoughts or feelings, although Sethra had implied that someday she would "wake up." I wondered what that would be like. It could get awful crowded inside my head, what with one thing and another.

I got up and said, "Klava. I must find klava."

A few minutes later I was dressed as Sandor. I didn't see anyone as I left the inn, and not too many as I made my way to a klava vendor down the street. He also had fresh muffins. Ten minutes later, I was ready to face the world, more or less.

"Okay, Boss. What's the plan? Or am I asking too much?"

"You're asking too much."

It was just a few steps back to Six Corners and the little shop. I walked in and called out, "Jakoub!"

He emerged from the back area, frowned at me, and said, "What is it?" I thought his tone rather brusque, almost impatient.

I said, "I believe you have some things for me."

He looked at me from under the frown, I think finding something familiar about my voice. I took my beret off, and the change in his facial expression was quite gratifying; I guess I really can do a decent disguise. "My lo—"

"Yes, yes. Do you have my things?"

"They're ready, m'lord."

"Excellent. I'll wear the boots, but wrap the sheath up in something."

"At once, m'lord."

Sandor had never expected to be treated with that much respect.

Jakoub reached under the counter, and produced the boots, as promised, then went off to get my new sheath. I went around the counter and sat on his stool, pulled off my old boots, and put the new ones on. Even as I was struggling with the left, the right was fitting itself to me, adjusting to the form of my foot. It tickled, especially when it worked its way up my calf. Jakoub watched my face carefully to see if I was happy with them, or else to catch me giggling.

We hardened, cold-blooded killers don't giggle very much.

It took only about two minutes for both of them to finish their adjustments; Jakoub really was very good at what he did. He returned with the sheath. I inspected it, making sure all the nice little extras were in place and worked the way I expected them to. They did. I nodded and returned it to him. He bowed and wrapped it in the sort of paper they wrap fresh fish in at the market.

"Will that be all, m'lord?"

"Not quite," I said. He tensed only a little, and waited.

"On what day do you make deliveries to that house on Stranger's Road?"

"Homeday, m'lord."

"Do you ever run into anyone else making deliveries that day?"

"Occasionally, m'lord."

"So I can assume that there are several people showing up there with money every day. That is, you know nothing to contradict that?"

"No, m'lord."

I looked at him, trying to see if he was holding anything back. I can never tell, but I always look anyway. I nodded and tossed him a few extra coins, then left his shop.

A quick trip to the room to drop off the sheath was enough time to convince me I was going to like the boots. Jakoub did good work. I hoped I wouldn't have to kill him. I headed out, intending to go back to Stranger's Road to see who else would show up there. I made it about halfway.

"*Boss—*"

"*Hmm?*"

"*Someone's . . .*"

"*Loiosh?*"

"*I . . .*"

My stomach did a flip-flop and my brain shut down, but my feet took over, leading me into the first small side street I came to, and then into a doorway, so I was pretty much out of sight.

"*Can you come to me?*"

He didn't say anything, but there was a flutter of wings, and Rocza landed on my left shoulder, Loiosh on my right. I felt a little better for a moment, until I realized that I was picking up feelings of panic from Rocza. If Rocza was scared, I was scared.

"*Loiosh, what is it?*"

"*Fighting. . . .*"

He wobbled on my shoulder, and gripped it harder. I tried to think to Rocza, to ask her what was going on, but I didn't sense that she understood. I felt her fear and confusion, an echo of my own. I touched Lady Teldra's hilt. Then I must have drawn her, because she was in my hand, and I was looking around the empty street. A tingling—not unlike what I used to feel from Spellbreaker— -ran up my wrist, my arm, my shoulder, to—

"Thanks, Boss. That helped. I'm okay now."

"What helped? What did what? What happened?"

"Someone tried to find me."

"And you stopped him? How?"

"I don't know."

"I didn't know you could do that."

"Neither did I. And I almost couldn't."

"Can you tell me anything about what sort of spell it was?"

"You mean, on account of I know so much about magic?"

"Loiosh, you know how witchcraft feels."

"Well, it wasn't that."

"Okay."

". . . Exactly."

I sighed.

"It's hard to describe, Boss. It felt a little like that, but—"

"Okay. Back to the room."

I sheathed Lady Teldra as Loiosh and Rocza launched themselves into the air again. I took a couple of steps, then stopped; I knew what I wanted to do. I dug out a stub of pencil and scrap of paper, and scribbled out a note.

"Loiosh."

He landed on my shoulder and accepted the paper.

"Get this where it needs to be."

"Then what?"

"Then you act as guide."

I could feel some objections forming in my familiar's mind, but he left them unsaid, and just launched himself into the air. Rocza remained in the area, keeping a lookout for me. I wandered around a bit, as I figured it would take Loiosh a couple of hours.

I made it back to the room without incident. By the time I got there, Loiosh had completed his mission, as evidenced by the fellow floating cross-legged about six inches off the floor. I took just a second to close my eyes. The preliminaries were over; the meal was about to begin.

"Hello, Daymar," I said. "I hope I didn't keep you waiting."

7

FISH

There is a god named Trout who dwells in the Halls of Judgment. I know he's there, because I've seen him, but that's another story. In truth, I know very little about him, except that the way his name is pronounced and the symbols used to represent those sounds are identical to the fish.

No gods were brought to the table at Valabar's; just fish. But then, there are those who have claimed that tasting the fish is akin to communing with the gods. On reflection, that can't be true. I've communed with the gods, and eating the trout at Valabar's is a much richer, more rewarding, and more enlightening experience.

And certainly more pleasant.

I don't know any of the rituals that accompany the worship of the god named Trout, but the ritual for the fish at Valabar's begins with a young man who unobtrusively removes your soup bowl, then returns a moment later and sets down a white plate with a tiny blue flower painted on the edge that he sets away from you. When you see that plate, there is at once a slight quickening of the pulse; you don't yet know what sort of fish will be showing up, but the plate tells you: This is serious, it's time to get to work.

Next, after an interminable wait of perhaps half a minute, Mihi shows up holding a silver platter in his left hand and two serving spoons in his right. On the platter are two large fish and several spears of goslingroot.

Telnan looked curious. I sat back and smiled. Mihi winked at me, which was not part of the ritual, but that was okay.

"Freshwater trout," announced Mihi, "from the Adrilankha River, stuffed with carrot slivers, fresh rosemary, salt, crushed black pepper, a sprinkling of powdered Eastern red pepper, minced garlic, and sliced lemon wedges. Accompanied by fresh goslingroot, quick-steamed in lemon butter."

Then, wielding the serving spoons like tongs, he reverently delivered some fish and vegetable onto our plates.

I reverently started eating.

I can't tell you a lot about the trout, other than what Mihi said, except that Mr. Valabar had once let slip that it was double-wrapped in a heat-resistant parchment so that it was steam that actually cooked it. If I knew more, I'd make it myself, as best I could. A great deal of the art of Valabar's, of course, consisted in putting astonishing amounts of effort into making sure that each ingredient was the freshest, most perfect that could be found. It's all in the details, just like assassination. Though with a good fish, more is at stake.

"If you're going to be a hero," I said, "I imagine it's important to pay attention to the details."

"Hmmm?" said Telnan.

"Uh, nothing. I was just thinking aloud."

"Oh. This is really good."

"Yes."

"The most important thing about heroics is preparation."

"Hmmm?"

He swallowed and said, "If you're going to march into a place horribly outnumbered, the big thing is to work yourself into a state where you don't mind dying, but can work to prevent it, and to have all of your spells prepared in your mind, and to make sure, well, that everything you can do is done and ready. It's the preparation they talk about. Is that what you meant by heroics?"

I nodded, even though I hadn't meant much of anything. But my mind chewed over his words as my mouth did the same with the fish.

"The only thing I can't figure out," I said after a while, "is why."

Telnan swallowed and said, "Why?"

"Why put yourself in a position where you're unlikely to survive?"

"Oh." He shrugged. "It's fun," he said, and ate some fish.

I should tell you about Daymar. I should, but I'm not sure if I can. Daymar was of the House of the Hawk, and typified much of the House: perceptive, clever, and, as they say, with a head so much in the Overcast that it had seeped in. He was tall, lanky, and, stooped a bit when he walked. He liked me for reasons I've never understood, especially when I recall our first meeting. His skills—but you'll pick those up as we go.

"Hello, Vlad. A few minutes, no more. What can I do for you?"

"Loiosh."

"Beg pardon?"

"Loiosh. That's what you can do for me."

He raised an eyebrow, which is just about his only expression. "What about him?"

"Someone attempted some form of location spell on him."

"What form?"

"That's the problem. I don't know."

"It wasn't sorcery?"

"No."

"So you're thinking it was psychics?"

"Can that be done?"

"Well, no, not exactly. You can't use psychics to find where someone is. I mean, in a physical sense."

"But you can locate him in a non-physical sense?"

Daymar nodded.

I carefully kept my face expressionless. "What does that mean, exactly? I mean, if you can't locate him physically, what can you do?"

"Locate him mentally."

"Ah. I see. You locate him mentally, but that doesn't tell you where he is physically."

Daymar nodded. "Exactly."

"Quite vivid, Boss."

"Hmmm?"

"The image in your mind of Daymar with his intestines spread all over the room."

"Oh. *I didn't know you could pick up on that."*

"I usually can't, but that one was pretty strong."

"Yeah."

I cleared my throat. "Daymar."

"Hmmm?"

"Are you related to Aibynn?"

"I'm afraid I do not know him."

I nodded. "Okay, let's try again, and see if you can help me understand."

"Understand what?"

I sighed. "What it means to locate someone without knowing where he is."

"Oh."

Daymar looked faintly befuddled. I guess that's his other expression. After a moment he said, speaking slowly, "Well, you're familiar with the tendency of psychic accumulation to form a spiritual gridwork, yes?"

"I assure you, in the small fishing village from which I come, it forms almost the sole topic of conversation."

"That wasn't funny the first time you said it, Boss."

"Shut up, Loiosh."

"Good then," said Daymar, "Well—"

I sat down on the bed. "But it wouldn't hurt for you to review it for me."

He blinked. "All right." He folded his arms. Floating above the floor with his arms folded made him look slightly ridiculous. He said, "Each mind capable of producing a significant amount of psychic energy creates a sort of image that an adept can sense. Enough of them within the same psychic location create something not unlike a grid—"

"Hold on."

He cocked his head. "Yes?"

"I think that term, 'psychic location,' is somewhere near the heart of my confusion."

"Oh. Shall I explain?"

"No. I love being confused."

"All right."

I closed my eyes. "No, explain."

"Each mind that emits energy, does so with its own characteristics."

"Okay, I can accept that."

"One characteristic is how strong it is. My own is, well, rather strong."

"Uh huh."

"Another characteristic has to do with the feel of the mind— that is how you are able to reach someone telepathically after you know him well."

"All right."

"Another has to do with shape, or the way your mind grasps his, which is used . . . never mind. Still another is, well, call it flavor."

"All right, I will."

"You can think of it as relating to not what the *mind* is like, but what the energy it produces is like. The energy comes in waves, and when you train yourself mentally, you are training to detect and work with those waves. You're lost now, aren't you?"

"Not quite. Go on."

"Okay, when I speak of flavor, I'm talking about how much space there is between those waves. There are a large variety of possibilities for the amount of space, but it isn't an infinite number. All right?"

"Uh . . . sort of."

He nodded, paused, and said, "Okay, then. Imagine a building of many stories."

"All right, I can do that."

"Minds capable of emitting energy—that is, almost any mind—can do so on any of a number of stories. When there are enough of them on a particular story, that story can be seen by an adept."

"All right."

"Imagine each flavor as being its own story."

"You're hurting my head, Daymar."

"Sorry."

"Continue."

He nodded. "A psychic location means finding the story, and where on the story a particular mind is."

I considered. "Do you know, I think I understood some of that."

"I'm sorry. I'll try again."

"No, no. Go on."

"I know, Vlad. That was a joke."

"Oh. I didn't think you did that."

"I do sometimes."

"All right. So, is there a way to go from this, uh, psychic location to a physical location?"

"Certainly."

"How?"

He gave me a curious look. "I don't know, Vlad. You're the one who did it."

"I did?"

"Yes."

"When?"

"Not long ago. Remember, I mentally located someone? And you fixed his mental location in a crystal, so I could convert it to a physical location?"

"Oh. Right. That's what that was?"

"I thought you knew."

"Uh. I guess I did, in a way. But I didn't know about the building."

"The building?"

"With all the stories."

"Oh."

"All right, then. Let's get back to this thing that happened."

"The effort to locate Loiosh?"

"Yes. If they can't go from, uh, the building to a physical location, then what were they doing?"

"I don't know."

"Can you find out?"

"I could take a look into Loiosh's head."

I nodded. "That's sort of what I was thinking."

"*Boss . . .*"

"*It doesn't hurt.*"

"*You've had it done?*"

"*Well—*"

"*Okay, Boss. You owe me one.*"

"*Yes.*"

"Go ahead, Daymar."

Daymar frowned. "I need him to move a little away from you."

"*Boss—*"

"I know. But do it anyway."

My familiar flew over to the windowsill. Daymar nodded and glanced at him; then a look of surprise spread across his features, and he said, "That's interesting."

"What, you did it already? What did you find out?"

"That was it?"

"I'm not sure," said Daymar.

"I admit that gives me a certain amount of satisfaction."

"Hmmm?"

"Nothing. What can you tell me?"

"Someone attempted a spell I've never encountered before." He sounded almost pleased.

"Can you determine what it was supposed to do?"

"Well, to find Loiosh. But I don't understand how she intended to make the transition from ment—"

"She?"

"Yes."

"You know the caster was female?"

He blinked. "Certainly."

"What else can you tell me about her?"

"What would you like to know?"

"Does she like trout?"

"Yes."

"Was that another joke?"

"Yes."

"Okay. I want to know if she is in the Left Hand of the Jhereg."

"What's that?"

"Okay. Then can you tell me anything about her state of mind?"

"Cold rage," said Daymar.

"Really? You can tell that?"

He nodded.

"Cold rage," I repeated.

"Boss, that makes it sound personal."

"Yeah, that's just what I was thinking."

"Who have you offended lately?"

"Daymar, I think."

"Daymar, if she had succeeded in locating Loiosh, could she have attacked me, through him?"

He frowned. "Maybe. I suppose that is possible. I don't know enough about the nature of your connection to Loiosh."

I nodded. "Okay, anything else you noticed?"

"Well, I can find her again, if you wish."

"Um, yes. But for definitions of 'find' that don't include an actual location?"

"Well, yes. Unless—"

"Unless what?"

"Unless you can do that thing you did before."

"What thing?"

"When you used that Eastern magic to find someone—"

"Oh, that."

He shrugged.

"Unfortunately, that's impossible just now."

"Oh. All right."

I sighed.

"Okay, Daymar. Thank you for showing up."

"Why?"

"Uh, why? Well, it helps me to know what—"

"No, why is it impossible?"

"Oh."

I tapped the pendant on my chest. "As long as I wear this, I cannot perform witchcraft."

"Oh. Is that why I can't feel your psychic presence?"

"Yep."

"Oh. Uh, why don't you take it off?"

"Valid question, Daymar."

"And?" I think "and" and "yes" must be Daymar's favorite words; he lingers over them the way I linger over Valabar's trout.

"If I remove it, I die."

"Oh."

I waited patiently for the inevitable question after he'd chewed that over. I could have gone ahead and answered it before he asked, but I guess in a sick way I was enjoying myself.

"What will kill you?"

"The Jhereg is trying to find me and kill me."

"Oh.

"Morganti."

"Oh."

I nodded.

"Why?" he said.

"I annoyed them."

He nodded. "You must remind me," he said, "not to annoy the Jhereg."

"I'll have Loiosh make a note. He handles things like that."

"*Shut up, Loiosh.*"

"*I—*"

"Of course," said Daymar, "if you want to, I can shield you while you perform the spell."

"You can?"

"Certainly."

"You can do what this amulet does?"

"Well no, not exactly. But I can keep your location from being known."

"I don't understand. What, exactly, are you talking about?"

"I mean that I can keep them from finding you if you take that thing off."

"Finding me in the, uh, building? Or in this room?"

"Both," he said, with more confidence than I felt.

"It also blocks sorcery; can you keep them from finding me that way?"

"Oh," said Daymar. "No, I'm afraid there my skills fail."

I pondered. "I suppose I can separate the two parts of the amulet, and just leave—"

"Boss—"

"Hmmm?"

"This is Daymar."

"What's your point?"

"Boss, what is he good at?"

"What's your point?"

"And what will happen when you take the amulet off?"

"Oh. Good thinking, chum."

"Daymar, I have an idea."

"Who had the idea?"

"What's the idea, Vlad?"

"Tell me if this will work. When I remove the amulet . . ."

I explained. He blinked. I couldn't tell if it was the "I should have thought of that" blink, or the "I've never met anyone so stupid" blink.

"Well?"

"I can do that."

"You're sure?"

"Yes."

I leaned back. "Well."

"But what about sorcery?"

"We take our chances. Make it fast."

He nodded. "Fast it is. Would you like to do it now?"

"Give me a moment."

He nodded.

I leaned back and considered the various ways this could go

wrong. Other than the possibility of a horrible death if Daymar had overestimated his skill, I couldn't come up with any. And I did trust Daymar; often in spite of myself, but I did trust him.

I did trust him.

"Okay," I said. "Let's do this thing."

Daymar nodded. "Take the amulet off," he said.

8

STEAMED GOSLINGROOT

When steaming, less is more, and this applies more to goslingroot than, perhaps, to anything else. Of course, it isn't that easy, especially because you can never find two spears that are the same thickness, not to mention length, which means that steaming them to perfection requires, in its own way, as much feel as is required of a broiler-man.

The flavor of this root is subtle by nature, and, to be frank, not all that interesting. But it's wonderful for absorbing butter, or for taking one of those cheese sauces that are so popular in certain kinds of Eastern cuisine. But too much of anything can turn it into mush.

Valabar's didn't put a cheese sauce on it; just lemon-butter and salt And it goes without saying that they didn't over-steam it. And its very simplicity made it a perfect accompaniment for the fish.

The whole business of finding the right vegetable, or side dish, to accompany each of the major elements of the meal is its own art, and deserves more discussion than I'm competent to give it; that is still another area where my abilities as an eater outshine my abilities as a cook.

Telnan took pleasure in this perfect contrast without being aware of it, which gave me the chance to feel superior to him. One must never pass up the opportunity to feel superior to a Dzur.

We didn't speak for a while as, each in our own way, we relished the skills of Valabar and Sons.

I took the amulet off, and slipped it into its box. As I closed the
box, I kept watching Daymar's face, looking for—well, I'm not sure
what I was looking for. What I saw was a slight furrow to his brow,
and then he closed his eyes—not tightly, but the way you close
your eyes when you don't want to be distracted by what's in front
of you. It helped to be touching Lady Teldra's hilt, though I don't
remember deciding to do so.

Daymar settled to the floor.

I was trying to decide if that should worry me, when I noticed
perspiration on his forehead. Yes, I decided, this should probably
worry me.

I heard his voice in my head saying, "*Put it back on.*"

I opened the box, removed the amulet, and slipped it over my
head.

Daymar opened his eyes and exhaled long and slow.

"My," he said.

"Not as easy as you'd thought it would be?"

"It took some effort." He frowned. "I have a headache."

"You have the right to one. There's a bed here; perhaps you'd
like to lie down for a while."

"I don't believe I can move," he said, and lay back onto the
floor.

I sat on the bed, staring at the prostrate Hawklord and trying
to think of what to say. He solved the problem by saying, "Her
name is Crithnak."

"You got the mind-probe off?"

"Barely."

"Crithnak," I repeated.

"Yes."

"She must be very strong."

"Yes."

He closed his eyes, opened them, and sat up, moaning. "And she really hates you."

"It *is* personal."

"Oh, yes."

"Hmmm. Any idea why?"

He nodded. "You destroyed her sister's soul."

"I what?"

"You killed her sister. Morganti."

I stared at him. *"Loiosh, have I been sleepwalking?"*

"Nope."

"How about sleepkilling?"

"Not so far as I know."

"Uh, Daymar, did you get any details on that?"

"She doesn't know how it happened."

"But she thinks I did it?"

"Oh, yes."

"Why?"

"Well, her sister was going after you right before she died."

I tried to organize all the questions in my head, but there were too many. For no special reason, I started with, "Why was her sister going after me?"

He frowned. "I'm not sure. It seemed to be impersonal—"

"Business?"

"I suppose. But I didn't pick up any details."

"Were you able to tell if she was trying to kill me?"

"Who?"

I stared at him.

"I mean," he said. "Do you mean Crithnak, or her sister?"

"Her sister."

"Sorry, I wasn't able to tell. It wasn't going through her mind that way. I can only pick up what she's—"

"All right. I wonder—"

"Hmmm?"

"Well, yesterday, someone came after me. Appeared out of nowhere. I killed her, but it wasn't Morganti."

He tilted his head at me. "I don't suppose you can make a mistake about something like that?"

"You mean, make a mistake about it being Morganti?"

"Yes."

"Uh, not likely."

He glanced at the hilt of Lady Teldra protruding from my belt. "You didn't use, uh, that, then?"

"Actually, I did. But she—that is, the weapon—never came within fifty feet of the sorceress who attacked me."

"So?"

There was a wealth of information contained in that "So?" and most of it consisted of things I didn't want to know. "You mean, Lady Teldra could have destroyed her soul from a distance?"

"Certainly, if the right combination of circumstances existed."

"Even if I didn't tell her to?"

"Did you tell her not to?"

I glared at him. "Okay, what constitutes the right combination of circumstances?"

"Hmmm. Good question."

"Thanks. I was proud of it."

He frowned at me. "Vlad, are you angry?"

"No, I'm overwhelmed with joy and love for all humanity, but I'm working very hard to conceal it."

"That was sarcasm, right?"

"Right."

"Okay. Are you angry with me?"

I sighed. "Yes, but I shouldn't be. I should be just angry in general. I'll work on that. In the meantime—"

He nodded. "To answer your question as best I can, it has to do with the exact nature of the weapon, and with, well . . . I presume this sorceress cast a spell at you?"

I tasted my own fear again as I remembered standing in that alley, holding Lady Teldra and staring at the sorceress as she—

"Yes," I said.

"Then it has to do with the nature of the spell. If it was one that opened a channel through the etherium, and there was nothing preventing reverse influx, then it would be possib—"

"You understand, Daymar, that I have no idea what you just said?"

He blinked. "No, I suppose you wouldn't."

"What's the short version?"

"There's no way to tell for sure, but it is possible that your weapon was able to take her soul because of the spell she cast at you."

"Well." I swallowed. "That's wonderful."

Daymar slowly rose, until he was floating, cross-legged, a foot or so off the ground again.

"Feeling better?" I asked.

He nodded.

I let out a long, slow breath. "Okay. Where was I?"

"You were just using a Morganti weapon on a sorceress."

"Yeah, I guess I was."

"Well, Boss, you could explain that you didn't really mean it."

"Now isn't the time, Loiosh."

"Sorry."

"What you said about asking her not to . . ."

"Yes?"

"How do I do that?"

"I'm sorry, I don't know. I'm told it can be done, but—"

"Okay. So this . . . what was her name?"

"Crithnak."

"Yeah. This Crithnak wants to kill me because I killed her sister."

"Because you destroyed her soul."

I shuddered. "Okay. And she tried to locate me?"

"Yes. It was very difficult to block."

"How was she doing it?"

"Pretty much, pure psychic energy."

"Oh. I thought there wasn't anyone as good as you at that."

"That's what I thought too."

"Did it hurt your feelings?"

"A little."

I sighed. "Okay, now what?"

"Hmmm?"

"Sorry, was mostly talking to myself. Uh, thanks for all your help."

"Of course."

"May I buy you a drink?"

He shook his head. "I think I'll be heading back home."

I nodded. "Where do you live, anyway?"

"Hmmm? Loiosh knows."

"Yes, you told him, but he's never told me."

Daymar laughed, which didn't happen often. Then he vanished, leaving me to contemplate many things.

I drew Lady Teldra and studied the elegant lines of the slim, dark blade. "Did you really do that?" I asked her. She didn't answer.

I put her back in the sheath. Loiosh nuzzled my neck.

She had destroyed someone's soul.

No, I had destroyed someone's soul. It wasn't the first time, but the other times I'd been paid a whole lot of money, and had reason to believe it was justified, at least by the standards of the Jhereg.

This was different.

What would Cawti say? What would Aliera say?

Why did I care what Aliera would say?

"Take some time, Boss."

"Hmmm?"

"Take some time. Get over it."

"I'm not sure it's that easy."

"I know. Take some time anyway."

It seemed like good advice. I lay down on the bed with the intention of taking some time, but after about a minute I couldn't stand it anymore, so I got up. Inactivity isn't one of my favorite things.

I paced around the room for a bit, but the room wasn't nearly big enough to pace in effectively.

"We going out, Boss?"

"Yeah. I need to walk."

They went out the window, I went out the door.

Walking around while people were trying to kill me and my head was filled with things other than how to avoid them probably wasn't all that smart, but it's something I've done before. This time, at any rate, I knew I'd be hard to find, and I had Loiosh and Rocza flying around and keeping an eye on me.

In any case, I got away with it; I spent a couple of hours tromping aimlessly around South Adrilankha without anyone trying to kill me, or, indeed, taking any notice of me.

At one point, I found myself back again at the place where my grandfather had lived for so many years, but I didn't stop. I thought about picking up some food, then realized I wasn't hungry. I tried to remember when I last ate, and, after working it out, decided it was probably a bad sign and I should eat something anyway.

I picked up some food at one of the stands and ate a bit while I walked. I tossed the rest into an alley for Loiosh and Rocza, who enjoyed it more than I did. I remember an old woman walking past me, wearing an off-white knitted scarf over her head, and thick, heavy shoes. Three or four children went running past me. Old people and children; you didn't seem to see either one in most of Adrilankha; in the Easterners' quarter, it seemed like they were the only ones around.

I walked past the shops of those who were wealthy by the standards of South Adrilankha, and the carts and booths of those who were not. I stopped occasionally, pretending to be interested in something, then moved on.

I wondered if I was the only guy in history to destroy someone's soul without even being aware of it. That would be a first, wouldn't it? I suddenly thought of Napper, whom I had watched fall to a Morganti weapon in the middle of a battle. I'd known him, and even liked him, and he hadn't deserved to die that way. And neither had this sorceress of the Left Hand whom I had killed, and destroyed, and to whom I had forever denied Deathgate and rebirth.

"You'll pay for that."

It took me a moment to realize that the voice was real, and not in my head. I focused on the fellow talking to me, and remembered I was still Sandor.

"I beg your pardon?"

"You'll be paying for that."

"For—?"

"That."

He pointed to the remains of a small blue ceramic cup that was in my hand. It had broken cleanly, and I was bleeding a bit, just below the fourth finger. "How much?" I said.

"Six and eight," he told me.

I nodded, and managed to dig out seven orbs, which I handed to him then walked off without waiting for change.

"You're bleeding, Boss."

"Just a little."

"But you're dripping it on the ground."

"So? Oh. Right."

I cupped my hand, and bought a piece of cheap fabric to wrap it in. I think someone asked what had happened; I don't remember answering.

I felt better after a few hours. There was a comforting anonymity in being Sandor, maybe because he hadn't destroyed anyone's soul. In any case, it finally penetrated that I wasn't making progress toward any of the things I needed to accomplish: figuring out what the Left Hand was up to, getting Cawti out of this mess, or figuring out how to keep myself safe from an irate sorceress.

Once more, I felt the desire to just walk into the house on Stranger's Road, start hacking away with Lady Teldra, and see what happened. Looking back, I have no idea why I'd been so shaken up by what I did to that sorceress yet was able to contemplate letting my weapon loose on the inhabitants of that house. No, it doesn't make sense, but I'm giving it to you as I recall it.

In any case, no, I didn't go charging into the house; I just wanted to.

"Ready to go back, Boss?"

"I'm ready to do something constructive, if I can figure out what."

"If not, you can always go kill something."

"I've thought about that. But, you know, I sort of want to have an idea of who to kill."

"Oh, anyone."

"Just now, that isn't funny."

"Yes, it is."

"I'll demonstrate funny for you."

"When?"

"Later."

"You're almost back to the room. Are we going in?"

"I don't know. Why? Nothing to do there."

"It's safer than out here."

"When have I given the least thought to my personal safety?"

"Okay, Boss. I'll give you that one. That was funny."

"I am fulfilled. Let's go back and observe that house some more. That's not quite as useless as anything else I can think of."

So we did, and watched for a few hours as another courier or two made drop-offs. If nothing else, I was getting a pretty good feel for how much money was involved in this operation. It was a lot. It was certainly enough that they wouldn't hesitate to brush aside an inconvenient Easterner. In a way, that thought was more annoying than either the Jhereg wanting my soul, or that sorceress who was after me.

"*By all means, Boss, don't let them insult you.*"

"*Shut up, Loiosh.*"

Between the pointless walking and useless observation, I was feeling a bit better as I headed back toward my room. I stopped and picked up a good loaf of bread, some peppers, and some sausages. There were a number of people queued up for the sausages, from which I concluded they must be all right. The woman in front of me, a frail-looking grandmother, glanced at me and said, "Jancsi has been getting busier and busier. Word must be getting out."

I nodded.

She said, "I've known about his sausages for thirty years, you know."

"Maybe you shouldn't have told all your friends."

"Mmm?"

"Never mind."

She gave me an odd look.

A little later she said, "Why are you wandering around in the middle of the day?"

"I'm permitted to leave for lunch."

"Oh? What do you do?"

"I keep the books for a slaughterhouse."

She nodded. "That isn't bad, I suppose, if you must work for someone."

"What else is there? I'm not the type to run a shop, or sell sausages in the street."

"My son is looking to buy some land. Grow some maize, maybe raise some sheep and some chickens."

I nodded. "How is that looking?"

"He's a hard worker, my son. He'll get there."

"He works in the slaughterhouses?"

She nodded. "And we save everything, he and I."

"Ah. I wish him the best of fortune."

She smiled, her whole face lighting up like I'd just given her the farm. "Thank you," she said. Then Jancsi asked what she wanted and I was saved from further embarrassment.

I ate the bread, peppers, and sausages as I walked. The sausages were dry, but good and peppery, with a bite on the lips and the front of the tongue. And there were people walking by who weren't any taller than I was. In fact, I was taller than a lot of them, and I rather liked that.

I remembered when there were Phoenix Guards all over these streets, facing off against Easterners holding kitchen knives, hammers, sticks, and the occasional rusted sword. There were no signs of that now. Had all of the anger vanished, or was it still there, where I couldn't see it, waiting to explode again? I had no idea. Nor was I certain if I cared, except that Cawti cared, and was likely to be involved if something happened.

I didn't know these people—people who dreamed of things like buying land.

I wrapped the remnants of the sausage in its butcher's paper to give to the jhereg later, and slipped into a place called Ferenk's. I treated myself to a Fenarian peach brandy called Oregigeret, and sat down at a table to drink it. It stung my tongue and burned my throat, and filled my nose with a harsh smokiness and something almost like pitch. It was wonderful. The Dragaerans have brandy, too, though they don't call it that. And it's right that they don't call it brandy, because if you like brandy, you won't like the stuff they distill. When it came to brandy, I was an Easterner.

Ferenk's was nearly empty, save for a couple of old men who looked like they drank professionally. Well, why else would you be here at this time of day? The one at the table next to mine nodded and gave me a half-smile full of yellow teeth. I nodded back. Maybe I should take up drinking professionally.

"Is the brandy good?" I asked him.

"I'm drinking oishka."

"Oh. How is that?"

He grinned, and I tried to avoid looking at his teeth. "Does the job," he said.

"Helps you forget your troubles?"

"I don't have troubles. I have oishka."

"Good answer."

Yes, there was a lot to be said for being a professional drinker. Of course, wandering around in a drunken cloud would mean I'd certainly be dead within a couple of days. But they'd be pleasant days.

"You're retired?" I asked my companion.

He nodded. "I hurt my leg pretty good, and now my daughter and her husband support me." He grinned. "I don't mind a bit. I worked hard enough and long enough."

"Doing what, if you don't mind my asking?"

"We had some land we worked for Lord Cerulin."

I nodded. "What happened?"

"The mare kicked me, bless her heart."

He laughed and held up his glass for a moment, silently toasting the mare, then drained it and wandered up to get another.

I finished the brandy and thought about having a second glass, but ended up walking out onto the street.

I returned to the room long enough to give Loiosh and Rocza the remains of the sausage. While they ate, I pondered. Having rejected drinking as a way of life, I was now back to trying to

figure out how to approach my problem. Or all of my problems.
Or any of my problems.

What I wanted to do was get hold of Kragar and have him
collect information on this Crithnak. But I couldn't lower my de-
fenses long enough to reach him. It was frustrating.

"*You could walk over there.*"

"*Yeah, I've been thinking about it.*"

"*And?*"

"*This disguise is pretty good in the Easterners' quarter. I don't
know if I want to bet my life on it in my old area.*"

"*You've always been good at sneaking around without being noticed.*"

"*Yeah, good enough for most things, Loiosh. But the way they're
looking for me now—*"

"*Well, you could break into the house and see what you can find.*"

"*I could, if I leave Lady Teldra behind.*"

"*Oh. Right. I imagine that's not going to happen.*"

"*Doesn't seem likely.*"

"*This is good sausage.*"

It was strange that, after years of wandering around the coun-
tryside, completely out of touch with everyone except the occasional emotionally damaged Teckla (there's a story there, but skip
it), I felt more alone and isolated here, now, than in all that time.
I suppose it was because I was physically close to so many of the
people I had missed, but was still out of touch with them.

Once again, I touched the hilt of Lady Teldra. There was that
feeling of presence again. It made me think of the time I had spent
in the East. Not the unpleasant part, which was actually most of
it, but the feeling of standing with my eyes closed, face up toward
the Furnace, like a shower-bath of warmth. And yes, she had
saved my life; but she had destroyed a soul in an action so auto-
matic to her, so instinctive, that I hadn't even been aware it was
happening.

Or was I reading too much into it? Very likely. There were

probably, I don't know, mechanics involved—things that she just
sort of did. Putting any kind of moral weight on her actions was
perhaps like blaming the rock that someone throws at your head.

I badly wanted to be able to be able to communicate with
her, but all I got was a vague sensation; pleasant, but frustrating.

*If I'm not around when she wakes up, you'll remember to say hello
for me,* Sethra had said, or something like that.

"*Hey! Lady Teldra! Wake up!*"

She didn't.

I wanted to go to sleep, or get drunk, or something. What
I *needed* was my old Organization, with all its sources of information, and legwork; but I couldn't reach Kragar or even Morrolan's
network. I was isolated, and frighteningly helpless. Which was
odd, considering that I still had all of my skills, my familiars, a lot
of money, and a Great Weapon. If I could just—

Hmmmm.

I *did* have a lot of money, didn't I?

"*Boss? You have something?*"

"*Yeah,*" I told Loiosh. "*Yeah, I think I do.*"

"*Is it something stupid?*"

"*Oddly enough, no. There was something I'd forgotten.*"

"*Which means—?*"

I checked the time. It had made it to evening; there would
now be people starting to fill the streets.

"*Come on, Loiosh. It's time to move.*"

"*Sounds good. Does that mean there's a plan?*"

"*Just watch me.*"

9

CHILLED DEFRINA

Mihi removed the wine and replaced it with a new bottle, providing us with new glasses, as well. Again the feather, the glove, the tongs.

Defrina is a white wine with just a hint of, of all things, cherries. The sweetness, which would normally have been too much for me, was cut by an extra chill that Mihi had put on it just for me. The first sip said a merry hello to the flavors already dancing around my tongue, and then it slid down my throat still leaving behind it the taste of the trout, but brightened just a little, if that makes any sense.

I leaned back and studied my dinner companion. "Fun," I repeated. He grinned and nodded.

The first several things that came to mind were all sarcastic, but sarcasm didn't really go with Valabar's trout and a good, chilled white wine. I said, "Can you explain that?"

He frowned and considered for a moment, then said, "You know, I don't think I can. I'll try."

I drank some wine and nodded.

"You see," he said. "There's this feeling you get when things are happening almost too fast for you to handle, and if you make a mistake, you're dead. You'd be scared out of your mind if you weren't too busy. Do you know what I mean?"

"Well, I know how I feel at times like that. I don't much care for it."

"Don't you?"

I ate some more fish and drank some more wine.

"In fact," I said, "I don't remember enjoying it, or not enjoying it. Like you said, I'm too busy."

"Well, there you are."

I grunted. "Afterward, though, I hate it."

He grinned. "I guess that's the difference."

"As long as there is one."

"That's just what I was thinking, Loiosh."

"Of course," he added, "the cause enters into it as well."

"The cause?"

"The reason you're fighting."

"Oh. It isn't just to fight?"

"Well, sometimes it is."

"You mean, most of the time it is?"

"Yeah, most of the time."

"Uh huh."

"But not the important times."

"Mmm. Care to explain that?"

"It isn't difficult. When you do something big, you want it to matter." He looked at me. "Well, don't you?"

"I don't usually get into things by my own plan. I get dumped into them, and then I'm too busy trying to stay alive to think about the importance of the cause."

He nodded as if he understood.

I had another bite of fish, and another sip of wine.

I remembered a friend I'd had named Ricard—one of the few people I knew who weren't involved with the Organization. He was an Easterner, a stocky fellow with thin hair, and we'd eaten dinner together, gotten drunk on his boat on the bay, and argued about matters great and small. He worked ten hours a day, four days a week, doing what I pretended to do—keeping the books for a slaughterhouse—and two or three evenings a week would play obscure music on the cimbalon

at an obscure house in South Adrilankha. Every couple of months he
would have saved up enough silver to take me out for dinner at Val-
abar's, and I'd take him a month later; we might or might not have dates
with us. He enjoyed good food more than anyone else I've ever met,
which made him a very pleasant companion. Right about this point in
the meal, he'd look up at me with a big grin and say, "This is why we
work so hard."

Sandor—that's me, if you've forgotten—made his way generally
southward, to the area where the streets start running downhill toward the eastern docks of Adrilankha. The streets were, indeed,
more crowded now as evening fell. As people passed me by, I was
struck again by a little thing I'd noticed before, when comparing
people in this part of Adrilankha to those in "the City": Scars. I
don't mean anything big or grotesque, but, like, one guy I passed
had this little scar on the corner of his mouth; another had a slight
white mark above an eyebrow. And, yes, here and there were missing limbs, or obvious, dramatic scars that spoke of someone who
had a story to tell his grandchildren; but even the little ones
you'd never see among Dragaerans, among those who could just
pop over to a physicker and make the injury look like it had
never happened.

Dragaerans: the scarless people.

"What's funny, Boss?"

"Nothing, Loiosh. I was just imagining walking up to Morrolan
and saying, 'Greetings, oh scarless one.'"

"And that was funny?"

"Imagining the look on his face was funny."

The streets in this part of the city were very narrow indeed,
and twisted even more than in most of South Adrilankha; I was
once told that this was done by design, and had something to do
with water runoff. While I won't claim to understand it, I have

vague memories of being here once or twice as a child during heavy rainstorms, and that I enjoyed playing in the water that rushed down toward the sea.

There was nothing here to indicate the names of any of the streets, but I recognized the one I wanted, took it, and started climbing again. Except when the street widened now and then to make room for a market, everything was the same: cheap, wooden houses, each one with a single door, a stairway around the side, two windows on each floor, and rooms for four families. One after another, just like that, as if some peasant had planted them in rows, watered them, and they'd grown up and were just waiting to be harvested.

I found the one I wanted and walked up the stairway on the side.

"*Remember, Boss. Pound, don't clap.*"

"*I remember.*"

I pounded on the door with my fist.

After a moment, the door opened, and Ricard was standing there, wearing a raggedy white shirt and a pair of shorts. "Yes?"

"Hey there, Ricard."

He tilted his head at me, then his eyes widened and I got a big grin.

"Vlad! Come in! Mornin'!"

For Ric it was always morning, no matter what time of day it was. I'd never asked him why because I was afraid of the answer.

"Brandy?" he said.

"Always."

It is very difficult to say no to Ricard.

His place, two rooms hung with pastoral watercolors, with a sort of kitchen attached to the main room, was comfortable enough, and I don't know what sort of brandy he brought me, but it was much silkier than what I usually drink, maybe not as complex, but there was no question it had been made from peaches, and it was just fine. We drank some and smiled.

"You're in disguise," he said, as if it were a joke.

"Yes, I am," I said, as if it weren't. "I half thought you'd be playing somewhere tonight."

"Tomorrow."

I nodded. "How have things been?"

"With me? Glorious. Ever heard of Bastrai?"

"The violinist? Sure, even I've heard of him."

"I went over to hear him at the Twisted Sheet, and when he was done, I ended up playing all night with his backup musicians."

"That must have been fun."

"It was wonderful." He grinned.

"I need to introduce you to a fellow I know named Aibynn. He's from the Island."

"He play?"

"He's a drummer."

Ric nodded, but didn't seem terribly excited; I guess he knew a lot of drummers.

We drank some brandy. Ricard sat back and looked half serious; which is about as serious as Ricard gets, barring catastrophe. "What's going on, Vlad?"

"I need help."

"Does this have something to do with your business?"

"No. Well, yeah, among other things. It's pretty complicated."

Ricard knew what I used to do, at least some of it, but we never talked about it. He nodded. "Could it get me killed?"

I considered carefully. "I don't think so. Not for what I want you to do, and if you stay out of the rest of it."

"Okay. What do you need?"

"I take it you know a lot of people."

He frowned. "I'm not sure what you mean."

"What with playing and all that, you meet a lot of people, that's all."

"Well, yes."

"Friends, acquaintances, just folks you run into, get their names, maybe hang out in an inn, or on the boat."

"Uh huh."

"I need to speak to some of them."

"Uh . . . what sort of people?"

"People who need money, and don't mind taking some risks for it."

"So, this could get them killed?"

"Yeah."

He nodded. "How much money?"

"Enough for each them to buy a little piece of farmland."

His eyes widened again, then he grinned. "Can I get in on this?"

"No. It can get them killed."

He drink some more brandy. "How likely is it?"

"To get them killed? I don't think very, but I might be wrong."

"Well—"

"No, Ricard. If you need that much money, I'll give it to you, but I don't want you involved in this. I couldn't stand it if, you know."

He sighed and nodded. "Okay, then. Other than wanting money, and me not caring too much if anything happens to them, are there any other qualifications you need?"

"Well, it would help if they aren't complete idiots."

"Most people are, you know."

I grinned. That was one of the things we liked to argue about when too drunk to be coherent. "Find some of the exceptions," I said.

He smiled. "I can do that. Where is Loiosh?"

"Flying around. If he's seen with me, there goes my disguise."

"Well, give him my best."

"I will. I have. He returns his reptilian regards, admitting that he is unworthy of your attention, yet eternally grateful for the honor you show him."

Ric laughed. Loiosh said, "*Boss, you are so going to get it.*"

"All right, then," I said. "Can I buy you some dinner?"

"Sounds good. Let me get dressed."

"When we're out, call me Sandor."

"Sandor," he repeated. "Okay. I'll try to remember."

We went out and down the street, to a place that catered mostly to dockworkers. We each had a roasted fowl covered in wine, and dark bread. It was simple, but good. Ricard didn't say much during the meal. I finally said, "Something bothering you, Ric?"

"Hmmm? No, just thinking about that list you want."

"Ah. Good. Think you can come up with names for me?"

"Oh, yes. Easy. Do you just want the list, or should I get them together for you?"

"Good question. I think I'd like to see them one at a time."

He nodded, and flashed me a grin. "I could get to enjoy this sneaking-around stuff."

"You remind me of that last guy I ate with."

"Oh?"

"He was a Dzur, so it isn't his fault. But he liked Valabar's."

"You ate at Valabar's and didn't tell me?"

"It was sort of last-minute."

"How was it?"

"Just like you remember it, only better."

He nodded. "Next time?"

"You bet. On me."

"Other than that, how have things been?"

I don't know why I said what I did, because I've always thought

of Ric as the sort of friend you had good times with, not the sort
you dumped your troubles on. But he asked, and I heard myself
say, "I've discovered, or maybe realized, that my Goddess has been
messing with my memories."

"Huh?"

"My Goddess—"

"The Demon Goddess?"

"Yeah. Her."

"What did . . . I mean, what's happened?"

"Memories have been going away and coming back. It's been
going on for years, I guess, but something happened, and I've
managed to put some of it together. Mostly little things, but the
Demon Goddess did it, and it makes me very badly want to kill
her, and I'm not entirely sure that I couldn't do it. In fact, I think
I could. I want to. I—"

"Vlad!"

"Hmmm?"

"Do you hear what you're saying?"

I sighed. "Yeah, well. With luck, she isn't listening. Actually,
the way I'm feeling right now, I half hope she is."

"Not before I have a chance to get clear of the neighborhood,
please."

I shrugged.

He said, "About this memory stuff. How do you know the
Goddess is behind it?"

"I just know."

"You just know."

"Yeah."

"What sort of things—?"

"It's little stuff, but it's stuff that . . . well, did I ever tell you
that I had been to the Paths of the Dead?"

He stared at me, a piece of bread halfway to his mouth. "No,
you somehow didn't mention that."

I nodded. "It was several years ago, and—"

"*Why?* Not to mention, how?"

"It was business-related."

"Some business you're in."

"Yeah, I've had that same thought from time to time. Anyway, I visited the Paths of the Dead, and there are pieces of that journey that keep going away and coming back. Pieces I shouldn't be able to forget."

"Heh. Go figure."

"Another time, I got into a jam, and called on her."

"I've done that. Did she answer?"

"Yes."

He stared at me again. "Vlad, that isn't a joke, is it?"

"No."

He sat back in his chair. "You have some sort of life, my friend."

"I guess. Anyway, there are pieces of that visit—"

"Visit?"

"Yeah, odd word choice, I guess. She brought me to her halls. Or else she made me think she had, which comes out to the same thing, I suppose. And there are pieces of that visit that I've only just started remembering."

"Like what?"

"She cut my palm."

"Huh?"

"While I was talking to her, she took a knife, had me hold out my left hand, and made a cut on my palm. Then she collected some of the blood in a sort of vial or something. I don't know what she did with it."

"So, she has some of your blood."

"Yes."

"She is supposed to be a goddess of witches."

"No, that's one of her sisters."

"You sure?"

"Sure? Dealing with the Demon Goddess? I'm not sure about anything."

"The beginning of wisdom. What else?"

"Isn't that enough?"

He flashed a smile and waited for me to continue.

"Near Deathgate Falls is a statue of Kieron the Conqueror, a general from the early days of—"

"I know who he is."

"Okay. Well, the fellow I was with—a Dragon—prostrated himself before the statue. Then, a little later, he started talking, mumbling, like he was having a conversation with it. Then he got up, and said he knew how to get through the Paths, which he hadn't before."

"Hmmm. Okay."

"Well, you see, I didn't remember any of that until a couple of years later."

He nodded. "I can see where that would be upsetting."

"Yeah, well, so that's what's been going on."

"Is there more?"

I shrugged. "Now and then, a few little things come back. It's—"

"Upsetting," he said.

I nodded. "You tend to think of what's inside your head as your own, no matter what anything else is. Even Kiera can't steal that."

"Who?"

"Never mind. The point is, it keeps messing with me. Every time I think about it, I get distracted, and mad, and I want to find the Goddess and, well, you know."

"Any practical effects?"

"Hmmm?"

"Other than how you feel about it, have you forgotten anything that mattered?"

"Well, that's just it. I don't know. I need to. . . ." I tried to find the words. He waited. "With what I do, I need to have confidence in my decisions. I need to find out everything I can, and then come up with a plan of action that's as good as I can contrive. That's how I operate."

"I understand that."

"Well, but the thing is, now I can't be sure if there are important things I don't know. And worse, what if it isn't just memories? What if the, I don't know, the mechanism of my thinking has been messed with? How can I commit to any sort of action, when I can't be sure if the Goddess hasn't been screwing around with how I make decisions?"

"Why would she do that?"

"Why would she do anything? How should I know? Maybe she has plans for me."

He gave a humorless laugh. "That's a comforting thought."

"Uh huh. But, you see the problem."

He nodded. "Did you know my people were peasants?"

"Hmmm?"

"When I was boy, we worked the land not twenty miles from here, for Lady Drenta."

"Okay. . . ."

"One day Pa sent me out to plow a furrow. He put me at the right spot, then pointed to our old nag, Chalkie. He said, 'Start here and aim at for where Chalkie is. But Rico—' I said, 'Yeah, Pa?' 'If Chalkie moves, you're going to have to change your mark.'" He laughed, and I gave him a courtesy chuckle.

A little later, he heaved a contented sigh, and pushed back from the table. I nodded, and we headed back to his place, where he made up a list with names, addresses, and best time to find each one.

"Thanks, Ric."

"Will you let me know how it all turns out?"

"If you hear I'm dead, it didn't work so well."

He shook his head. "I guess, all in all, I'm glad I do what I do, not what you do."

"Proving," I said, "that you aren't a Dzur."

"I'm not sure what that means, but guess it's good."

"It's good," I said. "And good to see you again, Ric."

"You too. And Vlad—"

"Yeah?"

"It's easy to consider everyone a sucker who cares about things you don't care about. So who does that make the sucker?"

"Uh, I don't see what that connects to."

"No, but you probably will before I do."

I wished him a good evening.

I ducked into the first public house I came to in order to read the list. The first thing that surprised me was that I knew South Adrilankha better than I thought I did. I mean, he had notations like, "Third house south of Wrecked Bridge, on the east," and I knew at once where that was.

There were a couple I could see right now, and I had no reason to delay.

"Still staying with me, chum?"

"What else is there to do? I don't like this business of you wandering around without me."

"I don't like it much, either. Once this is over—"

"Yeah."

Someone named Ernest was usually home in the evening, and didn't live too far away. In the City, there were globes at various points to provide light; I'd gotten so used to them that I never thought about them. Here, though, the only light was what spilled out from houses, public and private. It was enough to keep me from tripping over ruts and dips in the road and from stumbling into people, but not much more. Still, from Ric's description, I was able to find it: one of those place built to hold ten families of Easterners in the same space that would hold maybe three Dragaeran families. And families of Easterners are usually bigger.

I went to what should be the right door and hit it with my fist. After a moment, the door opened a crack, a pair of eyes peered out, and someone said, "Yes?"

"Ernest? My name is Sandor, and I'm a friend of Ric."

"A friend of who?"

"Ricard. The cimbalom player."

"Oh!"

The door opened more and he grinned. "Come on in. If you're a friend of Ricard, you must have brought something to drink."

"Actually, I didn't, but I'll buy you one, if you'd like."

"I'll get my coat."

It crossed my mind that if I kept buying drinks for people at this rate, I wasn't going to be good for much by the end of the day. But if you're going to be dealing with Ricard, and people Ricard knows, you had best be ready for serious drinking. If I dared remove the amulet, I could do a sobering spell. If I dared remove the amulet, a lot of problems wouldn't even exist. I mentally shrugged; I was all right at the moment.

We found a place, sat down in a back corner, and I bought him a brandy and water. I had a mug of bad pilsner, so I could nurse it.

"Thanks," he said.

I nodded. He was short and stocky, with big shoulders that made his arms hang out, and had the same look in his eyes as those Orca punks who used to beat me up just because they could. I instinctively didn't like him. To the left, there must be something decent about him, or he wouldn't be Ric's friend. But then again, maybe Ric was hoping he'd get killed.

"My name is Sandor. Ric gave me your name, because I need some help with a project, and I have some money to throw around to get it done."

"Oh? How much money?"

"A fair bit."

"What's—"

"Maybe we should talk about what I want you to do, and then, if you think you like the idea, we'll try to work out the money."

He shrugged. "All right."

"I know you know who the Jhereg are. Have you ever heard of the Left Hand of the Jhereg?"

"No."

"Good."

"Who are they?"

"They're sort of like the Jhereg, but they use magic, and are involved in different sorts of things."

"Like what?"

"That's what I want you to find out."

"Huh?"

"I need someone—actually, a few people—to find out what they're up to."

"I don't know," he said. "I've never—"

"I hadn't thought you had. I'll tell you what to do."

"What sort of, I mean—"

"I need you to ask around, without making a big deal out of it. But, you know, talk to friends, pick up gossip, that sort of thing."

"Uh, how exactly? I mean, who do I talk to? Who would know?"

"I'll point a few people out to you, people called runners. Once you—"

"Runners?"

"People who run errands for them, and deliver things to them. Once you know who they are, you sort of hang around them, see if they feel like talking to you. Or you find people they are talking to, and talk to them. Pick up whatever you can."

"Yeah, okay. I know what you mean."

"Do you think you can do that, without letting anyone know you're trying to get information?"

"I think so. What happens if I get caught?"

"You don't get paid."

"I mean, will they do anything to me?"

"No, I wouldn't think so. They aren't like the Jhereg, they aren't inclined to hurt people. Also, there is the matter of getting the information to me."

"Hmm?"

"Well, I can't have you and several others just coming to me in the open, one after another. It will attract attention."

"Oh. What do we do then?"

"Do you know your symbols?"

"Sure."

"Then what you do is write out anything you need to report, and you leave it outside of your bedroom window, pinned in place with, I don't know—"

"A stickpin?"

"That would work."

"Then what?"

"I'll arrange to have it picked up."

"Oh, so I get the glamorous work again?"

"Shut up, Loiosh."

Ernest nodded.

"I think that's it, then. Interested?"

His mouth worked. "How much?" he said at last.

There are advantages to having a lot of money. He agreed.

Over the next couple of days, I had that same conversation eleven more times. None of them said no. After that, it was a matter of pointing out the runners to them, emphasizing the importance of not letting it be apparent what they were doing, and setting them to work.

By the time I had finished instructing the last of them, information was only starting to trickle in from the first of them. It would be a while before I had enough to be useful, and, by that time, I needed to have a more solid background. I did something I'd never had to before: my own research. I crossed over to the City, and, still in disguise, I made my way into the Imperial library.

I worked my way down to the history section, settled in, and started studying.

10

SALAD

A young man I didn't know came by and removed the plates with the remains of the fish, then returned a moment later and gave us each a slightly smaller plate. Then Mihi returned with a large wooden bowl, and a pair of wooden spoons.

Valubar's has several salads. Today's was a combination of the round and the tall, broad-leaf kinds of lettuce, along with flatnuts, blanched tomato wedges, soul of palm, pimentos, scallions, and artichoke heart marinated in sweet vinegar, which functioned as a dressing. A grated nithlan cheese—sharp and musky—was shredded over it, and the whole thing was topped with candied rose petals.

Mihi dished it up with his usual matter-of-fact fluid elegance, and my mouth was watering.

"What are those?" asked Telnan.

"Candied rose petals."

"Candied rose petals?"

"Yep."

"Is that a term for something, or are they actually rose petals?"

"They're actually rose petals. Candied."

"Very lightly candied," said Mihi. "They aren't too sweet."

"Uh . . ."

"Just eat it," I said. "Trust me."

165

"All right."

He took a forkful, a dubious expression on his face. I blissfully dived into my own.

After a while, I said, "Well?"

"Hmmm?"

"How is it?"

He swallowed. "It's wonderful."

I wished I had someone like Kragar to kick the information around with; he was always an excellent sounding board. In some ways, that's what I missed the most. I could always talk to Loiosh, of course, but Loiosh's job involved keeping my emotions balanced, not working over information and helping me look for patterns. Something about the way the reptilian brain works, I suppose.

But I didn't want to bring Kragar in on this, which not only left me on my own as the information trickled in, but left me spending hours at the Imperial library learning things I could have had him get for me. It did give me a bit more of an appreciation for the sort of legwork I always used to assign him. If I ever spoke with him again, I'd have to mention that.

No, I wouldn't.

But I did learn things.

The Imperial library is not, in fact, organized so you can, say, go to the far corner of the third subbasement and find a book called *Here Is What the Left Hand of the Jhereg Is Up To*. It isn't even organized so you can find the history of the Left Hand of the Jhereg. In fact, I'm told that in comparison with various university libraries, it isn't even organized. And, to make matters worse, the librarians tend not to be excessively helpful to Easterners; I got looks that ranged from the mildly puzzled to the downright unfriendly.

But, eventually, after wandering aimlessly for a while, I found myself among piles of unsorted manuscripts where I ran across a very tall and, for a Dragaeran, portly fellow with wispy hair and heavily lidded eyes who didn't seem to notice my race. He seemed to be involved in making notes on these manuscripts and moving them from one pile to another.

When I told him I was trying to track down the history of the Left Hand of the Jhereg, he got a sort of feral gleam in his eye and nodded to me.

"This way," he said, and led me off.

His name, it turned out, was Deleen, or something like that. He was a Tsalmoth, and I think loved his work. He never asked why I was interested, never appeared to notice that I was an Easterner and never even gave me lectures on how he did his work—something that's pretty much endemic to specialists forced to work with amateurs. I got the impression that sifting through disorganized documents and obscure books in order to pull scraps of information out of them was what he lived for.

I didn't especially care for it, myself.

I noticed him performing spells from time to time and asked about them. He grunted and said something about finding recurring patterns of symbols within documents. I had never known sorcery could do things like that.

We spent about eleven hours a day at it for three days, most of it with him digging through documents and making notes, me standing there, occasionally holding things for him, or taking notes to colleagues of his which resulted in them handing me a manuscript or document of some sort, which I would deliver to Deleen. Every day I would offer to buy him lunch, and every day he would decline and shuffle off to eat on his own. We'd meet an hour later and resume. He spent his time about evenly between historical records and contemporary reports—most of these latter being in the form of quasi-legal gossip sheets. I observed at one point that I was surprised the Imperial library collected such things. He muttered something incomprehensible and I didn't bring it up again.

It was not the most exciting time I've ever had. Loiosh didn't like it much either—we weren't used to being apart, and he complained of boredom a great deal. I knew exactly how he felt.

In the evenings, I would speak with my "investigators," if I can call them that, and try to figure out if they'd learned anything.

Those are three days I would not care to live through again. On account of I'm such a nice guy and all, I'm going to give you what they call a *précis* instead of making you live through them with me. I accept gold and silver tokens of gratitude.

First of all, it turned out that Kiera was right—there was no history whatsoever of the Left Hand interfering with anything the Jhereg did. They were, or, rather, had been, entirely their own organization, with the only overlap being that they sometimes used the same contacts within the Imperial Palace. Next, I learned (or rather, Deleen deduced) that while the Empire monitored the activities of the Left Hand as best they could, they had never had much luck in actually prosecuting them for anything, except for the occasional individual who was caught with an illegal artifact in her possession. And third, it seemed that the Left Hand was even more loosely organized than the Right; they almost never exercised any control over their members.

Deleen kept digging away.

He'd occasionally ask me a question, like, "Ever heard of someone called Daifan?"

"No."

He'd grunt, nod, and go back to work.

Then he'd ask about some incident in the history of the Jhereg, like the Shay Market Slaughter, and I'd tell him what I knew. He'd grunt and go back to work.

On the second day he said, "Who was Curithne?"

"Was?" I said.

He nodded. "He's dead. Who was he?"

"When did he die?"

"About a year and a half ago."

"Murdered?"

"No. At least, not as far as anyone knows. Who was he?"

"According to rumor, the number-one man in the Jhereg."

"Do you believe the rumors?"

"Yes."

"I see."

"He died, eh?"

But Deleen was already back running his fingers through sheafs of something called the *Adrilankha Town Crier.*

Curithne had died while I was gone. Interesting. Who was sitting at the head of the table now? The Demon? Poletra? Curithne dying would set off—

"Can you ask Dotti for the *Candletown Flame* for the last year?"

"On my way," I said.

By the time—early the next day—that he informed me that there appeared to be some sort of power struggle going on in the upper echelons of the Jhereg, I had just about come to the same conclusion myself.

"It looks," he said, "like no one has yet taken the place of Lord Curithne, within the Right Hand of the Jhereg."

"Have there been bodies turning up at an unusual rate?"

"No. One sorceress from what you call the Left Hand was killed with a Morganti weapon not long ago. That's been the only murder associated with the Jhereg lately."

I kept my face expressionless and said, "Then there's no war going on."

"That would seem to be the case. There are certain actions that the Empire takes when Jhereg start killing each other, and—"

"Actions?"

"Certain departments within the Phoenix Guard are increased in size. Others are moved to the area where there is trouble."

"I see."

"Yes, and the Empire hasn't done those things."

"So, all right. A bunch of the bosses of the Jhereg are trying to get into position to run the thing. Have you found names, yet?"

"I'm looking for that, but it's difficult. Even the small local sheets don't like to give the names of high-level Jhereg."

"Go figure."

"But there is one who is known as Poletra."

"Uh huh."

"Another named Daifan, usually called 'the Demon.'"

"Oh."

"Hmmm?"

"I thought his name was . . . never mind."

He started to say something, then stopped, then said, "There are at least two others, maybe three. I'm still trying to find out who they are."

"But no bodies turning up."

"So far."

"All right," I said. "But what does that have to do with the Left Hand?"

"Nothing that I can tell."

"Oh."

"Although—"

"Yes?"

"Have you heard of someone named Terion?"

"Sure."

"Would he be one of the contenders?"

"Probably."

Deleen shuffled a few copies of some gossip rag, and said, "There's a story that he has a mistress who is in the Left Hand."

"You get a name of the mistress?"

"Triesco."

"Ah ha."

"Hmmm?"

"That means something; I just have to figure out what."

"Oh. All right. What can you tell me about her?" I won't add that I felt like an idiot for not starting with her, the one name I had. Deleen did a bit of checking around and got me what little there was; then I headed back out onto the streets, and made my careful way back to South Adrilankha, Loiosh and Rocza watching over me.

"Hey, Boss. How was the library today?"

"Boring, but I may be getting closer to knowing a part of what some people think might be an aspect of a bit of what is going on."

"So everything is solved, then. Good. What about the Irregulars?"

"The which?"

"The Jhereg Irregulars."

"Loiosh, I'm not sure what—"

"It's easier than calling them Those Friends of Ric Who Are Wandering Around Trying to Find Things Out for You."

"Oh. Them. I'll be meeting with a few of them tonight."

"Good. That might get you closer to knowing a part of—"

"Don't start, Loiosh."

I did meet with several of them. We'd arrange to get together in some local inn, sit in a back corner, and talk for a while; then I'd move on to a different place and meet with another. It kept me busy, and I discovered to my annoyance that I was now thinking of them as the Irregulars. I was also starting to get a pretty good feel for the scope of the Left Hand's involvement in the area.

They were trying to determine the outcome. They wanted to be the ones to decide who held the top seat on the Council of the Jhereg.

Which, of course, begged the question why.

Because Triesco was Terion's lover? Was that all there was to it? Could all of this nonsense have its source in nothing but a love affair?

Well, but then, that's what had gotten me involved, hadn't it?

Well, yes, but I was an Easterner.

Which meant what, exactly?

I mentally scowled and put that thought away for a while, along with the additional and related question of why that sorceress had shown up and done, well, whatever it is she had tried to do to me.

I had been figuring that last to be connected to the Jhereg's intense, burning desire to make an empty pair of boots out of me, even though it made no sense. It occurred to me now that it could be part of the power play within the Jhereg, only that made even less sense.

I returned to my room from the last meeting, scowling and muttering as I walked.

"*Boss!*"

I stopped, about forty feet from the entrance to the inn. "*What is it?*" I was in an inset doorway, my hand on the hilt of Lady Teldra, which was comforting in a couple of different ways. I wasn't certain of exactly how I got there.

"*Someone is in the room. I think. I'm outside, and I smell something.*"

"*Wonderful. Can you check it out without getting yourself fried?*"

"*I think so.*"

"*Don't take chances. There's nothing I need to go back there for.*"

"*Understood. I'll just sort of peek in the window.*"

Two minutes later I pushed the curtain aside, walked into the room, and said, "Hello, Kiera. How did you find me? Did you track Loiosh?"

She stood up and smiled. "I had a friend do it."

Loiosh flew over from her shoulder to mine. "Sit down," I said. "You gave me a start."

"Yes. Sorry. There's no way to reach you, you know."

"I know. And I wish it weren't so easy to find me."

"It isn't easy."

"Still, if your friend can do it—"

"That doesn't mean someone else can."

"Maybe."

"Well, first someone has to think of it, which isn't as likely as you might think."

"Actually, it's a certainty. Someone tried not long ago."

"Oh."

"You seem surprised."

"I am. It requires either a very close knowledge of Loiosh, or some object connected to him. And then it requires a skill in witchcraft. And that's after even thinking about it, which surprises me to begin with."

"I know, Kiera. It makes me nervous. Speaking of witchcraft, how is Morrolan?"

"I don't know him that well."

I felt myself flushing a little. "When you said witchcraft, I assumed—"

"You were right, but it was a favor for my friend Sethra, who then communicated the results to me."

"Oh. I see."

"I'm told that Morrolan is still in mourning for his friend Lady Teldra. He took her death hard."

"Well, she didn't die. Exactly."

Kiera the Thief stole a quick glance at me and didn't answer. I touched Lady Teldra. *It's all right*, she seemed to say. Or else I imagined it. I might have imagined it. I might have imagined—

"The Demon Goddess has been messing with my head, Kiera. My memories, maybe my perceptions, possibly even my, I don't know, my thinking."

"Yes. I'm told she'll do that, now and then, when she needs someone to do something."

"Oh. Well, that's all right, then."

She laughed. "What, Vlad? You don't accept that there are those who may know what's best, and use you for the good of everyone?"

"Not hardly," I said. "Do you?"

"Only when I have no choice."

"And I have no choice. Yeah. That's what I love about it."

"I imagine."

"Actually, I do have a choice." I touched Lady Teldra again.

"I suspect, Vlad, that that may not be the best option."

"For whom?"

While she tried to work out an answer to that, I said, "In any case, that isn't what you came to see me about. What's on your mind?"

"Blood, death, friendship, the Jhereg, the Left Hand."

"Odd. Those are the same things I've been thinking about. Care to be more specific?"

"You keep forgetting you have friends, some of whom are willing to help you, and some of whom worry about you."

"Which are which?"

"I'm almost tempted to answer that, just because I know you don't want me to."

"Okay, one for you. But, Kiera, the Jhereg is after me. They want it Morganti. I can't—"

"I know."

"—get other people involved in this."

"What would you do if someone were threatening Morrolan with a Morganti weapon?"

"Laugh at the stupid son-of-a-bitch."

"Vlad—"

"All right, all right. But—"

"Do you know that Kragar has sent a message to Aliera?"

I blinked. "My word. Has he indeed?"

"He wants to know how to reach you, so he can offer to help."

"I didn't think he had that much nerve."

"He does."

"I mean, the nerve to risk a snub from Aliera."

"I knew what you meant."

"He's nuts."

"Maybe."

"Kiera, he is *in* the Jhereg. He wouldn't last three minutes."

"So am I, and I'm not worried."

"You should be."

She smiled.

"Yeah, well, all right. Maybe not."

"To answer your question, I'm here to see if you need any help."

I sighed. "I'm not sure. My biggest problem is trying to figure out what's going on, why the Left Hand is here. And I already asked you about that."

"Yes. Have you learned anything?"

"There is a sorceress named Crithnak who doesn't like me very much."

For just an instant a flicker crossed her face. Either my reading skills are way off, or she knew that name, but then remembered that she wasn't supposed to know that name.

"What else?"

"Power struggle within the Jhereg."

She frowned. "Are you sure? I knew that Curithne had died—"

"How?"

"How did I know? Or how did he die?"

"The latter."

She shrugged. "He was an old man, Vlad. His heart failed."

"Are you sure?"

"One can never be sure, but I'm pretty well convinced."

"All right."

"You hadn't known about him?"

"No. I've been away."

"Sorry. I should have mentioned something. In any case, I haven't seen signs of a power struggle; it's just there isn't anyone yet who has taken his place. It isn't like there's a big hurry; business goes on."

"It always does. But, yeah, there haven't been any bodies turning up, but there are signs of various people, including my old friend the Demon, trying to get into position to take his place."

She frowned. "Are you certain of that?"

"I wouldn't say certain. I don't have access to the sources I used to. But I guess I can say there are good indications."

"I hadn't known that. They must be keeping things pretty quiet."

"Yes. No bodies. For a Jhereg power struggle, that counts as pretty quiet. Does it change things?"

"Well, yes. No. I think so."

"What I can't figure out is, what that has to do with the Left Hand."

She sat back and considered.

I said, "Terion."

"What about him?"

"Do you know him?"

"We've met. I don't send him salutations on the new year. How does he fit into this?"

"He's the only Council member I've heard of with a connection to the Left Hand."

"He has a . . . what is his connection?"

"Triesco."

I could see the name register. "I see. Yes. That would do it. What's the connection? Family?"

"His mistress."

"Oh, grand. What do you know of her?"

"She's a sorceress, born into the House of the Athyra, left it and became a Jhereg some years before the Interregnum."

"Why?"

"For love."

"Oh good grief," said Kiera.

"Yeah."

"This Triesco is, I take it, high up in the Left Hand?"

"I would imagine, but I know pretty much nothing of their structure. In any case, it's another name to dig at."

"Dig at?"

"I've been spending time at the Imperial Library, trying to figure out what's—"

"That's where you've been hiding? In the Imperial Library?"

"Well, not hiding exact—"

She threw her head back and laughed. "Vlad, you are price-
less."

"Uh, okay, what am I missing here?"

"Oh, nothing at all, I'm sure."

"Kiera—"

"Aside from the idea of you just gallivanting across the Chain Bridge, or whichever one you use, twice a day—"

"I'm in disguise, you know."

"—you can't have failed to notice that Imperial Library pretty much stares at the Jhereg Wing of the Palace."

I shrugged. "No one who matters ever uses that wing anyway. Stop grinning, Kiera."

"I'll try."

"You—"

"I'm just admiring, Vlad. The Imperial Library, forsooth."

I shrugged.

"I take it, at least, that it's been productive?"

"I'd say so, yes. I mean, I learned about the power struggle in the Jhereg, and the connection between Terion and Triesco."

"Good. So, what do you need?"

A list began to form in my head, but not one I was inclined to share with Kiera. "Mostly," I said, "someone to kick ideas around with."

"I can do that. Start kicking."

She was in the chair, so I sat on the bed. "Okay, then. We know there is a power struggle within the Jhereg—the Right Hand—and we know that the Bitch Patrol is involved. We're pretty sure that this Triesco is trying to see to it that Terion gets the head seat on the Council. So, the question is, how does the Left Hand being involved in South Adrilankha help Terion in his maneuvering?"

She shook her head. "I think you have it backward."

"Oh?"

"South Adrilankha is the price Terion is paying for the support of the Left Hand."

I frowned. "I hadn't thought of that. Payment in advance?"

"That's the usual method."

"True. That's going to create conflict in the Jhereg—I mean, the Right Hand—and in South Adrilankha. And I have no idea if it'll do anything to the Left Hand."

"No more do I."

"But the conflict in South Adrilankha itself might create an opening for me. I can do things here that most Jhereg can't."

"What sort of things do you mean?"

"I don't know yet; I don't know enough about what's going on. But something could open up. I need information sources."

"For South Adrilankha, I can't help with that."

"I understand."

I considered what she'd told me. "Okay, then the question becomes, exactly how is the Left Hand, or maybe just Triesco, helping Terion? And, secondly, what does this have to do with the sorceress attacking me? Oh."

"Oh?"

"Well, I got a piece of that."

"Yes. Now that I think of it, me too. The Jhereg wants you badly enough that Terion delivering your head will put him in a good position."

"Yeah. Or else it was part of the deal to begin with. Either way, it means that sorceress was planning to kill me. Good. That makes me feel better."

"It does?"

"Yeah, a little anyway."

"Uh, you'll have to explain that to me."

"I haven't told you what Daymar learned."

"Daymar? Yes, I remember him. What did he learn?"

I told her.

"Okay," she said. "Yes. That makes sense. And the sorceress is called Crithnak?"

I nodded.

"I should see what I can learn about her."

"I would certainly appreciate that. Then, I have to see how I can get her to attack me on ground of my choosing."

Kiera frowned. "Get her to attack you?"

"Why, yes," I said innocently. "Sethra Lavode once told me that defending is stronger than attacking."

"Ah. I see." Her face gave away nothing. "Well, I wouldn't know, but I imagine that, first of all, she was speaking tactically, not strategically. And, second, that she would tell you that this depends on the particular tactics involved at the time. She might mention that there are times—such as when offensive battle spells have acquired an advantage over defensive battle spells—that the reverse is true."

"Oh. You think she'd say that?"

"I'm just guessing, but yes."

"I've never been clear on the difference between strategy and tactics anyway."

"Haven't you? Tell Sethra that. She'll probably make you a general."

"Because of what I don't know?"

"Because you don't have the preconceptions that tactics are always tactics, strategy is always strategy, and the one never turns into the other."

"I didn't realize they did turn into one another."

"But you didn't assume they don't, which is a problem Dragons tend to have. Strategy only remains strategy, apart from tactics, in our heads. Once you get into battle, into war, they may turn into one another at any time. Dragons often have trouble with that. That's why Dragons always try to recruit a few Dzur. Or, at any rate, that's what I think Sethra would tell you."

"At which point Sethra would have lost me entirely."

"When a Dzur sees an opening, he'll take it."

"And Dragons don't?"

"Some do. But too often they get an idea into their heads and just plow through with it, regardless of what the obstacles are, or if a better way has appeared."

"I think of Dzur as just charging in, no matter what."

"They do that, too, but in different ways. The Dzurlord will charge into a fight without thinking, because they do their think- ing in the middle of the fight."

"I'm not sure if you can call that thinking."

"Maybe. Sethra would tell you it's the purest form of thinking."

"Well. Good thing Sethra isn't here. I never win arguments with her."

I considered Morrolan and Aliera and what Kiera had told me about preconceptions. After a moment, I decided to file it away for future thought. I said, "Dzur are more complex than they appear."

"Yes."

"But then, everyone is."

"You've changed, Vlad."

"Have I?"

"Yes. You talk different. You, I don't know. You're different."

"Maybe. I suppose it was going back East. That was—"

"You went back East?"

"Yeah. Scouting for Sethra the Younger."

She gave me a courtesy smile and said, "How was it?"

"It managed to be nothing like I expected. Which was odd, since I went in with no expectations."

"What happened?"

I let my memory drift for a moment, then said, "I lost a finger, and gained . . ."

"Hmmm?"

"Nothing. Another time."

Kiera nodded. "One more thing."

"Yes?"

"There's another who wishes to know if you need his help yet."

"Anoth—oh. Mario?"

She nodded.

"Not yet," I said. "Perhaps soon, though."

She stood up. "I'll be back tomorrow."

"You really shouldn't risk "

"I promise, Vlad. I won't show my face in the Imperial library."

"Ah. Well. That's a great load off my mind. Really, Kiera. I've got you, Mario, and Lady Teldra working for me. What could they come up with that even presents a good challenge?"

"I assume that's intended as irony."

"Well, yeah, maybe a little."

"Be well, Vlad."

"Kiera—"

"Yes?"

"Thank you."

She nodded and went through the curtain.

11

DESCANI WINE

Mihi came and replaced the wine with a Descani, which is something like what you'd get if you poured half a glass of white into half a glass of red. It sounds awful, but it really isn't that bad. And this, whatever it was, produced a very mild tingle on the tongue that went well with the sweetness of the candied rose petals.

"They seem to like you here," said Telnan.

"Hmmm?"

"Just, the way that guy—"

"Mihi."

"Yes. The way he always smiles at you."

"Well, I've been a regular customer for a long time. And, of course, I'm an Easterner like they are."

He nodded. He was right, though. I was pretty popular with the staff here. I'd found that out some years ago. I had accidentally come across Vili at an inn in South Adrilankha, and he'd been drinking. We talked a bit, and it turned out that, well, they sort of knew what I did, and they knew I was successful at it. In other words, I was an Easterner who walked around the upper echelons—or, the middle echelons at least—of Dragaeran society. I was one of them who'd made good, and the exact way I had either didn't matter, or maybe even added a little spice to it.

And, in turn, knowing they felt that way made eating at Valabar's all the more pleasant for me.

But I didn't care to explain all of that to Telnan.

"How you doing, Boss?"

"Better. It was good of her."

"It doesn't scare you that she found you?"

"Not as much as it should."

"So, what now?"

"I'm thinking about sending you to the Imperial library to continue my research."

"That's really funny, Boss."

"Okay, then how about you find out everything you can about Triesco and Terion."

"Sure, Boss."

"Okay, then. Skip that. You'll just keep guarding me when I step outside, and I'll . . ."

"Yes?"

"I haven't worked that part out, yet. Fortunately, however, I'm hungry and tired, so I can get some food, then sleep, and put off the decision for a while."

"I knew I could count on you to have the answer, Boss."

Having made a plan, I promptly put it into action. It worked perfectly.

The next day I returned to the Imperial library—albeit a bit more worried thanks to Kiera—and spent another day with Deleen. I didn't expect him to turn up anything new, but I couldn't think of anything else I should be doing instead.

In fact, he didn't turn up anything new. As the long day drew near its end, he said, "I'm starting to think we've found what there is to find."

"I imagine you're right," I said. "And I'd like to thank you—"

"It's what I do," he said. "I've enjoyed the challenge."

"Good. It's helped."

"Helped?"

"I mean, you've found some information that will be of use to me."

He frowned. I think it was just entering his head for the first time that I wanted that information for a reason. For a moment he looked at me, as if seeing me for the first time. Then I could almost see him mentally shrug, dismissing the notion as having nothing to do with him or his life.

"Well," he said, "Good, then."

"If there is anything I can do for—"

"No, no."

He nodded and turned away, off to be about whatever business he had. I think he'd forgotten I existed before I left the building. On my way out, I gave one nervous glance at the gray slate Jhereg Wing of the Palace, rising over my head. No one seemed to be looking for me.

Kiera did have a point though. I was glad I wouldn't be coming back this way. Just to be safe, I took the Five Mile Bridge. Most likely it didn't make me any safer, but it gave me a few extra hours to walk and think.

The streets of Adrilankha, even South Adrilankha, were first dug out, I suppose, from whatever paths people happened to make, so long ago that I can't conceive of it. They were paved with stone, and then trampled down farther into the ground, and new stones laid on top of the old ones. They tell me that the entire city has sunk several feet since it was first established; the streets sinking farther than the buildings, but both of them dropping. I don't know if that's true. I do know that by the time I got back to Six Corners, my feet hurt more than they had from walking hundreds of miles across the continent. It's funny how, after being cut, stabbed, and beaten by professionals on both sides of the line of justice, one can still be deeply annoyed by a pair of sore feet.

I was certainly grateful for my new boots, though, or it would have been much worse.

Eventually I reached Devon's House, a public house about a quarter of a mile east of Six Corners. I was early, so I sat in the corner and drank a white wine that was too sweet and not cold enough. My feet appreciated it.

The place began filling up—mostly workers from the slaughter-houses, to judge from the smell that accompanied them. There were a few tradesmen as well. And all Easterners. I felt safe, maybe safer than I should have, in disguise and surrounded by Easterners. I cautioned myself not to let myself feel too safe, especially when I didn't have Loiosh and Rocza in the room to watch for me.

An hour or so later my man came in. It took him a while to spot me, which gave me a certain amount of pleasure. He was a stocky guy, not unlike Ric, balding, with thin lips and a nose that looked like it had been broken. "Sandor."

I nodded. "And you're Vincent, as I recall."

He nodded.

"Please," I said. "Sit down. Wine?"

"Sure."

I poured, and passed him the glass, along with a pair of gold imperials.

He nodded and said, "I'll give you what I have."

"That's all I can ask."

He gave me a list of three names, Easterners, who ran small operations and paid off the Left Hand. Nothing surprising, and not exceptionally useful.

Then he said, "You know about the guy they're looking for, right?"

I frowned. "No. Tell me."

"The word is to keep an eye out for a guy, an Easterner, who walks around with a pair of jhereg on his shoulders."

"Is that right?"

"It's worth a hundred imperials to whoever spots him and gets word back."

"That's a lot."

"You don't seem interested in the news."

"No, actually, I am. It's good to know, and I'm glad you told me about it."

He nodded. "You seen him?"

"No. How are they spreading this, uh, word?"

"The runners were told. The guy who mentioned it to me said if I spotted him, he'd split it with me."

"Generous of him."

Vincent shrugged. "I haven't seen the guy."

"All right. Anything else going on?"

"Nothing that would matter."

"What does that mean?"

He shrugged. "The Ristall Market was closed, but that doesn't have anything to do with—"

"It was! When! I was just there yesterday."

"Today. I went by there to pick up something to eat, and it was shut down. The whole market. Carts gone, tarps over the stalls, everything."

"Why? Did you hear a reason?"

"Just gossip."

"I love gossip."

"Well, they say someone threatened to beat anyone who opened up."

"Someone? And you say it doesn't have anything to do with what's going on?"

"This is some local thing."

"What do you mean?"

"There are, you know, gangs here, that like to collect from the merchants, and when the merchants don't pay—"

"Yeah, I know."

"Well, I've never heard of the Jhereg operating like that."

"What, you think the Jhereg wouldn't muscle in on merchants?"

"Not on this scale, no. And they wouldn't be so clumsy about it. Making a whole market shut down and drawing attention to themselves."

"You know something about the Jhereg."

"A little. A few years ago I was a runner myself for a while. That's how I know so many runners."

"I see. Yeah, you know almost enough to get in the way of finding out anything useful."

"Eh?"

"But not quite."

I passed him five more imperials.

"What's that for?"

"Useful information."

"Well, okay. I'll look for more."

"Don't look so hard you become some."

"What?"

"Never mind. Just be careful."

He nodded, finished his wine, and walked out.

"*Hey, Loiosh. I think we're in business.*"

"*Is that good? It sounds like it should be good.*"

"*Yeah, I just got a big piece of the puzzle.*"

"*Oh?*"

"*Oh.*"

"*How big?*"

"*Big enough that I have an idea of what to do next.*"

"*Does that mean you're going to need rescuing in the next hour?*"

"*Not until tomorrow, I think.*"

"*Oh, good. I can rest up.*"

I had, of course, overstated things to Loiosh—nothing was yet certain. But I was pretty well convinced, and, more important, I knew how to make sure.

My next appointment was a quarter of a mile away, and I was early. The guy was named Claude, and he was big and hulking and bowlegged, with an extraordinarily large head. He was about two sentences into his report when I said, "You know the Ristall Market?"

He stopped in mid-sentence and said, "Sure. Just follow Cutback Lane to—"

"I know where it is. You know anyone who has a shop there, or a stall, or anything? That is, you know a name, and maybe an address?"

He considered, then said, "Yeah. There's a guy named Francis, uh, Francis Down-something. He has a fruit stand. I don't know exactly where he lives, but it's within a few steps of the market, I know that."

"Good. Anyone else?"

"Well, I know a couple of them by first name. You know, like, 'Good morning, Petrov. How is your bread today?' and like that."

"Okay, never mind the others. That's good enough." I paid him and sent him on his way. I sat there for a while and thought about things. I had that familiar feeling in the pit of my stomach—a good feeling, the feeling of, *it's happening*. I hadn't had that feeling in some time; I gave myself a moment to relish it.

It took a little bit of work to find Francis Donover, but not too much. As promised, he lived right at the market, above the shop of a cobbler who made a little extra renting out rooms because he wasn't as good as Jakoub.

If Francis Donover had been a Dragaeran, he'd have been a Teckla. I mean, I was being Sandor, who is about as harmless in aspect as it is possible to be, but Francis was still terrified of him. He opened his door just the barest crack, and seemed ready to slam it again.

"My name is Sandor, and I mean you no harm. Might I trouble you for a few minutes' conversation? It may be to your advantage."

The "no" that was forming on his face changed abruptly at the last word. Did I say Teckla? Maybe Orca.

"What is it?" he said.

"May I come in? I assure you, I mean you no harm."

He hesitated, looking at me carefully. Either he could see through my disguise that I wasn't as harmless as I looked, or else he was scared of his own shadow.

Yeah, Teckla.

I showed him my almost-empty hands, as a demonstration of harmlessness. Almost empty, because there was a bright gold imperial in one of them. He let me in.

His place was small and packed with more furniture— mismatched chairs and small tables—than wanted to fit into it easily. All those chairs, and he didn't offer me one. "What is it," he said, his eye on the hand that held the coin. I handed it to him.

"I'd like you to answer some questions for me. I have another one of these for you when you're done."

"What do you want to know?"

"You've shut down your stall. The whole market is shut down."

"Yes, well, there have been problems."

"Yes. I have a pretty good idea of what the problems are. There's someone—no, you needn't tell me who—who is trying to pry money out of all of you."

He hesitated a long time, then said, "Maybe."

"Do you want that imperial, or not?"

"Okay, yes. Someone—"

"Good. What I want to know is, who had the idea to shut down the whole market?"

He turned slightly pale. "Why do you—"

"No, no. You don't get to ask questions. I can tell you that I have no plans to hurt whoever it is. I have no plans to hurt anyone. I've never hurt anyone. I just get paid to collect information. My principal—that means the fellow who is paying me—doesn't plan to hurt whoever it is, either."

"It isn't that. It's—"

"Oh. You mean, can we protect you from him?"

He nodded.

"He'll never know you told me."

He still looked hesitant.

"But," I said, "if it's someone who scares you, I'll make it two imperials." I gave him Sandor's friendliest smile, which is even friendlier than my friendliest smile.

He hesitated again, then said, "It was one of, you know, of them."

"A Dragaeran?"

He nodded.

"Male or female?"

"It was a man. A male."

"How was he dressed?"

He frowned. "I didn't really pay much attention."

"Think. This is important. Try to remember the colors of his clothing."

"I don't know. Non-descript. Gray, I think."

Go figure.

"And what did he say?"

"He said that he had heard about our problems and he wanted to help."

"I see."

"He said they couldn't do anything if we all just shut down."

"How could you afford that?"

"He gave us money to survive on."

"I see. How much money?"

He looked worried again, but said, "Enough to get by."

I nodded.

"Have you seen him again, or just that once?"

"Twice. Once, about three days ago, when he suggested the idea, and then yesterday when he showed up with the money. He went around and saw everyone."

"Three days ago was when he first suggested it?"

"Yes."

"And when did you first hear from the guy who was muscling you?"

"Pardon?"

"Whoever wanted you to pay up, and threatened terrible things if you didn't."

"Oh. Uh, I guess that was a week ago."

I nodded. "One last thing."

"Yes, sir?"

Sir? When had Sandor become a "sir"? I suppose when he started flashing gold imperials. I said, "I'd like to speak to a couple of your colleagues."

"My . . . ?"

"Others who work that market."

"Oh."

"Just a couple of names, along with where I can find them."

He gave them without hesitation. I wrote them down.

"Okay," I said. "You've been very helpful." I gave him three imperials because I like to leave people happy in case I need them again, and because I could afford it. There had been a time when I would have done all manner of things for those imperials I was now throwing around. There was a time when I had.

"With this," I said as I opened the door, "you're liable to turn a profit."

He looked a bit embarrassed, as if I'd discovered a secret. Which I had, but not that one, and it was one I had expected to discover. I headed back out onto the street.

I was only a little worried, and that was because I always get nervous when I go to collect information and learn exactly what I expect to learn.

Yeah, he'd gone right down the line with what I'd been looking for. No surprise; I'd been pretty sure from when Vincent had first given me the information.

You see, Vincent was right.

When I was young, sometime before Loiosh, some people had run an operation like the one Vincent had described, and had tried to muscle in on various local merchants, "shredding the carrion," as the saying is. I knew about it even then because one of the merchants they'd gone after was my grandfather, who, while not exactly a merchant, made a good enough income to attract their attention.

Things got a little complicated, but they had eventually learned not to mess around with an old witch and a young punk. So, yeah, I was familiar with that sort of operation. My grandfather, in a futile effort to keep me from being involved, had told me that this sort of thing happened from time to time in South Adrilankha, when the greedy had no one to prey on but the desperate.

But Vincent was right; the Jhereg didn't operate that way. Putting pressure for a few coins on a few merchants was small-time, and involved more risk of attention by the Empire than the payoff could ever be worth. Sure, once in a while some independent operator might do something like that, and the Jhereg would either absorb him or crush him, as the case may be. When I was running an area, I wouldn't have put up with anything like that for more than about five minutes. No one else I'd heard of would have either; it's just bad for business.

So, the fact that it was happening now was either a hell of a coincidence, or it meant something else entirely, and you can guess which way I'd bet.

I made two more calls, and spent another eight imperials, and didn't learn anything new, but confirmed what Goodman Donover had told me, and got a name, description, and address for at least one of the Easterners who were putting the squeeze on the merchants in Ristall Market. His name was Josef; a good, Eastern name.

I had never put a shine on an Easterner; I hoped I wouldn't have to this time. Chances are I wouldn't. But I might have to mess him up a bit.

"Well, Loiosh. We now know everything we have to know in order to go out and get killed."

"Oh, good, Boss. That's just what I was hoping for."

"Okay, almost all. I need to reach a couple of the Irregulars for another piece, but it ought to be easy enough."

It was. It took being patient for a few hours, but I got it.

I got back late that night after picking up a celebratory bottle of a wine I'd never encountered before. Lying on the bed I found a brief note from Kiera saying she would look for me tomorrow. I was pleased that my friends were watching out for me, and sorry that I'd missed her; especially as I'd have had the chance to brag a bit about having solved the puzzle, or at least a big chunk of it.

What would I have told her if she'd been here? Maybe something obscure and epigrammatical, like, at some point, every complex situation will resolve itself into something simple and straightforward. The trouble is, by then it's usually too late.

Maybe this time it wasn't.

"You sure, Boss?"

"What does that mean?"

"Well, I'm just thinking, if the Demon Goddess has been messing around in your head—"

"Loiosh, are you trying to be funny?"

"No, Boss. I mean it. I'm just a little worried. You have a plan, you've figured out what's going on, only what if—"

"This is just what I need right now. I desperately need to have my confidence shattered by—"

"Boss, I'm just—"

"Yeah, okay."

Well, he's my familiar. That means that it's his job to worry about stuff like that. It also means that, if I have something niggling around in the back of my head, sometimes it's his job to bring it to the front. But I didn't like it much. I didn't like thinking about it, and I particularly didn't like it that he might be right. If you can't trust your own thoughts, what do you have?

"Uh, did that help, Boss?"

"No, but it didn't hurt. It was lousy wine anyway."

I went downstairs to borrow a broom and cleaned up the broken glass. The wine-stain on the wall I left there, figuring it would make a good reminder, though of what I wasn't exactly sure.

What if Loiosh were right? What if everything in my head was planted there by the Demon Goddess for her own reasons— reasons which I no longer trusted, if I ever had? Or what if it was just the product of illusory logic and warped perceptions?

And what if I spent all my time so worried about that I couldn't do anything?

Well, okay then. Sometime, there was a reckoning due between me and the Demon Goddess. But for now—

"You're right, Boss. I shouldn't have brought it up."

"Don't worry about it, Loiosh. You're just bouncing back what's in my own head. We move on. It's time to make it bloody. And if some of the blood is mine, so be it."

I took out my daggers and sharpened them up.

Tomorrow was liable to be an interesting day.

12

CHICKEN WITH SHALLOTS

Mihi cleared away the salad plates, and topped off our wine. I only knew in general what was coming next—it would be some sort of fowl. In the past, there had been the old standard capon in Eastern red pepper sauce, duck with plum sauce, pheasant stuffed with truffles, skirda in wine sauce, and what Valabar's modestly called—

"Chicken with shallots," said Mihi, holding a platter and those wonderful spoons he wielded so deftly.

"What are shallots?" said Telnan.

"Something like scallions," said Mihi, before I could say the same thing.

As Mihi served us, steam rolled up like a beckoning hand.

I can't tell you everything about how they build it, but I know that it involves de-boned and skinned chicken (which is unusual—Valabar's generally prefers its fowls with bone and skin) and then sliced up, and pan-fried in butter, along with minced garlic, shallots, and the delicious (in spite of its name) Imperial fungus. There is salt, of course, and I'm pretty sure there's white pepper. They pour a sauce over it, and I'm afraid I can tell you little about the sauce, except that it's built with the chicken, and so has a lot of the same flavors, along with a bit of tomato, the ubiquitous Eastern red pepper, and wine.

Along with the chicken, they served us baby steamed carrots and miniature red tubers with clarified butter.

I had to just sample things; there was no way to eat it all if I were planning to even taste the next course. But that's the sort of decision you have to make—less of one thing to have some of another. I wish all of my decisions were as painless.

"This is very good," said Telnan after his first bite of the chicken.

"Yes," I said. "Yes, it is."

We ate in silence for a while. I was communing with the chicken— the slight sting on the tongue, the surprise of the fungus, the way the hint of wine and the red pepper bounced off the shallots. Separate flavors, which suddenly come together in the mouth producing an amazing combination that isn't inherent in any of the parts, but, after a few bites, you realize was there all along.

Whether Telnan was having the same joyful discovery, I couldn't know. I decided I was glad he was there; it really is more pleasant to share a meal, even with a comparative stranger. And I'd certainly had less pleasant dinner companions. It occurred to me with a brief pang that I had never shared a meal with Lady Teldra, and now I couldn't. I wondered if she were able to take vicarious pleasure.

"Do you think your weapon enjoys the meal, Telnan?"

"Hmmm?"

"I mean, you're enjoying the meal, right?"

"Oh, yeah! This is great!"

"Well, you have this link to a weapon. Do you know if it can share any of the pleasure from—"

"Oh, I see." He frowned. "I've never thought about it. Maybe. My communication with Nightslayer isn't all that—"

"Nightslayer?"

"My sword is called Nightslayer."

"What is the Serioli name for it?"

"Um . . . I think it was something like—" He made a sound that,

if it had been louder, might have made the staff think someone was choking to death.

"Okay. And that means what, exactly?"

"Sethra said it means something like, 'Loci for different levels of energy from various phases of existence.'"

"Loci for different . . . How did they get Nightslayer out of that?"

"Oh, they didn't. I call her Nightslayer because I like how that sounds. You know, dangerous, and evil, and like that." He grinned.

Dangerous, and evil, and like that. "Okay."

Which didn't tell me if Lady Teldra were able to enjoy my enjoyment of the food. I hoped she could. Well, maybe someday I'd know.

$$\mathcal{B}\mathcal{D}$$

I woke up fast the next morning. Not fast in the way I wake up when Loiosh screams a warning, or when I hear some sound that makes me reach for a weapon, but fast in the sense that I was instantly wide awake, thinking, "Today I'm done waiting. Today I can move. Today I can start to act."

You see, it's all about contrasts: I don't usually get that excited just because I'm about to go charging into a situation where I might get sliced up into my component parts. And, to be sure, there was an element of fear in my belly. But after days of the sort of drudgery I despise it was such a relief to know that I was going into action at last, that I could almost understand how a Dragonlord felt before a battle, or a Dzur before a duel. Or, well, maybe I couldn't, but I thought I could, and that's almost as good.

"In a mood today, eh Boss?"

"A good mood, Loiosh. For the first time in longer than I care to remember."

"I'm not sure I believe it. So, what are we going to do first?"

"Kill the Demon Goddess."

After a moment, he said, *"Boss, any other time, I'd say, 'ha ha.' But—"*

"No, you can say 'ha ha.' We aren't really going to put a shine on the Goddess—"

"Good!"

"—today."

"Then what are we doing?"

I outlined the plan. He didn't make any remarks about how stupid it was. Since every time in the past that he'd told me my plans were stupid I had survived, the fact that he liked this one gave me a moment's pause. I put some things in a bag, slung the bag over my shoulder, and headed out.

For the first order of business, I went out into the morning and had myself a fresh, warm langosh from the cart down the road. I went into the inn across the street from it and drank a cup of mediocre klava. Don't think I'm complaining about that klava, by the way—I enjoyed it thoroughly. Living without any klava at all was still fresh in my mind.

In any case, the langosh was magnificent.

I left the inn and walked around to the back.

"Loiosh, is—?"

"You're clear, Boss. No one is watching."

Sandor went into a neat little package behind a trash container, and Vlad was back for a few hours. Loiosh and Rocza appeared, waited, hovering uncomfortably with much flapping of wings until I had adjusted my cloak, and then landed on my shoulders.

"Good to see you, Boss."

"It's good to be back."

I checked to make sure this and that were accessible and loose enough to get at, then said, *"All right. Let's do it."* Lady Teldra, her sheath slapping at my leg, almost seemed to agree.

It was a long walk to Falworth Square, most of the way to the

Five Mile Bridge. The air was sweet with the ocean and no trace of the slaughterhouses.

"*Always best to get killed on a nice day, eh Boss?*"

"*That's more like it. I was missing your cynicism.*"

At one point, I noticed that I was humming, and stopped.

Loiosh and Rocza took turns flying above me, circling, sometimes landing on my shoulder. I had the feeling that Rocza, too, was glad to be back with me. I was glad to have her back, too. I reached up and scratched under her chin.

"*Okay, Loiosh. The action gets going on Falworth Hill.*"

"*I thought we were going to that place on Harmony.*"

"*We are. That's first. But the action doesn't start until we get to Falworth.*"

"*Oh. So I can nap through this first part?*"

"*Actually, you probably can. But just to be safe—*"

"*Right, Boss. So, what now?*"

"*Now we get to spend several hours bored out of our skulls.*"

"*I can hardly wait.*"

I was right, too. I found the place easily enough, on Harmony about a quarter of a mile northeast of Six Corners, positioned myself across the street from Number Four, ducked into a shadow, and waited. Loiosh went around to the other door. He waited, too. About three hours and a little more, which is what you get when you start early in the morning.

"*Check me on this, Boss: An Easterner, a little taller than you, clean-shaven, short blond hair, gold ring in his left ear, wearing a sort of short sword in a brown leather sheath?*"

"*That's our man. Score one for the Irregulars. So he went out the back?*"

"*Yes, and he's heading north.*"

"*On my way. Don't lose him.*"

"*That's not likely.*"

I fell in about a hundred and fifty feet behind Josef. The streets

curved too much for me to see him, but Loiosh was there. The guy's
first stop was useless to me—he just stood out on the street, talking
to someone in a doorway. That was all right; I had plenty of time.

He headed off toward Ristall Market, which was no surprise.
About halfway there, he stopped at a blacksmith shop.

"What do you think, Loiosh?"

"He might just need some nails."

"I mean, does this look like a good place?"

"From the outside, it seems good. Not too much traffic, anyway."

I had actually already made the assumption that he didn't
need nails. Loiosh and Rocza landed on my shoulder as I entered
the place, about two minutes after Josef. As I walked in, I wasn't
holding a weapon, because I can get to one fast enough if needed,
and because once, long ago, I walked into a place wielding and
stepped straight up to a pair of Phoenix Guards who didn't think
it was funny at all.

It was four walls with no ceiling, and a door in the back that
I suppose led to his living quarters; and even with no ceiling, the
heat struck me at once. The forge was huge and glowing orange,
there were two long tables, one on each side, and they were full of
weapons. Excuse me, tools. The blacksmith—at least, I assume he
was a blacksmith; he was wearing an apron, anyway—had olive
skin, a neat little beard, and bright blue eyes. As the eyes shifted
to me, I nodded a greeting and told him, "I need to speak to this
fellow; would you mind leaving us alone for a minute?"

Josef turned around. "Just who are you suppos—"

I slapped him hard enough to rock him back on his heels, and
by the time he recovered I was holding a knife at his throat—a
nice stiletto with about nine inches of skinny blade and a wicked,
wicked point. The blacksmith retreated through the door in the
back of his shop. A little part of me observed that I was enjoying
this more than I should.

"We'll just be a moment," I told the door the blacksmith had gone through.

The place smelled like sulfur and charcoal. Josef's head was tilted back away from the knife and he was glaring at me. I said, "How do you do, Josef? My name is Vlad. I'm just here to give you a little information. And don't glare at me, I have a knife at your throat. When you have a knife at my throat, then you can glare at me. As I said, I have information for you. Do you want to hear it, or do you want me to find out if I can tickle the top of your skull from the inside?"

"Say it, then," he said, just barely not spitting.

"You need to find honest work. Or a different kind of dishonest work. But your scheme for Ristall Market is over as of now. Tell your associates, unless you want me to talk to them."

"Who—?"

I pushed a bit with the dagger, forcing his head further back and breaking his skin a little. "No," I said. "You aren't talking yet. I'm still talking. When I ask you questions, you can talk."

I cleared my throat.

"As I was saying, you're done. You don't need to tell the merchants, they'll figure it out. And you don't need to tell the Jhereg who set you up in this, I'll take care of that."

A flicker behind the eyes? Oh, yes. I'd known anyway, but the confirmation was nice.

"Now, to my question: Who was it. I need a name, and I need to know where he can be found."

He hesitated. I moved the knife just a little bit away from his throat before hitting him in the stomach with my left hand. Then, when he doubled over, I smacked the side of his face with the hilt of the knife. Loiosh flew down from my shoulder and hovered for a moment in his face before landing on the floor in front of him and hissing.

"I'm sorry," I said. "I didn't quite catch the answer. What did you say his name was?"

He coughed, which wasn't responsive, but I didn't hit him again. He spat out some blood and said, "I'm going to—" and I kicked him in the face. He was tougher than I'd expected, but the kick finally did it.

"Vaasci," he said.

"How do you get hold of him?"

He hesitated only a second, then said, "Back room. The Twig on Falworth Hill."

"Good. Now listen. I'm going to talk to your friend Vaasci. If it turns out that he's expecting me, I'm going to come back here and decorate Ristall Market with your intestines. By the time I'm done talking to him, you might want to be out of town, because I'm going to tell him you gave me his name, and that might irritate him, if he's still alive."

"You—"

I hauled my foot back to kick him again and he shut up.

I said, "In case you haven't picked up on it, I don't like you very much. You're better off not giving me any reason to like you less. Feel free to tell your buddies about me, though. If they leave town, it'll give me less to do. And if they come after me, I'll enjoy it enough that I won't care about the extra work."

Loiosh resumed his place on my shoulder. I turned my back on Josef and walked out.

South Adrilankha smelled unusually sweet.

"*Boss, you know you're a bully.*"

"Yeah."

"*And worse, you enjoy it.*"

"Yeah."

"*You've missed being a bully all these years.*"

"Yeah."

"*I'm proud to know you.*"

"Uh huh."

I headed generally west until I found a market that was open. I got some klava from a street vendor, paying an extra few coppers for a glass to drink it out of. I stood there drinking it. Right out in the open, looking like me, two jhereg on my shoulders. The klava was wonderful.

"So, okay, that was the easy part, right, Boss?"

"You nervous?"

As I said it, Rocza shifted on my left shoulder. "A little," said Loiosh.

"What about?"

"Standing here like this."

"Okay. We'll walk."

We did; aimlessly, but generally west, veering a bit northward now and then. It was still early, and I didn't figure Vaasci to be the early type. At least, I never had been when I'd been with the Organization.

"Okay, Boss. Can you explain something to me?"

"Probably not, but I'll try."

"Are you deliberately giving that Easterner time to do what you told him not to?"

"You mean, time to alert Vaasci? Yes."

"You didn't explain that part of the plan to me."

"It was a spur-of-the-moment thing."

"Mind telling me why?"

"I don't think I can explain."

"Oh."

"I'll try, though. First, I want to know if he will. I mean, if Josef actually gets the message to Vaasci, that will tell me whether there's a loyalty, or maybe just that Josef is more afraid of Vaasci than he is of me. I need to know that."

"At the mere cost of walking into a trap?"

"Heh. Like we've never done that before?"

"Not on purpose. Well, not often on purpose."

"Second . . . it's harder to say."

"You're hoping for the chance to kill someone?"

"Not exactly."

"You're hoping someone will try to kill you?"

"That's closer."

"Boss—"

"Kicking that bastard in the face gave me a taste, Loiosh. I need more than a taste."

"Boss, I don't understand."

"I know."

"But I don't like it."

"I know."

"It's not like you to make decisions based on—"

"I know. Have you ever been half asleep, where you aren't sure if you're dreaming or not?"

"I don't dream, Boss."

"Yeah, well, I said it was hard to explain."

"Boss—"

"The thing is, if you're in a situation where you don't know if you're dreaming, you try to wake yourself up to see."

"I'll take your word for that."

"And if that doesn't work, you play it as if it's really happening, because what other choice do you have?"

"Half asleep is no time to make decisions."

"I never said it was."

"That's reassuring."

"Besides, there's still useful information to be gathered. So there's a practical side of this."

"Right. Useful information. Okay, Boss."

"Then again, I could get to the Demon Goddess, wave Lady Tel-dra in her face, and say, 'You caused this problem, now fix it.' I have to admit, I like the idea of the Demon Goddess appearing in the middle of a Council meeting and setting the Jhereg straight."

"I like it too, Boss. But I doubt it's practical."

"Yeah. I don't know how to get to her Halls, for one thing."

"That's a relief."

"Uh . . . come to think of it, maybe I do."

"Boss—"

"Never mind, Loiosh."

I finished my klava and handed the cheap glass to an old beggar, along with a couple of copper pieces. You see a fair number of beggars in South Adrilankha; I've never seen one in the City. Maybe Dragaerans kill their beggars. I wouldn't put it past them.

I walked the streets aimlessly for a while. At the time, I was just thinking about giving Vaasci time to show up. On reflection, maybe I was tempting fate and the Jhereg. But no one took a run at me.

"I'm trying to decide if it's time to cross over to the City and have that talk."

"Boss, what's the point in pulling a weapon before you have a target?"

"I have a target, Loiosh."

"Oh. I hadn't thought of that."

"The thing is, that's going to really set things popping."

"Yes, it will."

"The timing is going to be tricky."

"Yes, it will."

"Especially because I don't know how long the, uh, weapon is going to take. I mean, I have no idea. A day? A year? Something in between?"

"Well, you could always tell him to make it fast."

"You're funny."

"You make a good example, Boss."

"And then, really, when you're calculating how someone will react to something, you never know. I mean, I think I know what he'll do, but what if I'm wrong?"

"Yeah. What if."

"So I'm trying to figure out—"

"You're scared, right, Boss?"

"Not scared exactly. Call it nervous."

"Uh huh."

I juggled this and that in my head. It was a couple of hours after noon. I said, "All right, Loiosh. Let's head over there."

"To the City?"

"No. We'll hold off on that part."

"Oh, the fun part."

"Uh huh."

He and Rocza launched themselves into the air, and we set off.

Falworth Hill overlooks the Stone Bridge, which, someone once told me, is the bridge the Empress would take if she ever crossed the river. It is the place where the elite among Easterners live next to, or, at least, not too far from, Dragaerans in that odd in-between station in life where they are willing to rub shoulders with us. I've met a few of them; they are mostly Chreotha and Tsalmoth, with a few odd Iorich here and there. They're strange. To Easterners who live on Falworth Hill, they are either genuinely friendly or they fake it enthusiastically. To other Easterners, they are even worse than your typical Dragonlord, if you can imagine it.

"What's the play, Boss?"

"They have a glass window."

"Okay, so they're rich."

"Yeah. You and Rocza ready to break a window?"

"Can do."

"You sure? Remember—"

"I can do it, Boss."

"Okay, I'll let you know where I am. The better the timing, the more boring this is going to be."

"I'm in favor of boring."

"That's two of us."

Between Pear Orchard and Driftwood Streets in the Falworth Market is a great, square, red stone building that rents out space to several businesses. The front, where it faces the market, is a public house with a piece of wood painted on the sign. I think it was supposed to be The Driftwood Inn, but everyone calls it The Twig. It was a nice place; padded benches and chairs around dark hardwood tables, etchings on all the lanterns, and like that.

I got some stares as I walked in. The host frowned at me and might have said something about Easterners not being permitted, but I gave him a look before he could say anything, and I guess he thought better of it. Besides, I didn't sit down; I walked straight through to the back of the room and pushed aside a curtain.

"Straight to the back, and through a—"

"I saw, Boss."

Two Dragaerans sat at a table, looking at a ledger of some kind. Both wore the black and gray of House Jhereg.

One of them looked up at me. "Who are you supposed to be?" which would have been an interesting question if I were still being Sandor.

"You must be Vaasci."

"That wasn't the question."

"I'm a messenger."

"From?"

"Your friend Josef."

"Who?"

I suddenly got worried; he looked sincere. "Josef," I said. "Easterner? Ristall Market?"

"Oh, that. Well, what does he want?"

"He said that the operation is over and he's leaving town."

Vaasci frowned. "Why?"

"Because if he didn't, he was going to be harmed."

"Harmed?"

"Yeah."

"*Now, Loiosh.*"

"*We're on the way.*"

"By who?"

"Me."

I smiled.

His eyes narrowed, and I had the sudden feeling he might have recognized me. Then the curtains moved and Loiosh and Rocza came flying in. Or, actually, Rocza came flying in. I was going to ask Loiosh where he was, but then things happened quickly.

They both stood up, and Rocza flew into the face of Vaasci's friend, who lost his balance and landed in his chair again. I rammed a shoulder into Vaasci, drew a dagger, and shoved it into the one who was sitting. I caught him below the heart, left the knife there, and turned to faced Vaasci. It was like a dance. Pretty slick.

I drew Lady Teldra, and drawing her, felt a sudden rush of invincibility. I'd have to make sure not to believe that rush; it could get me into trouble. But this time, at least, it seemed justified: Vaasci made a little squeaking sound, very un-Jhereg-like, and flinched.

I heard myself say, "Drop it," which was when I realized he was holding a dagger.

He didn't hesitate; he just dropped it.

Lady Teldra, sweet and firm in my hand, had gotten a little shorter and a lot wider—a throat-cutting weapon. Perfect for the occasion. What a coincidence.

I said, "If I get so much as a hint that either one of you are attempting psychic contact, I will have your souls."

I had to admire Vaasci; there wasn't even a flicker. His friend moaned, but that was because of the steel sticking out of him. I spared him a glance and said, "You'll live."

He started to say something, but coughed, and there was a trickle of reddish foam around his lips. I might have been wrong.

"*Loiosh —*"

"*Be right there, Boss. You okay?*"

"*I'm fine.*"

"Okay," I told Vaasci. "Now, we need to talk. I'm—"

"I know who you are."

"Good. That saves time."

Loiosh flew into the room and landed on my right shoulder. Rocza took up a position on my left.

"*What happened?*"

"*Nothing.*"

"*I felt something. I couldn't pay attention, but you were—*"

"*Don't worry about it, Boss.*"

I studied Vaasci in silence while I thought things over.

"*Got caught in the curtain, didn't you?*"

"*Shut up, Boss.*"

"*Watch them close, Loiosh. I need to know if either one attempts psychic contact.*"

"*I'm on it.*"

"*There aren't any curtains in the way.*"

"*Shut up, Boss.*"

"Okay, m'lord Vaasci. We have a problem, you and I."

He glowered. Or maybe glared. I've never been too sure of the difference.

"I admire your cleverness," I said. "It was a nice move. But I can't let it happen. Personal reasons."

"You are so dead, Taltos, that it's hardly worth talking to you."

"Yeah, you're probably right. But there are things I can do before I lie down. And you probably don't want me doing them on you."

"Okay. Keep talking."

"That was my plan."

I cleared my throat.

"Like I said, the operation is over. You are out of South Adri-lankha as of now. I know who you're working for, by the way, and he doesn't scare me. Not much scares me at this point, since, as you said, I'm pretty much dead already."

"What aren't you telling me, and get on with it."

"You've got nerve, Lord Vaasci, I'll give you that."

"Spare me the compliments, dead man."

For just a second, I wanted to shove the blade home. But I didn't do it, and he knew I wouldn't do it, so—"You tell your boss that . . . no. Tell your boss to tell his boss that South Adrilankha is off limits. For you, and for the Left Hand. All Jhereg operations here are off. Whatever the Easterners want to do here, they do."

"Right, Taltos. And he'll listen because you said so."

"No, he'll listen because I'm very persuasive, and because it'll be much cheaper to leave it alone."

"And you're going to convince him of that."

"Yes."

"Okay, I'll pass the word on."

"Meantime, you get out of here. If I see you on this side of the river again, I don't have to explain what will happen, do I?"

His eyes never left mine. "No, I think I'm clear enough on that."

"Okay. Take care of your associate. He looks uncomfortable."

I turned my back on him and walked out. Smooth.

"Loiosh?"

"They aren't moving."

"Okay, I'm clear. Come on out. Careful of the curtain."

I walked through the room. The host glanced at me then quickly looked away. Two or three patrons were carefully not look-ing in my direction either. It was just like after an assassination, except that it had taken longer, and no one had died. Well, unless Vaasci's friend succumbed to the dagger I'd left in him.

I was shaking just a little when I got onto the street. Loiosh and Rocza flew through the broken window and joined me.

I felt bad about the window.

We moved quickly back east. Loiosh said, "*We survived.*"

"Yes. *Were you worried?*"

"*Me? Of course not, Boss.*"

"*I was. That was a risky move.*"

"*Well, I admit if there had happened to be a couple more there, it could have gotten interesting.*"

I made it back to Six Corners, and found the pieces of Sandor right where I'd left them. Loiosh assured me that no one was around, so I put them on once more, not without a certain regret mixed with the sense of relief.

Okay, I had certainly opened the dam; now I got to see whose fields got flooded.

13

DESCANI WINE (CONTINUED)

If you follow your waiter's recommendation, which I almost always do
at Valabar's, the wine that goes with the salad is also the wine that accompanies the fowl. I don't actually know the reason for that, though I
could speculate that it has to do with transitions.

Transitions are important in a good meal, whether the next flavor
has only the most subtle differences from the previous, like between the
fish and the goslingroot, where the butter and the lemon defined the flavor, or drastic differences, like between the salad and the chicken.

In this case, it was the wine that provided continuity, and reminded
my mouth that, however much things changed, and however one moment
was completely unlike the one that preceded it, they were both still moments in an endless stream, the product of all that has gone before, and
the producer of what will follow; the lingering chill of the wine, now par-
taking of the fullness of a red, now of the elegance of a white, making us
step back a bit from the irresistible now of the chicken, and declaring an
eternal context of life, or meal.

Yeah, if you haven't figured it out yet, food makes me philosophical.
Poetic, too. Deal with it.

But there's a point I want to make: The wine that you drink with
the salad is different from the wine that you drink with the fowl. They
are the same, but what is happening in your palate is so different that

the wine is different too. Like when you greet a particular gentleman with the same words and in the same tone the day before and the day after you've agreed to put a shine on him; the context changes the significance of the greeting.

The difference in the food made it different wine; it changed everything.

"This is some good stuff," said Telnan.

He's not as poetic as me.

The lack of a course is a course, just like the spaces between the notes are part of the music. Actually, I wouldn't know about that last part; it's something Aibynn told me. But I can testify that it's true of a good meal.

After the fowl, you know what is coming next, because it is the thing that you actually ordered—half a lifetime ago, it seems. Your order has been sitting in the back of the mind for the entire meal. Every sip, every morsel has been a delight in itself, and, at the same time, a preparation for what is next.

And so, of course, Valabar's makes you wait for it while you drink the wine that went with the fowl.

They clear off the table, leaving you half a bottle of wine and your glasses. Then they come by and give you a whole new setting. I can't think of any reason for them to do that unless they are deliberately delaying, building the tension. If that is the reason, I can only say it works. New plates, new flatware, new wineglasses. The sound—soft but unmistakable—of each item set on the table was like music. Or, I imagine, what music would be like to those who felt about music the way I feel about food.

"What comes next?" said Telnan.

"What you ordered."

"Oh."

He frowned. "I don't remember what I ordered anymore."

"Then you get the pleasure of being surprised."

He nodded. "That works."

"You pretty much take what comes, don't you."

"Doesn't everyone?"

"Not the way I mean it."

"Uh. I guess I do."

"Is that a Dzur trait, or is that just you?"

He blinked. I don't think he knew how to answer that. He eventually settled for, "Why do you want to know?"

"Good question. I'm not sure."

"You're trying to figure out what it means to be a Dzurlord, aren't you?"

"I guess maybe I am."

"Why?"

"Telnan—"

"Hmmm?"

"Are you trying to figure out what it means to be a, well, a me?"

"Sure."

"Why?"

"Fair is fair."

"Oh. All right."

"I wish the food would arrive."

"Enjoy the anticipation, my friend."

"My favorite part of anticipation is when it's done, and the action starts."

"Ah ha."

"Hmm?"

"Just made a discovery about Dzur."

"Oh. You still haven't told me why you care."

"Because I don't believe you guys."

"Beg pardon?"

"You could say that Dragaerans have been a sort of study of mine all my life."

"Why?"

"Necessity. Survival."

"Okay."

"And I can make sense of most Dragaerans, but not Dzur. You seek out situations that I work as hard as I can to avoid. I can't make sense of it."

"Oh."

"Answer your question?"

"I guess. But—"

"Yeah?"

"I wish the food would get here. I like it when the action starts."

⌘

"All right, Loiosh. Ready for another long walk?"

"We'll fly, if it's all the same to you. Where are we going?"

"Back to the City."

"Oh. Is it time for that errand?"

"Past time, I think."

"And who's going? You, or Sandor?"

"Sandor. I don't think I'd make it."

"That's just what I was thinking."

We took the Stone Bridge across the river, which added several hours to the walk; but it wasn't like I had anything else to do. The day was chilly and the breeze stung a little, but I enjoyed walking in my new boots. When I'd left town before, with the Jhereg after me and my life in a shambles, I should have taken the time to get new boots. But now things were different. Now my life was in shambles and the Jhereg was after me.

Yeah.

I did get a few glances from travelers on the Stone Bridge, but I kept my eyes lowered and nothing happened. The Stone Bridge, I've been told, is the oldest of the bridges connecting the two parts of the City. It is certainly the narrowest, and, these days, the least used. I don't know why it was put where it was, unless both parts of the City grew in different directions than anticipated.

Which doesn't make sense you'd think that, once the bridge was up, it would determine how the City grew. But that was a long time ago, and just goes on the list of things I don't understand.

The bridge has always felt solid, though; what more can one ask?

I took a wide detour around the Imperial Palace—or, more precisely, the Jhereg Wing—in part because of what Kiera had said. I am not entirely free of superstition. Loiosh was merciful, and didn't make any remarks about it.

It was getting on toward evening when I struck Lower Kieron Road and my old neighborhood. The hair on the back of my neck stood up, and I could feel Loiosh become even more alert. I kept wanting to rest my hand on Lady Teldra's hilt, but managed to restrain myself.

It was even hard not to stop outside of my old office and stare at it for a while. Again, I resisted. I went straight in; a harmless Easterner who couldn't threaten a norska, that was me. Or, rather, Sandor.

I think after about two months of being Sandor I'd have to cut my throat.

The proprietor of the herb shop politely asked me if I wished assistance. This was gratifying; evidently working for an Easterner for several years had left its mark. I gave him a big smile.

"I'm looking for a gift for my uncle," I said.

He didn't respond at once; I suppose that wasn't all that uncommon a phrase. He said, "What sort of herbs does he usually consume?"

I cleared my throat. "I'm looking for a gift for my uncle," I said again, very carefully.

"Oh!" He stared at me, but even looking couldn't see through the disguise. Which was odd; it wasn't much of a disguise. He said, "What sort of gift did you have in mind?"

"Anything you sell will be perfect."

He nodded, gave me a funny look, and said, "We haven't used that code in three years."

"Oh," I said. "Sorry. What's the—no, never mind. Excuse me."

He nodded, and I went past him into the next room.

The Shereba game was going, and I could swear the same stumps were in the same chairs in the same positions with the same piles of coins stacked the same way as the last time I'd been in there. If I'd looked at their faces, no doubt I'd have seen a difference, but it wasn't worth it. The muscle-on-duty gave me a glance. I differentially pointed at the far door, and gave a sort of bob of my head. He nodded, and I passed through to the stairway.

A Jhereg I didn't recognize was leaning against the wall at the top of the stairs. I stopped halfway up and said, "Is Kragar in?"

"I think so," he said. "Who should I say—"

"Tell him someone is here with a message from Kiera the Thief."

His eyes widened a little, and I think I gained some respect. His face went blank for a moment, then he said, "Bide."

I nodded.

A moment later he said, "Okay, go on up."

I climbed the familiar stairs, and it occurred to me that this place, that had once been my office, might be the only establishment in the Empire where an Easterner could expect to be treated politely. As a legacy, I could do worse.

I didn't recognize the fellow sitting behind what had been Melestav's desk before Melestav had succumbed to temptation. He nodded to me, and said, "It's that door. Go right in."

Yeah, I knew that door. It had been my door. I felt about a half a second of irritation at Kragar for taking my office, then realized how absurd it was. I was looking very carefully when I entered, and there he was, seated at the desk, looking at me with his general-purpose smirk, as opposed to his smirk of recognition.

"I'm Kragar," he said. "Sit down. You have a message from—"

"Yeah, I lied about that part," I said. "Mind if I shut the door?"

"Vlad!"

I took that as a yes and shut the door.

He said, "What are you—"

"Mind opening the window, Kragar?"

"Why? Oh."

He opened the window. Loiosh and Rocza flew in the window and took positions on my shoulders. Loiosh hissed a greeting at Kragar, who shut the window behind them.

"Okay, Vlad. Now. What are—?"

"You," I interrupted, "are just about the sneakiest son-of-a-bitch I know."

"Huh? What did I do now?"

"It's what you've been doing for years, and never told me about."

"Uh . . . Vlad, I'm not sure—"

"Tell the proprietor his shipment is ready, and he might need more space to store it all."

Kragar's jaw dropped, which provided me a measure of satisfaction.

"How did you . . . I don't know which question to ask first."

I nodded. "My life is often like that."

"Vlad—"

"Okay, we can get to your questions in a bit. But first, you have a job to do."

"A what?"

"A commission to fulfill."

"What commission?"

"Tell the proprietor—"

"You mean, you're serious about that?"

"What would make you think I'm joking?"

After a while, he said, "Umm, all right. You're serious. I need to—Verra's tits, Vlad! You just come in here and . . . all right. Do you have a name?"

"Sandor."

"Okay, where do I find this Sandor?"

"No, no. That's my name. While I'm in disguise."

"Is that a disguise? I thought you'd just changed the cut of your clothes."

"Shut up," I suggested.

"Nice beret, though. It suits you."

"Shut up."

"Okay, well, good, now I know what to call you while you aren't answering my question."

"You mean the name of the target."

"Yeah, that would be helpful."

"It's a sorceress named Crithnak. Left Hand."

"Okay. Any other information?"

"Her sister is dead."

"Okay. Is that important?"

"I doubt it."

"What else?"

"She's very good. She managed to find me when she shouldn't have been able to."

"I'm sure he'll be terrified. What else?"

"How long have you been his contact, Kragar?"

"About, uh, ninety years, I guess."

"How did you meet him?"

"A mutual friend introduced us."

"A friend? I didn't think Aliera even liked you."

He chuckled. "One for you, Vlad."

"Kragar, didn't you once tell me, in so many words, that you didn't know how to get hold of Mario?"

"Uh, I don't think I ever said that. I may have implied it pretty strongly."

"Heh."

"But I also asked him if he wanted to get involved that time. He didn't."

"Why not?"

"I didn't think to ask him. I usually don't."

"Okay."

He nodded. "Wait here. I have an errand to run."

"Yep."

I sat back to wait.

"*You think he's doing it, Boss?*"

"*You mean, as opposed to running off to arrange to get the bounty on my head?*"

"*Yeah.*"

"*I trust him. Don't you?*"

"*Yes, but mostly because if he doesn't get that message to Mario, Mario will kill him.*"

"*Good point.*"

I glanced at the open door, and wondered if I should shut it. But, no, it wasn't my office anymore. I looked around. Yeah, I missed the place. Maybe not all that much, but I missed it.

"Okay, Vlad. Now do I get to ask questions?"

I jumped about halfway to the ceiling and glared at Kragar.

"Don't ask why I've never killed you, because I don't think I know the answer."

He smiled. Maybe I've never killed him because he's the only one who always knows when I'm joking.

"*What about me?*"

"*You missed one just the other day.*"

"So, where have you been, Vlad?"

"You mean, for the past few years?"

"Well, no, I meant the past few days. But I'm curious about the past few years, too."

"All over. Went back East, northwest . . . all over."

"Okay. But, these last few days—oh. You've been in South Adrilankha, walking around like an Easterner."

"Right. How have you taken to running things?"

"I like the money."

"Yeah, that part is nice. Any problems?"

"Yeah. Finding someone so stupid that he's willing to do for me what I always did for you."

"That would be tough, wouldn't it?"

He nodded. "So what's been going on? I haven't heard—"

"You've been working for Mario all this time, you sneaky bastard?"

"Well, yeah."

I shook my head. "And the worst part is, you're really enjoying it that I'm so shocked."

He smiled innocently.

"Bastard."

"Does this mean you won't tell me what's going on?"

"Do you really want to get any more involved with my affairs than you already are?"

He shrugged. "Why not?"

"Well, for starters, they'll kill you."

"Okay. What after that?"

"Chances are, that's all."

"So only one thing to worry about? That's not so many."

"How long did you say you'd been Mario's contact?"

"About ninety years, and I prefer the term 'business agent.' "

"You mean, messenger."

"Something like that, yeah."

I shook my head.

"So, what's the plan, Vlad?"

I studied him for a little. He frowned. "Vlad, are you wondering if you can trust me?"

"Actually, no."

"Good."

"I know I can trust you. I'm having real doubts about getting you killed."

"Why? You never did before."

"This is different and you know it."

"What's so different about it?"

"Well, it's Morganti. And it's the whole damned Jhereg. And the Left Hand is involved. I'm gone. I'm out of here. If you're known to be in this with me, and you live through it, then you'll have to be gone, too. You can't come back from this and go on with business."

"Isn't that my decision?"

"It isn't that simple."

"Yes it is."

"Not to me."

"That's because you complicate everything."

"Oh. So that's my problem?"

"One of them."

"Going to give the whole list?"

He grinned. "Not unless you ask for it."

I sighed. "I've put things into motion that I can't control. Things have started. I—"

"Just now? With my errand?"

"A little before that, actually. It all centers around South Adrilankha."

"Yeah, I knew that part."

"Do you know why?"

He smiled happily. "Not even a guess."

"For one thing, Terion," I said.

"What about him?"

"He's pushing for the number-one spot on the Council."

"Okay. And?"

"He's enlisted the help of the Left Hand."

"How did he do that?"

"His mistress is one of them."

"Ah."

"How is—"

"By gaining control of South Adrilankha."

"Why there?"

"It's the most lucrative area that's up for grabs. They're already fighting for it. I mean, the Jhereg. I mean, the Right Hand."

"Bodies turning up?"

"No," I said. "But one of the parties tried to start up a little enterprise among the Easterners. Small stuff, but if it had worked, it could have eventually put the heat on the Left Hand, and maybe interfered with their business there."

"Could have?"

"I sort of squelched it."

"Okay, that leaves Terion."

"As far as I know. And I'm pretty sure I know the whole way."

"And Terion's connection to the Left Hand is his mistress. Who is—wait. Crithnak."

"Yeah."

"Terion won't be happy."

"With any luck, Terion won't be alive."

"You going after him?"

"Yep."

"How?"

"The usual."

"Vlad, the usual doesn't involve protection by the Left Hand."

"They aren't protecting him, Kragar. They're just helping him take South Adrilankha."

"How do you know that?"

"I—"

I frowned.

Crap.

"Damn you, Kragar."

"Me!"

"Yeah. Before you said that, I thought I had a plan."

"Uh huh. Like the guy who found his walls were hollow when he saw a chipmunk making a home in them, and said, 'Damn that chipmunk, I thought I had a nice place until he came along.'"

"Yeah. Just like that. I thought I had a plan."

"Damn good one, too. What exactly is the problem you just discovered?"

"I'm in disguise."

"So?"

"So the fellow I just tried to smoke out won't be able to find me."

"Can you explain that?"

"I'm not sure."

"All right. So, what's your next plan?"

"There's a house in South Adrilankha, on Stranger's Road. The Left Hand runs their operations from it. I've been thinking of walking in there and just seeing how many throats I can cut before they take me down."

"Hmmm. Been feeling frustrated, have we?"

"A little."

"How about a backup plan, in case you come to your senses before trying that one."

"You have something in mind?"

"Nope. Plans are your department. Blowing them up is mine."

"Okay. Glad to know we have the division of labor figured out."

He nodded.

Except for him sitting on my side of the desk, it felt a lot like old times. I'd have enjoyed it more if I hadn't been so busy trying to figure a way out of the mess I'd gotten myself into.

After a few minutes of contemplation, I said, "Things are already in motion. I have to take out Terion. Once his mistress gets shined, then the Left Hand will be after me in addition to everyone else." I sighed. "It's sad. "They all want me dead."

"That's true."

"And yet, I'm such a great guy."

"You are. Everyone says so. Can you tell me why you got involved in this in the first place?"

"Cawti," I said.

"Oh."

There were things Kragar and I didn't talk about it, and Cawti was most of them. He cleared his throat into the moderately uncomfortable silence, and said, "Okay. So, you need a new plan."

"Actually, maybe just a couple of small modifications to the old one."

"All right. I can accept that. What do you have in mind?"

"You've sold me on one thing: I have to ask you for help."

He smiled. He looked pleased. Sometimes I wondered about him.

"You want me to find out who on the Council has just gotten upset that his scheme in South Adrilankha has just been broken up."

"Yes. Can you do it without anyone finding out that you're working for me?"

"Don't worry about it."

I cursed under my breath.

"Anything else?" said Kragar.

"Maybe one other thing."

"Hmmm?"

"Can you find Terion?"

"I imagine so. It might take a little time."

"Okay. Just make sure no one knows you're looking."

"Just how do you imagine I'll be able to do that?"

"I don't know. I've never known how you do anything you do. But just be sure."

He shrugged.

"Dammit, Kragar, don't you get it? Don't you have any idea just how big this is? If they know you're helping me, they will kill you."

"Well—"

"They will kill you, Kragar. I don't know how they'll find you, but they'll manage, and they'll kill you. I will not wander around with that on my conscience. If you can't figure a way to find him without it being known that you're looking, then don't find him."

"And you'll do what, then?"

"I'll think of something."

"Right."

"That isn't an answer," I said. "I want your agreement."

"I don't work for you anymore," he said, smirking. "You can't give me orders."

I found a use for several of the more creative curses I'd learned from some Orca I'd briefly traveled with. Kragar waited. I said, "I suppose threatening to kill you would be counterproductive."

He nodded. "And carrying out the threat would be entirely out of line."

"Yeah." I drummed my fingers on the arm of my chair.

I leaned back. "Okay. Let's go back to the beginning and take another look at it."

He nodded and waited.

"What happens if I kill Terion?"

"He doesn't get the Council seat. There are rules about dead people—"

"Yeah, yeah. What else?"

"I don't know who does get it. Probably the Demon. Maybe not."

"What about South Adrilankha?"

"What about it?"

"Who takes it?"

"Without Terion getting the Left Hand involved, then I guess they get out of it. Probably goes as a prize to whoever gets the seat. Or else maybe he gives it to someone else who supported him."

"Yeah, either of those are reasonable. What else?"

"Well, they can't try to kill you any more than they already are, so no change there."

"True enough."

He frowned. "If you really want my help in figuring this out, you'll have to give me a better idea of what's going on."

"Yeah, I know."

"You keep saying things like, 'things are in motion,' but you don't say what things."

I nodded.

"So, you want to tell me?"

"Not especially."

"Vlad—"

"Okay." I took a deep breath. "The Left Hand seems to be—"

"Seems to be?"

"Kragar, I'm giving you my best guesses. If you're going to demand certainty, we need to give it up now."

"All right."

"The Left Hand seems to be backing Terion in his bid for the Council, because his mistress is one of them. They—the Left Hand—are trying to take over the action in South Adrilankha, figuring that will tip things in Terion's favor. With me so far?"

"Uh huh."

"Okay. Now things get fun."

"Oh, good. I've been waiting for the fun."

"Well, what happens when you send your forces against a particular part of the enemy's lines?"

"Vlad, have you been hanging out with Sethra?"

"Okay, sorry. Anyway, because Terion has gotten involved in South Adrilankha. It's become a battleground."

"Yes, you mentioned one other was involved. The one I'm supposed to find out about."

"How do I find you, once I know?"

"Ugh. Good question. There's a shoemaker named Jakoub. Leave a note with him."

"You sure he won't read it?"

"You're funny."

"I know. So, you were saying South Adrilankha has become a battlefield; so, while you're smoking out this guy—"

"Right. And, at the same time, I've just given Mario the commission—"

"To kill Terion's mistress."

"Yep."

"So, you figure, you'll find out who is running that operation in South Adrilankha, and kill Terion, and mess up the Left Hand when Mario kills that sorceress . . . uh, and then what?"

"That's the problem. I'm no longer sure."

"What if you do all of that, and leave Terion alive?"

"What does that do?"

"Gives you bargaining power."

"How . . . oh, right. Anyone else who's interested."

"You have something to give them."

"That could do it," I said.

"And it removes the problem of exactly how you get to him before someone gets to you."

"Yeah, that was a problem I hadn't solved yet."

"So we go with it?"

"I admit there's a lot to be said for it."

"But?"

"But I'd really like to kill Terion. He's a bastard."

"No shortage of those."

"Yeah. No, you're right. That just might be the one number that might work for getting Cawti out of this jam."

"It gives you a wedge, but how to use it—"

"Oh, that part I have worked out already."

"Oh? Well, now you've gotten me interested. What's the big plan?"

"That's your other part."

"Uh huh."

"And at least one person is going to have to know you're working with me."

"Okay."

"And that isn't going to be safe."

"I got that part."

"Okay. Set up a meeting with the Demon for me."

He kept his face expressionless. "Are you going to kill him?"

"No."

"I just ask because I'm sure he's going to kill you."

"Yeah."

"Are you . . . okay."

"You'll do it?"

"Yeah."

"Not quite yet."

"Oh?"

"We need to wait for things to ripple in."

"You mean, for word to get out—"

"Yeah."

He nodded. "Is this going to work?"

"Maybe."

"Best shot, right?"

"Right."

He grinned. "It's good to be working with you again, Vlad."

"I hope you're still in a condition to say that in a couple of days."

He nodded judiciously. "That would be good," he said. "Oh, by the way . . ."

"Hmm?"

"What do I get for this?"

"I'll buy you a meal at Valabar's."

"Done," said Kragar.

14

BRISKET OF BEEF

Telnan shook his head in wonder. "How can they make food this good?"

"It's not actually all that difficult," I said, "if you know how to make pepper-essence and you're a genius."

I'd just given him a small bite of my beef. He had the look on his face of a man who had just discovered that food can be sublime. Yeah, I knew that look, and I envied him his epiphany.

I communed with the brisket for a while, which left me too busy to be envious. A little later he said, "What is pepper-essence?"

"Do you really want to know?"

"If it goes into that, yes I do."

"Melt a couple of spoonfuls of goose-fat, stir in a few spoonfuls of powdered Eastern red pepper. Stir it, don't let it burn. You get an intensified pepper flavor."

"Oh. Yes, it's very intense. It's . . ."

He groped for the word.

"Sublime," I suggested.

"Yeah."

They start with a brisket of beef. I don't know exactly what connections they had, but it was better beef than my father was ever able to get. *The sauce was built with onions, garlic, Eastern red pepper, salt, and just a little tomato. And then the pepper-essence with sour cream. That's about it.*

Amazing, isn't it? That simple, that basic, for such an effect. There's a moral in there, somewhere.

I made it back to South Adrilankha safely, and threaded my way through familiar streets, to Donner's Court. There weren't many people here, and the few who were, weren't paying any attention to innocuous little Sandor.

"Boss, what are we doing?"

"Now is when I kill the Demon Goddess."

"Now is when you reassure me you aren't joking."

"I'll be back in a bit," I said. *"Don't go too far."*

I drew Lady Teldra.

"Boss, what—"

I laid her blade flat against the top of the shrine.

Something *ripped* somewhere inside and outside of me, with a grinding sound and a feeling that wasn't painful, but seemed like it should have been. There was a space of time of unknowable duration where I saw only a terrible bright blue, and as it faded, my right hand seemed to have turned into a golden shimmering spear, which resolved itself almost at once into just my hand, still holding Lady Teldra.

"Hello, Goddess," I said.

It worked better than I'd expected: I was standing in her Halls, just as I remembered them, and she maybe four feet away from me; and Godslayer was naked in my hand. I could see her relax a little as she regarded me.

"I hadn't known you could do that. I must be certain to seal that portal."

"If you have the chance."

"If you'd planned to kill me," she said, "you wouldn't have spoken to me."

"It still isn't too late."

"I do not bargain with mortals."

"Even mortals who have the power to destroy you?"

"Especially those."

"How's that policy worked out for you?"

"Mixed. Where is your familiar?"

"Back in the real world steering clear of your wrath."

"Good plan. So, what put a burr under your saddle?"

"A what under my which?"

"Sorry. I still think of you as Fenarian. What put a notch in your blade?"

"Some memories have returned."

"From where?"

"From wherever you stowed them."

"I? You give me too much credit, Fenarian. Or too little."

"I don't think so. I've remembered that you've been messing with my head."

"That wasn't me—"

"You're lying."

"—exactly. And don't call me a liar. And would you mind putting that thing down?"

"I'd rather keep her in my hand. I find her reassuring."

"Even with that, I don't believe you can harm me. Not here, not after giving me time to prepare. And in these few moments, I have had time to prepare."

"Maybe you're right. Maybe I can't harm you. But while we consider the matter, let's chat. I want to know what happened to my memories. To my thought processes. I want to know what you did to me, and why. And unless you feel like testing that 'maybe'—"

"Taltos Vladimir, you cannot walk into the Paths of the Dead as a living man and expect to both retain all of the sensations you receive, and remain sane. I acted to keep you from going out of your mind."

"There's more to it than that, Goddess."

"Some."

"Well?"

"Well what?"

"You have a plan for me. Or I'm part of a plan involving something else, something too far-reaching for me to comprehend, and too sensitive to trust me with, and too important for me to risk."

"That's not impossible."

"Tell me about it. Make me comprehend. Trust me with it. Take the risk. One of us has to take a risk. If you won't, I will."

She considered me the way I might consider a brisket of beef into which I was about to stick sharp things. She was taller than a Dragaeran, which meant much taller than me. Her features were angular, her hair dark and swept back, and there was an extra joint on each finger. Eventually she said, "I have said all I choose to say, and threats will not compel me to say more. Attempt to carry out your threat, and I will destroy you utterly. You are in my Halls, Easterner. Don't make me show you what I can do."

It was odd. I had this terrible anger in my belly. I wanted to see about that "maybe." I wanted to in the worst way. I didn't care if I got her, or she got me, I just wanted to start the show. But there was something else going on; something that kept the lid on. Something that kept my voice calm. Something that—

Something that was Lady Teldra.

As if from a distance, I wondered if I was glad or sorry she was there.

"You owe me, Goddess. I'm not sure what for, or how much, but you owe me."

"That is a way of looking at it. There are others."

"Goddess, there are stories among my people about you and the Jenoine."

"What of them?"

"Would you treat me as they treated you? Or expect me to respond differently?"

"Don't even start. The cases are nowhere near each other."

"It seems to me—"

"But on reflection . . ."

I stopped and waited for her to continue.

"I admire your courage in coming here like this," she said after a moment. "It is unlike you."

"I've been hanging around Dzur."

"But you didn't come here to destroy me. What do you really want?"

"An explanation."

"You know you aren't getting that. What do you want?"

"I—"

"Don't play me, Taltos Vladimir. You need help, and you're too angry to beg me for it, as is traditional. Well, I'm inclined to help you for several reasons, mostly because, as you know, I have use for you. But you must cooperate. You must tell me what it is you want. Otherwise, I can't do it."

"Goddess, you don't know me as well as you believe you do."

"Were you actually intending to kill me?"

"What do you think?"

"What do you wish of me?"

"We're not finished with this, you know."

"I know that better than you. In the meantime, what do you wish?"

I actually hadn't thought about it. But . . .

"I'm not sure. If I were to walk into a house filled with sorceresses of the Left Hand, all determined to kill me, could you protect me?"

"I can't interfere with internal matters of one of the Great Houses."

"Great."

"At least, not directly."

She smiled, did the Goddess.

"If you know an indirect method for getting me out of there alive, I'd be glad to hear it. I had been thinking in terms of breaking a teleport block."

"No, that would be direct."

"Then I suppose a divine manifestation is out of the question?"

"I'm afraid so."

"Well then?"

"I'm rather good at sending dreams."

"Yeah. You've sent me a few, haven't you?"

"Yes."

"The last one sent me off East and cost me a finger."

"That wasn't the last one."

"Oh."

"Well? What about it?"

"I think I see what you're getting at."

"And?"

"All right."

"Then I'll return you."

"Well, tell me what's going to—"

That's as far as I got before Verra's Halls were gone from around me, and I was once more standing next to her altar in South Adrilankha.

15

DUMPLINGS

My father spent hours and hours trying to teach me to make good dumplings, but I guess there are just some things I wasn't cut out to do. On the other hand, even if they had been good, they wouldn't have had the perfect consistency of Valabar's.

The thing about dumplings, more than perhaps anything else I've ever tried to prepare, is that they take patience: patience to get the mix exactly right, patience to push out each individual dumpling, patience to make sure to pull them from the water at exactly the right moment. I used to put about the same amount of work into preparing to put a shine on a guy, but guess I must have enjoyed that more or something.

Since I've been spending so much time making analogies between murder and cooking, I ought to dwell on patience for a bit, because it really is a key factor in both. It's funny, but until I got into this line of work, I had thought I was by nature an impatient person. It turns out that, when it came to committing murder, I had no trouble sitting around waiting for the perfect moment before striking, or standing outside someplace watching for someone, or following some guy around for days and days to track his movements.

I'm not sure why it is that I'm able to exercise great patience with some things, but with others I get jumpy, jittery, and eventually just *curse under my breath and declare the task finished, or else convince myself that it's good enough.*

With cooking and murder, there really shouldn't be a "good enough." You need to get as close to perfect as possible, otherwise find another line of work. Which, in fact, I did.

I studied Telnan, who was working on his kethna, accompanied by Valabar's cabbage, about which I could say a great deal if I felt inclined. One of the arts of putting together a meal—and one that Valabar's has completely mastered—is determining what goes well with what. I guess it's like selecting the proper weapon to finalize someone; it goes along with all the other factors, like the individual's particular skills, and the right time and place.

So there is another similarity between murder and cooking, to accompany my thoughts about the need for patience when making death or dumplings. But these are my thoughts now—well after the meal and all that followed it. At the time, I was just eating, I wasn't thinking about murder at all—though I guess I did have a few passing thoughts about how I'd never been able to make dumplings to my father's satisfaction. Or my own, for that matter.

The reward for doing the dumplings right is that you have the perfect accompaniment for the Valabar's brisket of beef. I mean, you bite into one and you get an explosion in your mouth of the pure sauce that it's been absorbing. It's magnificent.

The only problem is that by this time, you really have to pace yourself; there's been just too much food in too short a time, and you are very much aware that soon you're going to reach the end of your capacity.

I think Telnan made a couple of comments that I didn't hear during all of this, or else that I heard at the time but no longer remember; I think they were about the way the sausages worked with the kethna, but I'm not sure. What with the beef, the sauce, and the dumplings, I just didn't have a whole lot of attention to spare.

Another similarity, if you will, between committing murder and indulging in supreme pleasure: Both take one's full concentration.

$\mathcal{B}\mathcal{D}$

"*Boss!*"

"Damn."

"*What is it, Boss?*"

"*All is well, Loiosh.*"

"*If you ever do that again, I'll bite you. I mean, really, really hard.*"

"Understood. *How long was I gone?*"

"*Forever. Almost an hour.*"

I checked with the Orb. I'd been gone about twenty minutes.

"Okay. *Let's go home.*"

I returned to the sanctuary of my room, and settled in to wait. The waiting lasted about three minutes before I realized that sitting there doing nothing would drive me nuts.

"*You know, it could be days, Boss.*"

"*It could be weeks.*"

"*You can't just walk around for weeks.*"

"*I'm not just walking around. I have a destination in mind.*"

"*Oh, all right. Where to, then?*"

"*Anywhere.*"

We went out and walked anywhere, Loiosh and Rocza staying above me, but pretty close. I guess Loiosh was nervous.

Mostly what I remember from that day are faces, passed in the street. The faces of Easterners, of my people: old and young, one who seemed pleased about something, a couple who appeared unhappy, several who were lost in thought, a couple who were looking around. One guy, about my age, made eye contact with me and gave me a nod. I remember nothing of where I saw them, or what I was doing—just walking, I suppose. But I remember the faces.

"There is a moment," Telnan had told me, "when you either attack with everything you have, or you do something else. That moment, right before you commit yourself, that's when you learn who you are."

"Okay," I had told him. "What if you don't like yourself?"

He'd laughed, like I was kidding with him. But what I ought to have asked was, how do you survive the interminable seconds, or hours, or days, that lead up to that moment? If I saw him again, I'd ask, but it was unlikely the answer would do me any good. Whatever I was, I wasn't a Dzur.

"*So tell me, Boss. Do you plan to just wander around South Adrilankha for however many days or weeks it takes?*"

"Pretty much, yeah."

"*Oh, joy.*"

A few hours later, I swung by Ristall Market. It was full of people buying and selling things. So, at least that part of the operation was working. While I was there, I picked up a bag of pecans and chewed on them as I walked. Pecans don't grow near Adrilankha, they have to be imported from, uh, from somewhere. They're ridiculously expensive. I think that's why I like them so much.

Eventually I returned to the room and got some sleep.

Then I was holding a dagger, then Loiosh told me it was okay, then Loiosh yelled, then I woke up. It was another one of those things where what I remember isn't what actually happened, only now those were beginning to bother me more than they used to. Was it because of Verra, or does everyone goes through that when his familiar wakes him in the middle of the night to warn that someone is about to kill him only to then tell him no, don't worry, it's only your friend the assassin?

Hmmm. Let me rephrase that.

On second thought, skip it.

"*It's Mario,*" said Loiosh. "*Sorry to scare you.*"

"*Better that than the alternative.*"

Aloud I said, "Come in, Mario."

The curtain moved and he entered. I lit the lamp and pointed to the chair.

He sat down and said, "Sorry to awaken you."

"I wasn't sleeping. What's up?"

"It's done."

I yawned and nodded. "Hmmm?"

"It's done."

"It's . . . oh." I wrapped my head around that. "What happened?"

"Excuse me?"

I cleared my throat. "What's the word on the street? Or, what will it be?"

"Oh." He considered for a moment. "The sorceress was stabbed to death by a person or persons unknown as she emerged from a teleport in the middle of the night at Di'bani Circle near the Imperial Palace. The cause of death was a single stroke by a large knife administered to the back of her neck, severing her spine. There were no witnesses. No doubt, after a thorough and lengthy investigation, the Phoenix Guards will shrug and say, 'Mario did it.'" He didn't smirk as he said it, which must have required great restraint.

I said. "Uh huh. I get it. No, wait. As she *emerged* from a teleport?"

"Sure. There's always an instant's disorientation when you—"

"Yes, but how did you . . . never mind."

Mario smiled.

"Thanks," I told him.

"Least I could do, under the circumstances. Anything else you need?"

Now *there* was a question.

"Feel like putting a shine on the whole Jhereg? And half the Left Hand?"

"Sometimes, you know, I do."

I nodded. "I can respect that."

"Anything you need that's within the bounds of reason?"

"Except for mass slaughter of the Jhereg, I don't think this one can be solved by making anyone become dead."

"Yeah, some things are like that. Odd, isn't it?"

"Sometimes I can hardly believe it."

After Mario left, I lay back down on the bed.

"Tomorrow, Loiosh. We move tomorrow."

"I know, Boss."

The next morning I didn't waste any time; I was up and out in minutes. It wasn't so much that I was in a hurry as that I was tired of doubts and second thoughts. I went to Six Corners and waited there, looking like I had nothing to do, watching. While I watched, I scribbled a note and folded it. On the outside, I put the address of the office, and directions for getting there.

In about five minutes, I spotted a candidate. I said, "Hey, boy. Come here."

I got a suspicious look from a kid who looked like I might have looked when I was nine.

"Come here," I repeated. "As long as you promise not to hurt me."

That turned out to be the right tack. He came up to me, and I flipped him an imperial. "Want another one?"

He stared at the coin, tapped it, pocketed it, and grinned. "Who do I have to kill?" His voice hadn't changed yet. He was dressed in a cotton tunic that had been bright blue a long time ago, and brown wool trousers.

"Never kill anyone for less than a thousand," I told him. "This is easier."

"What—"

"Run over to the City and deliver a message."

"I've done that before."

"Never for this much, I'll wager."

He shrugged. "I get the other one when I get back with a reply, right?"

"Right."

"And if he doesn't give me a reply?"

"Then you're out of luck."

"All right. You'll be here?"

I nodded and handed him the note. "Do you read?"

"A little." He frowned and stared at the writing, then he nodded. "I can make this out."

"Good. If you're back in less than two hours, I'll make it two imperials."

He set off at a walk, just to show me how independent he was. I'm sure he broke into a run the instant he was out of sight. I liked him.

"I could have saved you a few imperials, Boss."

"I know. But I want you around me right now."

"Expecting trouble?"

"No. I'm just . . . I want you around."

"Okay."

I returned to the room, put all that was Vlad, at least externally, into a sack, and said good-bye to the room. Whatever happened, I wouldn't be back there. That part didn't make me sad.

I returned to Six Corners and bought a pear. I took my time eating it. I rinsed my hands off at the market pump and left a copper for the poor, because it would have looked funny if I hadn't.

I spotted the kid about a minute before he spotted me. He handed me a note. I glanced at it, verified the signature, and gave the kid two imperials. He gave me an odd look.

"You're wondering what someone like me has to do with the Jhereg."

He nodded.

I smiled. I was briefly tempted to have him watch while I turned back into Vlad. Strange. Why would I want to impress this punk? Maybe he really did remind me of me. But I just gave him an enigmatic smile and said, "See you around."

"I doubt it," he said. I guess he wanted to get in the last word. Yeah, he was like me.

I wandered away from the market and found a quiet place where I could study the note more carefully. "Vlad there's a back room at the White Lantern I know the place and will have protection there for you be there at the sixth hour Kragar."

"*Okay, Loiosh. It's set.*"

"*I don't know the White Lantern, Boss.*"

"*I know where it is. And we either trust Kragar, or we don't.*"

"*Do I get a vote on that?*"

"*No.*"

"*Didn't think so. Who's going to cross the river?*"

"*Sandor.*"

"*Okay. When?*"

"*Now.*"

"*It's early.*"

"*Yeah. So just maybe they aren't watching all the bridges yet.*"

"*Which one are we taking?*"

"*Chain.*"

"*Because there's room to move around, or just to make my job harder?*"

"*Both, of course.*"

An hour later I was safely across the bridge. I thought about heading to Valabar's to wait, but there were a lot of reasons not to; mostly because it was no secret how much I loved it, and it was bound to be watched now that I was known to be around. So I went back to the Imperial library, picked up a book at random, and read for a few hours.

Just before the fifth hour, I left the library and found one of the coaches that served the Palace. The third one was willing to carry an Easterner. Or, at any rate, an Easterner who offered to pay double, and paid in advance. Sandor climbed into the coach and drew the blinds. Forty-five minutes later, Vlad climbed out in the middle of Malak Circle. I didn't give the driver a glance as I left his coach; I just lost myself in the crowd of the market. Loiosh and Rocza landed on my shoulders.

"*Do you have a plan when we go in, Boss?*"

"No."

"*What about us?*"

"*I want you both with me.*"

I found a place to watch the place that could watch the front door. I determined that no one was there, so I moved up a place. Did you follow that?

I became relaxed, calm, and much more confident than the situation called for; at which point I realized my hand was resting on Lady Teldra's hilt. *Thank you,* I thought to her, and was almost surprised that there was no response. What had Sethra meant about her "waking up"? It might become awful crowded in my head. I'd have to get them all to take turns. Maybe I could . . .

"*It's time, Loiosh.*"

"*I know.*"

I walked across the street, hands empty and at my sides, and walked through the front door as if it was perfectly safe. Well, maybe it wasn't, but no one attacked me. No one even particularly noticed me.

Malak Circle is not in one of the classier parts of town; it isn't somewhere to go if you want to rub elbows with the high end of the nobility. The exception is a public house with an outstanding wine list and barely passable food. There was no sign indicating a name for the place, but it was clearly marked by a bright, white lantern that was kept burning even during the day.

The inside of the Lantern had pale stonework with blue mosaic trimming, and there were no tables of the type I'm used to, just little things, suitable for setting a drink on, next to each of

the big comfortable chairs. It was a good place for me, because
Jhereg stand out there; mostly you'll find Dragonlords, Dzur, Lyorn,
and Tiassa. I stood out, but so would the Demon, as well as anyone
placed there with unfriendly intentions toward me. Also, killing
someone there was liable to bring on a lot more heat from the
Phoenix Guards than the Jhereg would like.

I got looks from everyone there when I came in. That was
good. I'd have been worried about anyone who didn't give me a
glance or two. I walked straight to the rear, where there were two
doors back-to-back. I glanced at the host. He pointed to the right-
hand door, and I took it.

It was a private little room, well lit, with no windows, and,
above all, no one in it. I left the door open and took a seat around
to the side, where I could see the only door well enough, but without ostentatiously placing myself in an ideal defensive position.
Loiosh and Rocza sat on my shoulders, unmoving, waiting, like
me. I caught the faint psychic whispers that indicated they were
having some conversation with each other. There was a steady,
quiet hum of conversation from the next room. No one was loud
at the White Lantern.

I checked the time. It was just the sixth hour. I waited.

About two minutes later, a Jhereg I didn't recognize came in,
glanced at me without acknowledging my presence, let his eye flick
over the rest of the room, and then nodded back toward the door.
The Demon came through next, followed by another bodyguard,
who closed the door. The Demon hadn't changed much. I didn't
stand.

He sat down across from me and said, "All right. Talk."

"Shall we get a drink first?"

"Talk."

"You don't want to be sociable?"

He looked at me.

"Damn," I said. "And here I thought we were friends."

"Talk," he said, with a sort of "this is the last time I'm going to say it before I have people kill you and I don't care what deal we've made or what the consequences might be you scum-sucking asshole" intonation to it. I'm good with intonations.

"A bunch of people want the number-one seat on the Council. I—"

"You applying for the job?"

I chuckled. "Thanks for the offer, but I'll pass. I'm thinking of going into dry goods."

"Uh huh."

"Terion's got the backing of the Left Hand, for reasons we don't need to go into. You—"

"You did it!" he burst out suddenly.

I raised an eyebrow and didn't say anything. He grunted. "All right. Go on."

"I can get you the game."

"You can, huh?"

"Yeah."

"How?"

"That's my business."

"If you think that's going to let you off the hook for what you did—"

"No, I don't. Me getting off the hook isn't part of the deal. But I do want thirty hours, just so I can finish this."

"I don't speak for the Jhereg."

"Thirty hours from your people."

"That would not be impossible. Let's hear it, then."

"South Adrilankha."

"What about it?"

"I want it to be hands-off for the Jhereg. All of it."

"For how long?"

"Let's say . . . until the end of the next Dragon Reign."

"That could be quite a while."

"Yes."

"You are unlikely to still be alive by then."

I chuckled. "That's something of an understatement."

"My point is, Lord Taltos, how do you expect to enforce it?"

"I trust you."

"No, you don't."

"Well, yeah, I guess I don't."

"So, then?"

"I have friends."

He look at me and waited.

I said, "I imagine you've already heard about who had a shine put on her last night."

He put a few things together in his mind and nodded slowly. "I see."

"Yeah."

"That would do it, I expect. You're asking a lot, you know."

"I know."

"The Organization will grow there on its own, and it will be crying out for someone to run it. There will be a lot of work involved in keeping the Jhereg out of there."

"That's how I see it, too. But you know what you get for it."

"Can you deliver?"

"I think so."

"You think so."

I nodded. "And, of course, if you don't end up in the number-one spot, you don't pay."

"And your life isn't part of the deal?"

"Nope."

"Okay. What else?"

"As part of leaving South Adrilankha alone, you negotiate with the Left Hand. They're the ones running it, and—"

"Your wife. That's the meat of the whole thing, isn't it?"

"Yeah."

"All right. I was trying to figure out why you got involved in this in the first place. Now I know."

"Uh huh."

"You dived into this whole thing for her."

"Yep."

"Like a Dzur hero come to save the maiden."

"You got it."

"How does she feel about that?"

"None of your fucking business."

"That's what I figured."

"Do we have a deal?"

"I gotta be honest. I don't know if I can call off the Left Hand at this point. They aren't under any authority but their own."

"No, but if they get, uh, called off, as you put it, I think you can negotiate with them to stay out."

He gave me a contemplative look. "I don't know what you have in mind, of course. But that would depend on exactly how they get called off."

"Yeah."

"Care to tell me about it?"

"No."

"Then I can't give you an answer, can I?"

"I'm negotiating with them."

"Negotiating."

"Uh huh. If you want, you can show up for the negotiations."

"Oh?"

"I'll be meeting with them around seventh hour, give or take."

"Where?"

"In South Adrilankha. There's a district called Six Corners. Not far from there is a house, Number Eleven Stranger's Road. We'll be meeting there."

"And I'm invited?"

"Yes. At least, that's where we're starting the negotiations."

"And when will these negotiations be concluded?"

"Like I said before, I'll need about thirty hours."

"Then I can't give you an answer before then."

"Sure you can. A conditional answer."

He nodded slowly. "You're asking a lot, you know."

"You're getting a lot."

"Yes, I am."

"And, as I said, feel free to show up."

"Yeah. I might do that."

I gave him some time to think it over. A part of me regretted that I wasn't still in the Organization, working for someone like him. He'd be a good guy to work for. And life would be so much simpler.

After a moment, he nodded. "Okay on the thirty hours. And, yeah, depending on how these negotiations go, I'll agree that if you get me the position, I'll keep us out of South Adrilankha until the end of the next Dragon Reign, or until I'm knocked on the head, whichever comes first."

"That works," I said.

"You know it won't make any difference, right?"

"Hmmm?"

"I mean, if you're thinking that you'll be doing something to help those people—"

"I'm not. If anything, it'll be worse for them, unless they find someone who knows how to run this sort of operation efficiently."

He nodded. "She must be some kind of woman."

"Yeah," I said.

"It's too bad things worked out this way, Vlad. I'd have liked to have you working for me."

I nodded.

"Good luck," he said.

"Thanks."

He got up and walked out, taking his bodyguard with him.

"Good going, Vlad," said Kragar. "Now, can you pull it off?"

"I hope so," I said.

16

RED WINE

There was a place I passed through when I visited the East a couple of years ago. It was sort of a meadow, extended downward from a bare, rocky slope, and ending in woods. It wasn't very big; standing on the top of the slope you could see the woods clearly enough. But in that place, there were an odd collection of berry plants and flowers, and I happened to hit it at a time when they were all emitting their specialized scents. There were wild roses, brittleberries, whiteblossom, honeykeolsch, and clover.

I mention this, even though at the time my mind was on other things and I didn't pay much attention, because, though it was of the type that is called "full" and "deep" and "strongly flavored," there were hints of most of those in the wine Mihi brought to accompany the beef.

I set the glass down and opened my eyes.

Mihi winked at me and walked away as Telnan drank some wine and nodded. "Goes good with the food," he said.

"Got lucky," I said.

He flashed me a grin. Only one meal, and he was already figuring out my sense of humor.

"I'll bet there's a whole art to that, isn't there? I mean, picking the right wine to go with a meal."

"There is," I told him. "I don't know how they do it, but I'm glad to reap the rewards."

He nodded. "Think you can really tell the difference, though? I mean, between a wine that goes perfectly with what you're eating, and wine that only sort of goes with it? Is there, I don't know, a lot more pleasure, or something?"

I actually had to think about that, for more reasons than to try to figure out what he was asking. "There are a lot of things," I said, "that you don't actually notice, but have an effect anyway."

"Yeah, that's true," said the Dzur. He looked lost in thought for a minute. "That really is true," he repeated, as if I'd said something profound.

I let him think so while I ate some more of the beef.

I said, "They chill it just a bit, for me, even though it isn't supposed to be served that way. Not chilled like a white wine, but just a little chilled. I just think wine is better when it's a little bit cold. Unlike brandy."

"And heroics," he said, grinning.

"Hmmm?"

"It's hardest to be a hero when you have to do it cold."

"I don't follow you."

"I was just making a joke."

"Oh, all right."

"But it's true, though."

"I don't—"

"It's one thing to go charging into a fight when you're outnumbered, and you just, you know, hack away as best you can. It's another when you have to just sit there, everything against you, and no one to actually attack. All the demons in your head start on you, and, it's like, you're giving yourself every chance to be afraid, but you have to keep on anyway. I'm not describing it very well."

"I don't think I've ever been in that situation."

"It's not as much fun as you might think."

I nodded and took another sip of wine. Just a little bit chilled, the way I like it.

βⰃ

"You were there for the whole thing?" I asked.

Kragar shook his head. "I arrived late."

"I thought you might do that. Were you expecting him to make a play for me?"

"Vlad, you aren't out of here, yet."

"True."

"I'll go out first."

"Just like the old days."

"Sort of."

"Hey, Kragar, I'm trying to remember something."

"Yeah?"

"You know, all those times I walked out of a door wondering if someone was on the other side waiting to put a nice pretty shine on my skin, was there ever anyone there?"

"You mean, has anyone come after you when you were looking for it? Not that I recall, but maybe I wasn't around."

"This might be the first time, you know."

"You're just saying that because you're a superstitious Easterner, and you think if you say it, it won't happen."

"Exactly."

"Good plan."

It worked, too. At least, no one took a shot at me when I left the Lantern.

"What now?" he asked. "You hungry? We should have gotten something to eat."

"Yeah, I'll just sort of hang out here for another hour or two, that would be smart."

He chuckled. "Office?"

"Sounds good."

We made it there with no trouble, but I'd be lying if said I wasn't nervous during the walk.

The guy running the game nodded to me as I went past. He ignored Kragar.

"How do you do it?" I asked him when we were in my old office, with him behind the desk.

"Do what?"

"Get people to obey your orders, when they don't even know you're there."

"Oh. I write a lot of notes."

"Dangerous."

"They get burned. And you know how it is: There's usually nothing incriminating in them anyway."

"I don't know, Kragar. All it takes is one that—"

"You want the job back, Vlad?"

"No, thanks."

"Then shut up."

"Right. Shutting up."

"What happens next?"

"The Left Hand comes after me."

"How are you avoiding them?"

"I'm not."

He studied me. "You're going to let them find you?"

"I'm going to them."

"Mind if I ask why?"

"Because I can't have them chasing me. Having the Jhereg chasing me is bad enough; having the Left Hand—"

"Wait. You don't want them chasing you, so you're going to give yourself up to them? I mean, in one sense it's logical, but—"

"I probably shouldn't have tried to explain."

"Yeah, that was a mistake. Where is this happening?"

"There's a house in South Adrilankha where the Left Hand has set up shop."

"Where exactly?"

"You don't need to know."

"A house full of sorcerocces, and you're going to just walk into it?"

"Pulling them out of it, actually. And there aren't as many of them as there were yesterday at this time."

"Ugh. Need backup?"

"You can't help with this one, unless you're a better sorcerer than I think you are."

"You aren't that much of a sorcerer yourself, Vlad."

"I have help arranged."

"All right. But if you want a spare knife, I don't mind—"

"No, thanks."

He nodded. "I knew you were going to say that. That's why I didn't mind asking."

"Uh huh. You hungry? I'm buying."

"How about if I send someone to pick something up?"

"Embarrassed to be seen with me in public?"

"Wouldn't you be?"

"Well, yeah."

He arranged for seafood soup with sour bread from the Locket. It showed up and we ate it. I'd never eaten at the Locket, though it wasn't far from the office. I don't know why I'd never gotten there. Too bad; they made a good soup.

While we were eating he said, "Aren't you going to ask me about that name you wanted?"

"You mean, you have it already?"

"Yeah, that's really why I showed up there. Finding a shoemaker in South Adrilankha seemed like too much trouble."

"Okay, I'm impressed."

He bowed.

"So, who is it?"

"Nylanth."

"I've heard that name. Who is he?"

"He's on the Council. He controls part of South Adrilankha anyway, so I guess he figured—"

"What part?"

"Shipping."

"Shipping? What is there to control with shipping?"

"Vlad, not everything shipped is exactly legal."

"Oh. Don't the Orca handle that?"

"Yeah. He buys Orca as he needs them. And he also runs some gambling by the piers."

I nodded. "Okay, makes sense, then. How is he reacting?"

"To you messing up his plans? Well, if he wasn't already trying to kill you, as was the whole rest of the Organization, I'm sure he'd start trying now. As it is, nothing much has changed."

"Yeah, that's the nice thing about the position I'm in: It's hard to make it any worse."

"I don't think that's true. You could make it worse. You could put yourself in the hands of a bunch of sorceresses who want to kill you; that would be worse."

"I'd never do anything that foolish."

"Oh. Good, then. Any steps to be taken?"

"Steps?"

"Regarding Nylanth."

"Oh." I thought about that.

"No," I finally said. "Let him keep chasing me around South Adrilankha; I don't think he has much of a role to play anymore."

"Okay."

We finished up, and left the crockery on Kragar's desk. I said, "Okay, I think it's time for me to move."

"Just a minute."

He closed his eyes for about a minute, then said, "I wouldn't go out the front, Vlad."

"Someone waiting?"

"My people didn't see anyone, but said they can't promise anything. Too much street traffic."

"Oh. If there is someone waiting, the back will be covered, too."

"Yep. Take the tunnel."

"Excellent. Good. Perfect. What tunnel?"

"I've made some changes."

"Why? I mean, why you of all people? You could walk out the front door and no one would notice."

"I figured you might be back, and I know you aren't teleporting much these days."

"So you put in a tunnel?"

"Just a short one."

"Where does it come up?"

"Behind the haberdasher's just this side of Malak Circle."

"Okay. Where does it start?"

"There was the room in the basement where an ancient people used to practice their heathen rites."

"My lab?"

"I had no use for it."

"I guess not. All right, lead the way."

"Oh, Vlad —"

"Hmmm?"

"Nice boots."

He lit a lantern and led the way down the stairs and into the basement. The musty smell and the feel of the dirt floor brought back a lot of memories. Most of my old gear was gone, but the brazier was still there, on its side up against the far wall. I didn't see any doorway, so I looked a question at him.

He smirked and gave one of the sconces on the wall a twist. Nothing changed, but I heard a faint "click."

"A secret entrance with a hidden passage with a secret latch," I remarked. "I don't hardly believe it."

"I couldn't resist."

"Did you go all the way and kill the builders?"

"I forgot that part."

He went over to the middle of the left-hand wall and gave it a push. It swung open without a sound. He led the way. It was narrow—just barely room to walk forward—but tall enough that Kragar didn't have to stoop. The walls looked finished, probably with tile, and his boots went clack against the floor. When I spoke, there were echoes.

"You left the basement floor dirt, but put a floor in this?"

"Well, when you turned things over to me, I had all this money I didn't know what to do with."

I didn't have an answer for that, so I shut up and followed the dancing light of the lantern he held. It seemed like a very long walk.

The tunnel didn't branch, but led straight to a stairway, which ended in a narrow door. Kragar put his face against it.

"A peephole?" I said.

"Of course."

He pulled on a rope that hung from the ceiling, and the door opened.

He stepped out, looked around, and nodded to me. Loiosh left my shoulder and flew out, then I followed. There was no one there.

"Thanks, Kragar."

"Good luck, Vlad."

I took the Stone Bridge back to South Adrilankha, feeling very exposed and vulnerable during the walk, although Loiosh and Rocza were alert to anyone even glancing at me. It was around the seventh hour when I reached the Six Corners district. I made my way to Stranger's Road and found the same observation point I'd used before.

"Okay, Loiosh. See what's up."

"*On my way, Boss.*"

I slid back behind the corner of the building, reassured by Rocza's weight on my shoulder.

"*Nothing yet, Boss.*"

"Be patient. If they noticed before, they'll have to notice now."

"*Oh, I'm patient. How 'bout you?*"

"Going crazy."

"*That's what I figured. Uh, Boss? Mind telling me what happens when they spot you? Or is it a secret?*"

"It's a secret. I can't trust you not to pass on the information to the Empire."

"*Right. Did it occur to you that the Empire doesn't much care if they kill you?*"

"The Empress likes me. If they get me, I'm sure she'll wear something white. At least for the afternoon."

"*That's a great consol—someone's coming out.*"

My stomach turned over.

"Okay."

"*Boss, can't you just tell me generally what we're going to do?—*"

"We're going into the house."

"*Going in? What—*"

"I have a plan, Loiosh."

"*How are we getting out alive?*"

"The plan doesn't extend that far. What is the sorceress doing?"

"*She's looking around.*"

"Okay."

"*Should I stay here?*"

"Yes. Keep watching."

"*Someone else has joined her. They're talking. Should I get close enough to listen?*"

"No. Stay where you are."

"*A third one, now.*"

I took a deep breath, and sent Loiosh a mental nod.

"Three of them, Boss. Just standing on the porch."

"All right."

Rocza squeezed my shoulder. I turned around, and there was a sorceress behind me, about ten yards away, dressed in black and gray, holding a dagger. If the dagger wasn't enchanted, I'd eat my new boots. I wanted to draw Lady Teldra so badly I could feel my hand twitching.

"Took you long enough," I told her. "I've been standing here for most of an hour."

Her grip on the dagger tightened in a way that looked like she might be about to do something with it, so I drew Lady Teldra, holding her in front of me. The dagger the sorceress was holding moved in a small circle. Lady Teldra glowed a little and I felt a tingle run up my arm. That's all.

"Now, now," I said. "No need for unpleasantness."

Her expression didn't change, but I got the feeling she didn't know exactly how to handle this turn of events. Or maybe Jhereg banter was exclusive to the Right Hand. I badly wished to know what spell had been cast at me. She had long limbs, rather light hair, and deep-set eyes. She carried herself with a relaxed ease.

"I'm Vlad," I told her. "You?"

"I'm not," said the sorceress.

"I didn't actually think you were. Feel like telling me your name?"

"Why? Can you use it in an enchantment?"

Okay, so Jhereg banter crossed the line to the distaff side.

"Probably not," I said. "I'm willing to try, though, if you wish."

"They usually call me Nisasta, which I was once told means 'seeker of truth' in some language or another."

"They're walking toward you, Boss."

"All right, Nisasta. Before your friends get here and I have to work up a sweat, how about if we just agree to have a peaceful conversation."

"You killed—"

"Yes, I did. How about my proposal? Your friends are getting closer, and if it looks like I'm going to be outnumbered, I'll have to do something about it."

Lady Teldra had taken the form of a short, very nasty-looking triangular dagger. I let her bounce a little in my hand. She felt solid and useful. Nisasta avoided looking at her.

"How close are they?"

"About thirty paces."

"Decide," I said. "Talk, or slaughter. I don't much care."

She still didn't look at Lady Teldra. I was impressed; that can't have been easy.

"It isn't my decision to make," she said finally.

"Then you'd best speak to whoever's decision it is. Fast."

She nodded, and her brows furrowed a little; she didn't close her eyes. That can't have been easy, either; closing your eyes when speaking to someone psychically is instinctive.

She said, "They say—wait."

"They've stopped, Boss. There's—"

"What? What?"

"The Demon is here, Boss. With two bodyguards. He's talking to the sorceresses. I can't hear them from here."

"Okay. So far, so good."

"What are we going to do if they don't want to talk?"

"Improvise."

"Oh, good."

"Not to worry. It's the same thing we're going to do if they do want to talk."

"Oh. All right. That's fine, then."

"I am told," said the sorceress who called herself Nisasta, "that they'll speak with you if you disarm yourself."

I laughed. "Oh, sure. That's real likely. I'll just walk with you into that house there, so I can be surrounded by a dozen sorceresses who all want to kill me, after giving up the one thing that might keep me alive. Do they have a second idea?"

"You think it will be enough to keep you alive? You should know there is now a teleport block over this entire area. No can gets in or out save by walking, and no one is close enough to help you."

I shrugged. "I expected that when I put myself into this situation. We can dance if you want. You'll probably get me eventually. How many of you will go down first, and what will happen when you do? You know what I carry."

She barely nodded, and was silent again for a moment.

"*They still aren't moving, Loiosh?*"

"*Nope. Just standing there, Boss. Talking with the Demon. Shall I get close enough to—?*"

"*No. We wait.*"

I briefly wondered why I felt so calm; then I became aware of the smooth, cool, reassuring feeling of Lady Teldra's hilt in my hand, and stopped wondering. Would Telnan consider this cheating? I'd have to ask him if I got out of this.

"Are you willing to, at least, sheath it?"

I hadn't expected that question, and I had to think about it. "If we talk out here, no. If we're going inside, then I will, until something happens that makes me feel threatened. I react badly when I feel threatened. It's a personality quirk."

After a moment, she said, "Inside, then."

I nodded. "After you."

"*Boss, you want to go inside?*"

"*Yes.*"

"*Why, for all the—*"

"*If spark comes to fire, I want them in a confined space.*"

"*But—*"

"*Not now, Loiosh.*"

She set off toward the house. I sheathed Lady Teldra, not without some regret, and followed her. Loiosh flew over to me. Nisasta, as much as I could tell watching her from behind, flinched just a little when he flew past her. She looked back at him as he landed on my shoulder. I wasn't calm anymore, which was good, because Telnan could no longer accuse me of cheating.

"Hey, Boss. How do you figure the odds that they're going to try to kill you once we get inside."

"Dead certain, more or less."

"Yeah, that's what I figured, too."

"Glad to know we're in sync."

"Yeah. Any idea how we're going to get out of it?"

"Some vague ideas, yes."

"Okay. Care to tell me why we put ourselves in this position?"

"It's been our plan all along."

"Oh. Well. All right then. And to think I was worried."

The sorceresses, along with the Demon and his bodyguards, were about forty paces ahead of the one called Nisasta, who was just a few paces ahead of me. The group of them opened the door, entered, and vanished within. Nisasta reached the door and held it open for me. I gave a nod toward it. She shrugged, and walked in front of me.

"Want me to scout?"

"No. Stay with me."

We stood in a wide entryway, with a hallway leading off to the right, an arch at the far end, a stairway next to the arch, and a door, presumably a closet, to the left. It looked pleasant and comfortable; the sort of place Jakoub might dream of buying. Or Sandor. The door swung shut behind me, from some sort of counterweight, or maybe a spell of some kind. It went "snick" with a sort of finality. I wondered how hard it would be to open it again.

"Boss, are we trapped?"

"*No, they are.*"

"*Oh. All right, then.*"

Nisasta looked back at me over her shoulder. "We'll talk in here," she said, and went through the arch.

"*Last chance to run, Boss.*"

"*Oh, shut up.*"

I walked through the archway like I hadn't a worry in the world.

17

PALACZINTA

Mihi came back to the table. He brought a bucket of ice on a stand, and in the bucket was a bottle I knew well. Mihi was all smiles. I think this was his favorite part; it was certainly right up there for me.

Dragaerans usually served a fruit at the end of a meal, but we Easterners like to serve a confection, or something sweet to finish off a meal. We call it "dessert" and no one does it better than Valabar's. Mihi gave a slight bow, refilled our wineglasses, took a deep breath, and began speaking.

"Today, Mr. Valabar has prepared an apple cheesecake with a mild cinnamon sauce topped with powdered chef's sugar and a finely ground pecan mix chocolate raspberry mousse cake in a chocolate shell sweetened with white sugar with jumpberry sauce and a selection of fresh berries vanilla-cinnamon custard lightly caramelized on top with brown sugar and a garnish of fresh fruit a six-layer dessert palaczinta consisting of a layer of rednuts ground to a fine powder a layer of sweetened chocolate a layer of raspberries a layer of walnuts ground to a powder and a layer of tartberries with a chocolate-brandy sauce dribbled on top."

Telnan stared at Mihi. Mihi looked smug.

At last, Telnan said, "What?"

"No, no," I said. "Don't make him repeat it. My heart couldn't take it. I'll have the palaczinta."

Telnan's mouth opened and closed a couple of times.

"Bring him the mousse cake," I said. "He'll like that."

"Uh, sure," said Telnan

Mihi nodded happily and walked off.

A palaczinta is nothing more than a wafer-thin griddle cake, suitable for having preserves spread on it, or maybe butter and sweetened cinnamon, or to be rolled up with meat and baked. But at Valabar's, they'd stack them in layers—with a delightful assortment of things on each layer—and then slice it like a pie. It is a joy and a delight; it's one of those things that makes life worth living.

I watched the sweat run down the side of the wine-bottle and waited for Mihi to return, meanwhile thinking pleasant thoughts.

He was back in a few short minutes. Holding a small white plate in his left hand, with another cradled in his left arm; from the expression on his face, you'd think he had not only prepared the delicacies, but had invented the whole concept of dessert. I've always liked Mihi.

♫

The sitting room was dominated by a long, dark table, with ornate, high-backed wooden chairs placed all around it. They were all standing, waiting for me; the Demon stood in a corner, flanked by his bodyguards and staring off into space as if he were bored by the whole thing. There were six sorceresses in the room, all of them wearing some form of black and gray. One of the sorceresses said, "Sit where you please, Lord Taltos."

I picked one of the chairs and sat in it, then gave them all a big smile, and said, "Well! Isn't this grand!" They all sat down as well, one of the sorceresses I didn't know sitting at the end to my right, the Demon on the end to my left. His bodyguards stood behind him.

"Tell Rocza not to grip so hard."

"We're both a little nervous, Boss."

"Why?"

"Couldn't say."

The pain in my shoulder went away.

The sorceress at the end of the table said, "My name is Caola, Lord Taltos. I would welcome you to my home, but I try to avoid blatant hypocrisy. Why did you wish to speak with us?"

"Which of you is Triesco?"

"Why?"

"Just curious."

"I am," said the one seated to the right of Caola.

"Okay."

Caola said, "I ask again, why did you wish to speak with us?"

"This area," I said. "South Adrilankha."

"What of it?"

"I'd like to propose a bargain."

"Very well, we'll listen. We're curious about what you believe you have to bargain with."

"That's a reasonable question."

She nodded and waited for me to continue. I wasn't sure what sort of relationship there was between her and the other sorceresses; I knew nothing about the structure of the Left Hand. But it was different than in the Right Hand, at any rate; none of them said a word, or even made a motion. They just sat there and stared, sometimes at me, sometimes at Caola.

It was actually pretty creepy.

"What I have to bargain with, is letting all of you out of this room alive, and with your souls intact."

A couple of the sorceresses stiffened, the Demon raised an eyebrow, and Caola shrugged. "I think it would be more to the point to ask how *you* are getting out of here alive."

"If you turn down my offer, I don't expect to." My hand was about two inches from Lady Teldra. I tapped the hilt. "How many of you will go with me?"

"I don't think you'd—"

"You're wrong," I said. "That's why I wanted the Demon here. You know him, he knows me. Ask him."

Caola turned him an inquiring glance.

He shrugged. "I believe he'd do it, yes."

"Interesting," she said. "All right, Lord Taltos. Let's hear your proposal."

"You pack up and leave South Adrilankha, and agree to stay out until the end of the next Dragon Reign."

"Go on."

"Your plan for the Council of the Jhereg—pardon me, of the Right Hand—has fallen through. You recognize that, and agree to make no objection to the Demon taking that position."

"I'm still listening."

"That's it."

"Okay. What do we get?"

"Like I said, that's it."

She stared at me. "That's it?"

"Yes."

"You ask us to abandon our projects, and, in exchange—"

"Your lives." She started to say something, but I interrupted. "Lady Caola, you never intended to let me out of this room alive to begin with, did you? So, what's changed? Let's start the dance."

She stood up and raised her hand, by which time I was out of the chair and rolling on the floor. Loiosh and Rocza launched themselves into the air. I stood up, Lady Teldra out and in front of me. My hand was steady as I held her; my breathing was slow and easy. What would happen, would happen—no point in worrying about it.

Now would be a good time, I thought.

"*Loiosh, wait!*"

"*Hunh?*"

"*Get back here, both of you.*"

"*We're not going to—*"

"No. We're not. We wait."

"You're the boss," he said.

They circled the room once, making everyone, even the Demon, flinch a little, then landed on my shoulder again.

I became aware that a spell had gone up somewhere in the area; a teleport block, no doubt; they didn't want to just seal the house, they wanted to seal the room. Lady Teldra could break it if I were willing to put some concentration into doing so, and then more concentration into the teleport, as well as removing all my protections.

Just how effective would the Phoenix Stone be? Of course, it wouldn't help at all if they decided to drop several hundred pounds of masonry on my head; the most obvious way to sorcerously kill someone protected from sorcery. I resisted the temptation to look up.

These thoughts were removed from me, though. I considered these things, but they didn't matter—what mattered was the waiting.

One of the sorceresses put herself between me and the door.

Now would be a very good time.

The Demon was watching me. He hadn't moved, but his bodyguards had shifted just a bit closer to him. The sorceress called Triesco made a very slight motion of her right hand. I shifted the point of Lady Teldra, and the motion stopped.

Now. Now would be good.

I tried to watch everywhere at once. Even with Loiosh and Rocza helping, that was difficult. Someone was going to move, and then I was going to move, and then there would be blood. They must know about the Phoenix Stone, they had to take it into account. Either they could get around it, or neutralize it, or outright destroy it.

I watched myself stand there, waiting, and wondered why I wasn't scared.

There was a sound somewhere behind me, outside the room; a scuffle, a muffled cry, a thud.

Could it be . . .?

I heard the door opening.

Everyone's attention was suddenly focused on a point behind my left shoulder. And then I felt the presence of his weapon, and there was longer any doubt: the pure raw essence of the predator. I had been in the room when Blackwand was unsheathed, and I had always thought of that as being some sort of limit—that nothing could strike the mind as more vicious, more powerful. But this was something new.

Everyone felt it; even the Demon tensed up.

All the sorceresses stood up, stepped back, and began making various sorts of motions with their fingers, in some cases with ornate-looking daggers.

"*Boss—*"

"*Is it him?*"

"*How did you know he—*"

"*He couldn't help it.*"

"*But did he find—*"

"*He had a dream. I made a deal with the Demon Goddess.*"

"*You know, Boss, you aren't as stupid as everyone says you are.*"

"Hi there, Vlad. How are things?"

"Well enough, Telnan. Thanks for dropping by."

"My pleasure."

Caola stared at him. I'm thinking she badly wanted to ask how he'd managed to get past her teleport blocks, but she of course wouldn't. I was still watching the sorceress; I didn't turn around to look at the Dzur.

"Now, Vlad," said Telnan, "you just make your way out the door, while I keep these charm—"

"No, I don't think so."

There was a very loud silence behind me.

After a moment, I said, "I think we're going out of here together."

They were all staring at him, except for the Demon, who was looking at me with an expression of wry approval, like I'd done something clever.

"Vlad, I came here—"

"I know, Telnan. It's a Dzur thing. But I'm a Jhereg. We go out together."

Caola said, "I don't think you go out of here at all." Caola looked at me, and I felt Telnan do the same. I hefted Lady Teldra.

"There are two of us," I said. "And a bunch of you. I like our odds."

"I don't calculate odds," she said.

I shrugged. "Up to you."

Me, I did calculate odds. I wasn't all that crazy about mine, but Telnan and I would certainly take some of them with us. The question was: Could Caola back down in front of her people? I knew that no one on our side of the Jhereg could afford to under these circumstances. Could she?

"Vlad," said Telnan. "I really wish you'd let me do this."

"Think of it as a good chance to practice not getting your own way."

"I'm not good at that."

"That's why you need the practice."

There was a sigh behind me. "All right. Think we can take them all? If I can't die heroically, outnumbered and all that, I'd just as soon win."

"Maybe. I wouldn't care to bet this one either way. What do you think, Demon?"

"Me? I'm just here as an observer."

"I know. But how do you like the odds?"

"Could go either way," he said. "Not that it matters. If they don't take you down here, we'll do it later. Nothing personal, but we aren't all that concerned about who puts the shine on you, so long as it happens the right way."

"Makes sense," I said.

I shifted my eyes to Caola and raised my brows. "Your call," I told her. "Doesn't much matter to me."

"Or to me, really," she said. "As your associate from the Right Hand pointed out, now or later. It's all the same."

"Yeah."

She studied me.

"All right," said Caola at last. "You can go. We'll postpone—"

"No!" said Triesco.

Caola turned to her. "Sit down."

"I—"

"Sit down, Triesco."

She sat. Caola said, "You—"

"He killed one of our sisters, and destroyed her soul. And arranged for another. He will die. At least."

I cleared my throat. "I'd like to point out that she was in the process of trying to kill me."

Caola ignored me and spoke to Triesco. "Yes, he will. But not just now."

"I want—"

"There will be another time," said Caola.

I do not doubt that Triesco had many talents; but one talent she didn't have was concealing her rage. At least, she couldn't do it just then. Eventually, she managed a nod.

"Okay," I said. "Another time, then. But for now, I want to be clear on this. You—" I nodded to Caola, "—and your people, are out of South Adrilankha, and out of the business of the Council."

"Agreed," she said coolly.

"Good."

"What else?"

"And my friend and I get to walk out of here."

"Yes. What else?"

"That's all."

"Agreed," she said.

There was an almost inaudible hiss from Trlesco, and the sounds of some shifting and moving, but no one actually said anything.

"Good."

"Don't think you've won," said Caola. "This isn't over."

"Do I look like I'm gloating?" I said.

"Then get out."

I nodded.

I turned and walked out the door, Telnan behind me. The air outside tasted sweet.

EPILOGUE: AILOR DESSERT WINE

"You know," said Telnan, "I really like this place."

"Glad you approve."

He belched. In some Eastern societies, I'm told that's a compliment. I was taught to excuse myself. Dragaerans just ignored it.

"Thank you, Telnan," I said.

"Oh, it wasn't for you. It's just the food—"

"No, not for belching. For helping me understand that I am not now, never have been, nor ever will be, a Dzur."

"You were worried about that?"

"Not especially."

"Oh. Well, you're welcome. I'm glad Sethra sent me along."

"Me too," I said, lifting my glass in his direction, and drinking.

The wine that goes with the dessert is always the same: an Ailor, served chilled. How can I describe the product of the Ailor Vineyards of Fenario? Poems have been written to it, and that isn't my skill. For my part, I'll say that I'd have thought it impossible for anything to be that sweet without being cloying. The saying in the East is "Ailor is not created with magic, it is magic." In the original Fenarian, that rhymes.

And it would take ten poets to describe the sensation of the wine with the palaczinta.

Words fail me.

I said, "Where is the child now?"

"With Norathar."

"Can I see him?"

"Vlad . . ."

"Hmm?"

"Are you certain you wish to?"

"Why wouldn't I?"

"Well, you're going to be leaving."

"I know. But still. Yes, I'm sure."

She nodded. "I will arrange for the child to be brought here so you can meet him."

"Here?" I chuckled. "I think Kragar will be amused to have his office turned into a nursery. What have you named him?"

"Vlad Norathar."

I swallowed. Something about hearing the name made it all real. "Does Noish-pa know?"

"Of course. I informed him by the post as soon as I was able."

"Able? Oh. Was the, uh, birth difficult?"

"No. Aliera was there. It was easy and nearly painless."

"Good. I wish I'd been there too."

"What are you going to do now?" she said.

"See my son."

She pretended not to hear what my voice did when I said that. "I meant, after."

"Oh. I'm going to keep moving, I guess. Nothing is resolved."

"Where to?"

"You really want to know?"

"No, I guess it's best if I don't."

I nodded.

"I understand Sethra's Dzurlord saved you."

"Yeah."

"How'd you like being saved?"

"About as well as you liked having me solve your problem for you."

"Yeah, that was going to be my point."

"I know."

"Vlad . . ."

"Yes?"

"Nothing. I'll go get the child."

I nodded.

I should go visit my grandfather. Vlad Norathar's great-grandfather. Yes, I could do that.

I could do a lot of things.

I could do anything.

Well, anything that didn't involve being in Adrilankha; and anything that I could do with that amulet around my neck. And as long as I stayed on the move.

I wondered how long I could stand it.

"Where is Cawti?"

"Hello, Kragar. I didn't notice you come in. Isn't that remarkable?"

"Amazing. Where is Cawti."

"Getting my son."

"Getting your . . . okay."

I nodded. "Put it all together, didn't you?"

"It wasn't that difficult. Can I meet the boy as well?"

"Sure."

"Thanks."

"Then I'll take you to Valabar's."

"Think that's smart?"

"Of course not."

"You can always go in disguise."

I shrugged. "I'll take the chance. It's the Dzur in me."

"Nothing personal, Vlad, but I don't think there's much Dzur in you."

"No, there isn't, in fact. Dzurlords are all about standing alone. I'm all about having friends. That's why I'm taking you to Valabar's."

"Okay."

"And I'll introduce you to my friend Ric. I promised to let him know next time I went. Assuming that you don't mind being seen with two Easterners."

"Who will notice me?"

"The waiters, I hope."

"Good point."

"You, Sethra, Kiera, Aliera, Daymar, Mario, Morrolan . . ."

"Hmm?"

"It's good to have friends."

"Uh huh. What will you do after that?"

"Get out of town. Alive, if possible."

"Have a destination in mind? Not that I'm asking what it is."

"Yes, in general, I guess."

"Sooner or later, Vlad, you'll have to settle things with the Jhereg."

"And the Left Hand."

"Yes, and the Left Hand."

"At the moment, I only see one way of 'settling' that might work out, and that isn't a way that pleases me much."

"I can't imagine why not."

"Heh."

"I mean it, Vlad. This will have to be settled."

"Not today. Today I have to meet my son."

He nodded.

I heard sharp footsteps outside of the door, and recognized them as Cawti's. Kragar stood up. "I'll see you in a while, Vlad."

I tried to speak, but couldn't, so I nodded.

My hands were shaking.